THIS BOOK SHOULD BE RETURNED ON OR BEFORE THE LATEST
DATE SHOWN TO THE LIBRARY FROM WHICH IT WAS BORROWED

RAWTENSTALL

24. JAN 03.

27. MAR 03.

ACCRINGTON

H RAC
517
RAWTENSTALL

- 8 MAR 2004   17. DEC 05.

17. JUN   RAWTENSTALL

ACCRINGTON

17. JUL 03

ACCRINGTON

AUTHOR

CLASS

F
A G

TITLE   BIRMINGHAM nouveau

D0540207

Birmingham Nouveau

Birmingham Nouveau

edited by
Alan Mahar

TINDAL STREET PRESS

First published in 2002 by
Tindal Street Press Ltd
217 The Custard Factory, Gibb Street, Birmingham, B9 4AA
www.tindalstreet.org.uk

Copy Editor: Emma Hargrave
Typesetting: Tindal Street Press Ltd

A CIP catalogue reference for this book is available from
the British Library.

ISBN: 0 9541303 0 8

Printed and bound in Great Britain by
Biddles Ltd, Woodbridge Park Estate, Guildford.

Acknowledgements

For all their help with *Birmingham Nouveau*, the editor would particularly like to thank Emma Hargrave, Penny Rendall, Charles Keil and Helen Cross of Tindal Street Press; Dan Mason, Ross Reyburn and Steve Harrison of the *Birmingham Post*; and Colin Walker and Joanne Swatkins of Arts & Business New Partners.

Photographs

Many thanks to the *Birmingham Post* for kind permission to use images from the newspaper's picture library.

Particular thanks are due to picture editor Paul Vokes and designer Steve Harrison for all their help.

Photographs are by photographers from the *Birmingham Post*, *Evening Mail* and *Sunday Mercury*: Andrew Fox, Alan Williams, John James, Simon Hadley, Neil Pugh, Adam Fradgley, Chris Furlong, Tim Easthope, Sam Bagnall, Darren Quinton and Edward Moss.

Contents

Introduction

Birmingham has been reinventing itself – once again. A new Bullring development for the new Millennium is meant to add to the modern city confidence which the nineties transformation of Broad Street so emphatically achieved.

There can't be much doubt that the city-boosting that started with Simon Rattle's Symphony Hall, the ICC and the City Council's (unsuccessful) bid for the 1988 Olympic Games, and manifested itself in a rash of hotels for those overseas visitors whom many thought entirely imaginary, created something remarkable. The relentless development of hotels, bars and canalside apartments around the Mailbox and Broad Street area has culminated in a city with a fashionable district where young people throng on Friday and Saturday nights, and where business types and city visitors drink cappuccinos in the daytime.

There's been a change in the city. It has a new public face. A street life now exists which Birmingham never really had before. The success of Centenary Square as a New Year and summertime Trafalgar Square for the West Midlands; the pavement cafés; the Ikon Gallery . . . Brummies are gratified that visitors are pleasantly surprised by this city-centre renaissance.

But is such evident newness illusory? Is it a PR ruse perpetrated by self-serving property developers? Perhaps

Introduction

Birmingham is still too stuck in its old self-image of grimness ever to seriously aspire to Barcelona status.

Just over a year ago, an enormous hole was carved out of the rock in Digbeth where the old (agricultural) Bull Ring had been and the concrete Bull Ring of the sixties used to be. Giant hoardings fenced it round, cranes towered over it. There was great curiosity to see what the bedrock of the city was really like. What was there next to the market, next to St Martin's Church, in front of Moor Street Station? After a few weeks it became hard to remember what had been there before. But there was a palpable, unsettling air of mystery about the hole back then – archaeologists were busy, next to the piledrivers, disturbing the earth beneath the concrete and the clay. That was a mystery which, sadly, the subsequent Cunard liner of a shopping mall has mostly dispelled.

This anthology began life as a newspaper competition. A project funded by Arts & Business New Partners in partnership with the *Birmingham Post* and Birmingham's fiction publishers, Tindal Street Press, placed a writer in residence at the newspaper's offices, with a brief to encourage creative writing from the *Post*'s readers. Six masterclass articles on short-story writing were published and a short-story competition on a Birmingham theme was announced in October 2001.

More than one hundred and sixty stories were submitted to the *Birmingham Post* Short Story Challenge. Yes, as expected, there were tales of pick-ups in Broad Street bars; and love on the building site. But there were subtler treatments of urban change, too. Not so much a knee-jerk nostalgia for old Brum, but a proper historical respect for a once-grand city.

It also turned out that many *Post* readers are proud of the new. Story after story name-checked the landmarks of the city: the Victoria Square water feature known as the Floozie in the Jacuzzi; Antony Gormley's formidable Iron Man; the television screen Tony Hancock; and Thomas Attwood (that surprisingly popular bronze figure reclining on the steps of Chamberlain Square, with his parliamentary papers sprawled on the concrete).

The stories chosen for this anthology reflect many diverse responses to the changes in the city. By no means all of them favourable. Writers, being so astute as a breed, aren't hoodwinked by the publicity of council spokespeople and developers. There's more to life than shopping. Sex, for instance. Politics, or at least the fading memory of political activism. The poverty of homeless street-people – in the hedonistic noughties it was surprising to come across such social conscience. The whirligig of relationships. Not so happy returns. Tragedy. Disappointment. Terrorism. The poignancy of failure in football (now, thankfully, a distant memory). But hope, too: contained in a positive sense of a city's cultural diversity; a markedly more comfortable feeling about its future and its past.

These stories provide twenty views of Birmingham. Glimpses of the extraordinary mix of life here – its cafés, museums and art galleries, its hotels and its synagogues, balti restaurants and market stalls. To complement this strong visual geography, twenty photographic sketches from the *Birmingham Post*'s talented team of photographers have also been included.

The Franglais title was chosen deliberately to act as an echo to a sister anthology – *Birmingham Noir* – of short crime fiction set in the city's 'dark, smoky' underworld, also published by Tindal Street Press. And because the phrase seemed to contain a built-in question mark. *Birmingham Nouveau?* Can the new Birmingham really be any different from the dour old city? What essentially is the difference? Who believes in this new Birmingham?

The twenty writers on view here – some for the first time in print – are not trying to answer that question directly. They are doing what writers everywhere do: they are responding to the world around them and telling their own stories.

Alan Mahar
November 2002

An Air Kiss

John Wagstaff

In the artificial light it was almost impossible to see him, even in the centre of the great wide water-stair that tumbled down from fountain to fountain in Victoria Square. The sodium lights neither sank into him nor reflected from him. So from out of his invisibility he stared down the steps at the straggling knots, and waited. He could sense the coldness of the running water as it tugged at the tips of his wings and parted around his ankles, but he was not chilled by it.

For the girl, it was the first time she'd spent all night in the city centre – actually out in the city centre all night long – and to begin with it'd been fun. It was easy while the evening shops were open, of course. Shops were the natural environment for a thirteen-year-old city girl. In her cargoes and hoody, she was perfectly adapted to her surroundings. One store was giving free tastings of cheese, and in another there were samples of some kind of exotic chocolate cake that was sweet but tasted funny. She went back and forth between them for a while, taking little cubes until she noticed the assistants looking at her. When the security men started to rattle the shutters and the malls began to clear, she found there were still some people in a bookshop. Some of them were queuing up, all with the same book under their arms, by a round table where a smiling woman was writing in each book in turn. Others were milling around with coffee cups. She found where the free coffee was, and drank a cup standing at the back of the queue, with a couple of biscuits on her saucer. As the function wound down and people started to leave, she saw that there'd be plenty of biscuits left on the plates near the used cups. She took four more for later, and made sure that she wasn't the last to leave.

As she strolled across to New Street, three hundred watches in a jeweller's window told her it was past her usual bedtime. She turned her face away from a pair of ambling policewomen, but she knew there was no possibility of anyone searching for her yet. Each household thought she was with another. It might be as long as two or three days before any of them even thought about her, let alone wondered when she would be back.

The girl was shy of the pubs that jangled and reeked as she walked past their doors, but she liked and understood the fast-food shops. She wandered into most of the burger bars and pizza restaurants that she came across, and made a show of looking around for her friends or family, sometimes giving a little wave to a distant table before making her way back into the thinning streams of people in the street. She collected some sachets of sugar and ate them like sherbet.

Her heels felt tender in her trainers as she reached the other end of New Street and emerged onto the tilted plane of Victoria Square. In the gap between the Town Hall's violet-lit columns and the Council House's orange froth, she could see neon glowing from a McDonald's near the library. She made her way up the steps beside the clattering water feature.

As she went by, the creature that crouched on the water-stair moved for the first time that night. It was only his eyes. Just the eyeballs swivelled slowly in their sockets, tracking her steadily as she walked from the mouth of New Street, across the square, and up the broad steps to his right. He measured the slight weariness in her calves each time she lifted her feet to climb. When she'd passed out of his line of vision he turned his eyes back to the undifferentiated passers-by below. They were of no concern to him for now. He waited.

In the blare and echo of Paradise Forum she idled beside a bar menu and watched the queue beneath the golden arches. Two boys, a bit older than herself, were dressed in baggy calf-length trousers and carried nonchalant, battered skateboards. On their shirts were sullen images from the inserts of last year's CDs. She watched them pay from chubby wallets and emerge into the main piazza where they hunkered down near an exit to eat: too cool to sit at a table. She strolled past them, made sure they looked up at her, lifted a hand and grinned as if they were acquaintances, then left through the automatic doors. Two beats and she retraced her steps. She sat down in the space between them and asked for a chip. The boys weren't certain that they didn't know her; and, flattered that she seemed on casual terms with them, were unsure how to respond except by feeding her. One of them held up his Coke and, without taking it from him, she took a long fizzy drag on the straw. The other one offered his drink, too. Before the fries were all gone she stood up again.

'Got to go,' she said, and walked off.

Encumbered by their skateboards, their food and their sense of dignity, they made no attempt to follow. Half an hour later, these pleasant, bright boys from King's Heath were upstairs on the number 50 when one of them realized his wallet was missing.

*

Ahead of her, along the walkway, the view was like peeping through the keyhole of a jewel box. Jumbled across the black velvet night were thousands of cold, sharp shards of colour. Some were still and steady; some went rushing past below her feet. Some lights spun and repeated themselves; some pulsed and changed their tones. There were beams and floods, spots and filters, flickers and bars. As she walked between sloping cliffs of glass reflections, she had little sense of what was far away and what was near at hand. It was just about midnight, and for half a mile in front of her Broad Street was starting to bounce.

She paused on the bridge above a rolling tide of lava, where the traffic slurred round Paradise Circus. To her left, a slim white column shot up into the darkness with a grace and vigour that made her gasp. From the side, this block of offices was just a wall of windows, but from here she could see it revealed as a fountain jet, a searchlight beam. It was angled to a vertical wedge like the bows of a vast liner surging out of an ocean night. This was what she had come to visit.

The naked warriors around the Hall of Memory rippled their muscles at her as she passed their floodlights. She turned her shoulder against the lure of Centenary Square, where the neon sculpture fizzed at the entrance to Symphony Hall, where indigo lifts slid up and down the Hyatt, and girls with bare shoulders wove arm in arm between the cars from Brindleyplace to Five Ways. She crossed the road and slipped down some steps to wide grey spaces at the foot of that slender pencil block. Then she crossed over to where the sharp prows came right down and stabbed into the flagstones. She put a hand out to rough wrinkles on the slabs that frothed and furrowed like a frozen bow-wave.

Four hundred metres away on the water-stair, out of sight behind city layers, a young drunk was pausing to spit into the fountain when he caught a sudden movement in the centre of the flow. He thought for a moment that someone had snapped their head round to stare straight at him. But there was no one there. At the top of the stair the river-spirit lolled plump and nude in her birdbath, pouring out the waters that tumbled down to the lower pool, where two slim adolescents knelt innocently naked, facing each other across a little fountain. None of them had moved. Someone pushed past him, and with his dull, defocused eyes the drunk was almost sure he thought he glimpsed . . . over in midstream . . . just in the instant that he was jolted off-balance. There was a sound then, too, like a purr in the throat of a bear, like the first threat of a snarl. The drunk turned and sat on the low stone surround. He swayed as his mind, lacking definition as much as his vision, toddled away on its own for a while.

Suddenly he lurched forward from his seat, sprawling and turning at the same time, his hands and feet scrabbling on the steps as he scuttered away from the water-stair and off into the knots and gaggles of the night. Across the paving of the steps, his shocked bladder had left a sudden dark drizzle. And at the centre of the River, the current swirled oddly and there was a gap in the water-curtain that tumbled from the lip of one step.

It was still too soon to start, thought the girl, and she'd tired herself with her wandering around the city. She found a little cave where the architect had left a cutaway behind the white prows of the tower. The concrete cradled her. The noise of traffic reached her like the rumble of someone running a bath at home, when she used to curl up with her big sister in their room at their old house. When things had been okay. Not great, but okay. She let herself start to doze.

No one heard the sound like a long sigh on the water-stair . . . The stillness in the centre of the flow became even more still, and even less visible. He did not sleep. He waited.

A couple of hours was all she needed. At thirteen, a body refreshes itself quickly when it needs to. There was no cramp or stiffness in her joints as she ducked out from her hideaway. Along Broad Street, one batch of clubs was closing and another batch was opening. The more domestic clubbers, with family homes and jobs to go to, were competing for taxis. A grimmer-faced, more hardy crew were queuing at loud doors for the approval of bouncers wearing suits and headsets. The city was breathing in a mild, clean breeze coming straight across the Shropshire plain from Welsh mountains.

The girl pulled her hoody off over her head and knotted the arms around her waist. She held an elastic band in her mouth while she bunched up her hair into a ponytail, her elbows poking bonily out of her T-shirt. Last week, the last time she'd been to school, she'd learned the only thing that had ever interested her in English. She was now the same age as Juliet Capulet had been when she'd married Romeo Montague and was buried alive in order to be with him. Then she woke up in her tomb to find her dead husband sprawled across her, and she poked a dagger through the flinching skin under one new breast, and between her ribs to skewer the pumping muscles of her own heart. Exactly the same age: two weeks short of her fourteenth birthday. It was time to do something.

She turned to look up at the column of offices rising into the darkness above her. There was a black line down the very tip of its pointed bow – a split in the white concrete. It opened into emergency stairs, and was just wide enough for a person to slip out through in order to escape – if any means of escape could reach as high as might be needed.

There were twenty-seven rows of windows – she'd counted them lots of times – then a roof-level crowded with satellite dishes and antennae. Add on a ground floor. Call it thirty storeys.

You couldn't get into the stair-split from the ground, of course. The first point of entry was as high off the ground as the roof of their old house. The façade of the tower's prow was made up out of big concrete blocks, with deep seams between them, just wide enough for toes and fingers.

As the toe of her right trainer nudged into the first seam, and the fingers of her left hand reached up for the second, a low rumble rolled out across Victoria Square. The surface of the water in the upper basin trembled. If anyone had been passing just then they would have glanced up at the sky, squinting past the lights to see if thunderclouds were blowing in from the west. The murmur died away in his chest. His nostrils widened as he snuffed at the air. It was not the broom of the Lickey Hills he detected, nor the free oxygen from Welsh waterfalls; not even the tang and metal of city traffic. He tasted only the garbled mass of sleeping souls in villages and towns, the occasional bored nightshift in a Black Country plant, the sour spirits who loitered nearby on Ladywood streets. And, out of them all, he found the scent of her bruised and weary essence. He caught the flavour of her damaged hope, and the savour of her fantastical adolescent ambition. Not long to wait now.

It was easier than she'd expected. The height of each block was a comfortable distance for her to stretch, the angle of her thigh when bent gave just the right leverage. There was a small lip in each joint, around which her fingertips could curl. She leaned back from the face, as they'd taught her on the climbing wall in the school gym. But with no ropes or helmets or teachers, it felt much simpler somehow. By the time she'd reached, stepped, levered, balanced and reached again three times she was as high off the ground as a bedroom window. Once more, or maybe twice, and she'd be able to swing herself round into the access gap and onto the stairs. *Reach, step, lever, balance.* She was breathing fairly hard now, and would welcome a chance to stretch. She shuffled a little to the side, her toes scuffing along the joint, and bent as far as she could to get one hand onto the edge of the vertical split. Then she swung sideways and dropped down clumsily onto a landing of the fire stairs.

It was dark on the staircase, and the bare concrete steps made her breathing loud and harsh. She felt like an intruder here: a burglar in threatening shadows. Her heart pounding, she listened for footsteps, she listened for alarms. She stood as close as she could to the opening, where the city seemed wide and friendly around her. She could look out at the now-sparse traffic turning onto Broad Street, at the uplit warriors protecting the Hall of Memory. It was stupid to be afraid of the dark stairs.

Biting her lip and clutching the steel handrail, she started to tiptoe up one flight. There was a landing with double doors, marked '2'. The second floor. Round windows in the doors revealed the shadows of desks and monitors. The absence of human movement in this place, made utterly for people, scared her and she hurried up the next short flight to another landing like the one where she'd climbed through. Standing right in the gap, she could see the top of the Hall of Memory's dome. She needed to get back into the open air again. She took a couple of deep breaths to steady her heartbeat, then stepped up onto the bottom rail and found one of the familiar joints in the facing blocks. With her head back outside, she felt better at once. The next floor up would be labelled '3'; more than a tenth of the way already. She knew she could get to the top.

On the third floor, the darkness of the stairwell was just too forbidding. She stood outside on the handrail for a couple of minutes to give her muscles a rest, then she carried on climbing up to the next landing. But the last *balance, reach, step, lever* took too much out of her. There wasn't much weight for her to lift, but she had so little power with which to do that lifting. On the fourth landing she had no choice but to tumble down over the railing and sit on the concrete floor, stretching her calves and unclawing her fingers. She huddled close to the opening. While she rested she undid her ponytail, shook her hair loose and then carefully remade it again. She forced herself to stay inside for about ten minutes. When she got to her feet her legs ached, but they no longer trembled. Her fingertips felt tender as she reached, stepped, levered up and out onto the sheer face of the building.

Now that she'd been inside twice, the escape stairs seemed less daunting, so she decided to stop for a few minutes at each floor. At the seventh floor she could make out the glassy pyramids of Paradise Forum. And was it her imagination, or was the sky lightening just above the building line, behind the warning lights on the Telecom Tower? She wanted to be at the top to see the sunrise.

Lever, balance, reach, step.

It was as she came back out from her rest on the fourteenth floor – where, for fifteen minutes, she'd sat nursing the hum of pain in her calves and shoulders – that someone saw her.

Beyond the roof of the Rep, high up in a block of council flats by the canal, but not as high up as the girl, a young father had pulled back the curtains so his unsleeping baby daughter could gaze out at the shifting landscape of lights. He stood sideways to the glass, his nose dipped to her soft, flaking scalp, breathing her scent into every crevice of his sinuses, humming it out again in lullaby. From the corner of his eye he saw a movement where there'd been none on any of the other nights he'd stood here. He stared so hard that he stopped swaying to and fro and the head on his shoulder wobbled back for a moment, then butted him with all its tiny weight and started to grizzle. He cupped her skull and tutted as he edged across towards the bedside phone.

At the lower edge of Victoria Square, wide-hipped women were climbing out of a minibus and off to start their cleaning jobs. The first sign of a new human day. Only one of them noticed the change in the fountain as they went up the steps beside it. Although the artificial lights hadn't been able to touch or rest upon him, the early wash of daylight was different. It settled in specks like a drizzle of diamond dust, like a mist of stars on the crouching creature in the water-stair. The woman tipped her head, creased her brow and reached for her friend's elbow.

The rhythm of her movements helped the girl ignore her pain. There was comfort and strength in the *step, lever, balance, reach, step* . . . It soothed the sandpaper just below the skin of her thighs and shoulders. It was ointment on her raw fingertips, on the bruised tendons of the arches of her feet. Not for a moment did it occur to her to fear the huge emptiness behind her back – the vacant air around the tower, the terrible narrowing of the concrete waterfall as distance dwindled it beneath her toes. With the dawn so clearly silhouetting the city's jumble to her left, she forced herself past the next landing without stopping.

When she dropped exhausted onto the seventeenth stairwell she knocked her knee against some pipework and was almost pleased at the feel of a different kind of pain. In the dawn light she could see the state of her hands: the rims of blood round the fingernails, and the mash of crushed blood vessels under the surface of the first two joints. Now that there was a thin web of day inside the stairs, the fire escape had become matter-of-fact and dull. If she was going to reach the top in time, she'd need to swallow her pride and do it the easy way.

But she soon realized that the stairs posed even more of a challenge. Her leg muscles were refusing to respond to normal commands; her knees groaned and wavered; her hands would not grip the rail. She found she was laughing at the comic spectacle of herself shuffling, bent double, staring at her feet with the effort of making them remember how to climb stairs. And as her frightened laughter echoed down the stairwell, another sound came up to greet it: a door clanging open, heavy steps, some distant male voices so reverberated that their words were harsh gibberish.

She threw herself up the next turn of stairs and leaned gasping on the rails at the escape gap on the nineteenth floor. For the first time she looked directly down, and there at the foot of the tower was a constellation of flickering lights – blue, orange, red – from the police cars, fire engines, ambulances pulled up on the plaza pavement. In an instant her head was full of official phrases and images, whose meanings were as shadowy and scary as the stairwell had been: trespass, burglary, arrest, risk, care, welfare, parental guidance, custody, guardian . . . She escaped the words in the same way that she'd escaped the shadows. She climbed back outside.

Few of the daybreak passengers through Victoria Square paused for more than a moment when they saw the extraordinary lighting effect the council had achieved in the River. It was some sort of 3D hologram thing, done with lasers or fibre optics. You couldn't quite see what it was meant to be, because it seemed to change all the time. Sometimes it looked like a bush of fire or a tangle of glowing wires. The next moment, a sort of crouching skeleton, and then it was more a milky white bird with huge wings folded around its head. Or maybe it was just a random galaxy of light points, which seemed to pulse and breathe. Still, as the volume of passers-by grew, more and more began to pause and watch.

In her alarm and shame, the girl found the strength to move on up the joints of the tower, returning to her old climbing rhythm. She was much slower now, though. It took longer to get her balance each time; the step and lever came with an effort; at each reach she gritted her teeth.

Twenty-one storeys below her, tiny figures with yellow helmets were spreading out something like a big mat across the paving slabs. They connected a tube, pulled on a lever and started to inflate the huge airbag. To the video news team hurrying with a tripod and mike boom, it seemed enormous as it writhed and spluttered into shape, but from the girl's perspective it was smaller than a thumbnail.

Voices were echoing on the stairs almost at her elbow. She bit into her lip and edged quickly sideways along a seam, as far away from the gap as she could. A walkie-talkie squawked inside the concrete and far below yellow dots were dragging the airbag sideways to track her progress.

There were only five or six more joints above her now. She had almost made it. Maybe she could find somewhere to hide among the dishes and antennae until they'd all gone away. She kept her eyes upwards and dragged herself through the slow agony of the rhythm: *lever, balance, reach, step, lever, balance.*

A movement above her. A yellow helmet and a white one, a female head with a chequered hatband, outlined against the sky. Panic clenched her stomach and she lost the rhythm. She faltered and could only move sideways, back towards the stairs. The dark slot seemed to offer some kind of refuge where she could perhaps try some doors, see if there was a way to get inside and give them the slip. She reached the side of the slot and started to lever up towards the rails on the twenty-third landing.

In her hip pocket, the wallet she'd taken from the skater had been edging upwards with her every movement. Now it shifted that final degree to the pocket edge, where a pound coin's centre of gravity tipped its angle just enough to take the wallet clear and away – spinning and tumbling, gathering speed as it went – reaching its terminal velocity with such force that it ripped open the seam of the half-inflated airbag as it struck, and still chipped a stone flag. She heard the shouts, but she didn't notice the wallet fall.

The shifting group of gawpers in Victoria Square gave a nervous jump and then a murmur of approval. A sudden band of brightness had shot out from the light sculpture, spreading from side to side of the water-stair in a vast sweep of humming power. 'Like wings,' said someone. 'Wings,' they repeated, and no one was sure if they were feathered wings like a bird or leathered wings like a bat.

'Hello, love, want a hand?' said a voice just above her head. Up and to her right, a man with grey hair was looking down from the rails. He had friendly laugh-lines at the corners of his eyes, and some kind of uniform flash on his shoulders. He was puffed from climbing all those stairs.

A foolish child, just a waste of everyone's time and money and emotion. A sudden rush of shame convulsed her face with self-disgust and made her eyes stream tears. She saw how ridiculous she was, and gasped and heaved with rage at how her body was betraying her. Her nose was running and great sobs shook her as she clung to the concrete.

The man was speaking. His face was soft and tender, but

there was terror inside his eyes. He was so frightened for her. She was still too far away for him to reach her, but his shiny toecaps were level with her chin, behind the railings. She swallowed her tears, blew away her sobs, and turned her face up to his.

'Don't be afraid,' she said.

Then she opened her arms and stretched them out at shoulder height.

She lifted herself onto her tiptoes in the concrete crack, bent her knees just a fraction, curved her spine and launched herself out backwards into the emptiness.

Horrified, the policeman on the stairs watched her holding that graceful diving pose as her body turned in the air until he saw the soles of her shoes plummeting away from him.

Light erupted on the water-stair, leaving only a column of spray falling back into the basin. He curved round to the left first, away from the tower, to gather speed by turning in the entrance to Eden Place, faster than anyone's eye could watch him; the snap of his wings cracked like cannon fire as his light-blur bridged above Paradise Forum. The dot that plunged from the tower fell as slowly as a leaf by comparison.

Somewhere at about the seventh floor, the sweep of brightness met the headfirst, stiff-curved, diving Juliet and soared up again out of the plaza away across the rooftops towards the west.

So there was nothing but her little bag of bones to meet the ground.

Tea at the Museum

Anne Dyas

The second Tuesday in February was a good day for a lovers' tryst in one respect, being close enough to the fourteenth. But in every other it was awful, since the weather was usually bad. The older Margaret became, the more the climate influenced her activity. After the hip replacement, she tended to keep indoors as much as possible between October and March. But this was one appointment that she forced herself to keep.

The train was on time at Snow Hill. Painfully and slowly, she ascended the steps to the concourse above. She hadn't trusted escalators since she'd lost her balance on one a year ago, but the alternative was almost worse. She had to stop halfway to regain her breath. Why was she doing this, silly old woman? She really should never have come.

At the top, she caught sight of her reflection: stooped, shabby, wispy grey hair escaping from her knitted hat. How different from the first time she'd taken tea at the museum. She recalled a rather nice little suit in grey wool, with a pair of black court shoes. Now it was sufficient that she could get upright in the mornings, never mind what she looked like.

As she walked across the concourse, her breath came in painful rasps, but the pain in the chest that had begun to trouble her was mercifully absent. She stopped out of necessity, and was almost knocked flat by a youth in a ridiculously wide pair of trousers and with a piece of chain threaded through his nose. She was surprised when an apology rather than an obscenity came over his fleeing shoulder.

Her breath regained, she moved slowly out of the station, past the *Big Issue* seller and into the street. It was a real *February Fill Dyke* day: the water was running in a grey-brown stream down the gutter and passing cars were a hazard to all on foot who preferred to keep the inside of their shoes dry. Margaret dug in her bag and produced a black umbrella with only a couple of broken spokes. It'd been a very good umbrella in its time, which was part of the problem. It steadfastly refused to blow inside out even when subjected to the Roaring Forties, so it hadn't been replaced even though it was nearly as antiquated as Margaret herself. Reduced income in recent years had developed a tendency for prudence into desperate penny-pinching, so an umbrella that was still doing its job, no matter how shabby, certainly couldn't be thrown away. She could hear Caroline's voice saying, 'For goodness sake, Mum, treat yourself. Get a new one. You can afford it.'

Caroline would no doubt have had something to say on the subject of Margaret's trip today. But Caroline didn't know. Nor would she.

This particular journey had changed less than most of the city. She could still pick out where the Kardomah had provided tea and biscuits at Formica-topped tables at the corner of the Great Western Arcade. Those railings around the cathedral were new; they looked like the massed spears of an oriental army. She struggled on against the deluge, trying to avoid stabbing unfortunates with the umbrella; from her viewpoint, she had little notice of their approach until their feet appeared below its frayed rim. And by then it was almost too late. The umbrella reminded her of a dead crow, all sticking out bone and the sheen long since gone from its feathers. Or perhaps it was she who more resembled the crow.

How life spun past, like a zoetrope – just a few moments frozen in memory, as if the thing had stopped for an instant, held by the finger of fate. Here she was, three score and ten aching years of trudging tedium, repetition and toil, encompassed by just a few fleeting frames: her first day at school, her father's dreadful accident and funeral, her wedding day, Caroline's birth, her mother's death, her own retirement, the day of the hip replacement, Lionel's coronary and his death. And, of course, the first time that she came here, thirty years ago. The whole story could be recounted in about fifteen minutes, she reflected. Amazing how some folk managed to pad it out into an auto-biography. The sheer effort of living, of keeping the head above water and the wolf from the door, had so occupied Margaret that there was little time left for anything interesting.

Apart from the reason that brought her here. She was quite proud of the fact that she'd conducted this clandestine, admittedly platonic affair under Lionel's nose for all those years. Not many women could claim such an achievement at sixty-nine. His sudden departure for the hereafter had left her with no reason for secrecy; indeed she could now, if she wished, make the whole business entirely public. But, instead, she wouldn't even tell Edmund that Lionel was dead. That just might add a complication which, in her seventh decade with one bad hip, she could do without.

She'd reached the steps of the museum, and she turned to look across the square before climbing upwards. This place had changed over the years. It was a bit like a serviceable set of teeth. Bits had cracked off here and there, there was a fair amount of bridgework and a filled cavity or two, but the underlying structure was still the same. It was a better place now that you were no longer at risk of being run down; she could remember when the double-deckers used to hurtle around Victoria's unsmiling black effigy. With a grunt, Margaret began to mount the steps.

Behind the great, heavy doors it would be warm and dry. She tried to get through them leaving as much of the weather outside as possible, but the umbrella somehow became tangled in the closing doors, and she suddenly found that her stiffened wrists weren't able to extricate it.

'You all right, dear?' asked the man at the desk, but it was a rhetorical question – he was already coming to help her.

'Sorry,' she said. 'Sorry, I can't open it,' but knew she was apologizing for being old. Don't be sorry, she thought, as the rain slowly trickled down her neck and slid like the pendants of a tiara from her hair.

Flustered and discomforted, she began the long haul up the inner stairs, with the commissionaire's voice over her shoulder: 'There is a lift, you know, love.'

Lift be damned. In thirty years of coming here, she'd never taken the lift, and that wasn't going to change now. That would be a real admission of the slide into old age. But the marble treads did rather resemble the slopes of K2 today.

At last the summit was achieved, and she pretended to study the display at the top while she caught her breath. She was ten minutes early, and Edmund had never been on time, so there was space to dry herself off a little. Could anything be done with the hair? She knew the cloakroom mirror would show her an aged crone, as she described herself these days, but underneath was still the eternal youth that lives on in all of us. Thus, with a minute to spare, Margaret sat herself in the round gallery at the entrance and waited for him to arrive.

She always sat in the same place, beneath Leader's picture: a Victorian study of a couple of rather hopeless serfs making their way home after heavy rain. The water in the ditches almost ran off the canvas. But on the horizon was a glimmer of watery sunshine. That was like her life really; mostly pretty miserable, with a distant hope of something better.

Twenty minutes became half an hour and then three quarters, and still he didn't come. He'd never been as late as this, not on any occasion in the last thirty years. She set to wondering why he'd come every year for all this time. After all, he'd not obtained what a man usually wanted from an affair. For herself, it'd been something secret from Lionel, something outside the restricting confines of her family, just one place where she was Margaret and not Caroline's mother or Lionel's wife.

And for Edmund, what? Duty, was it? Or friendship; or love, whatever that was. They'd been in love once, of course, when they were at school, but then destiny had parted them for twenty-five years until that chance meeting in this very place all those years ago. She knew little of his life outside their annual meetings, except that he had a disabled wife; or maybe that was in the past, for he hadn't spoken of her for some time, and Margaret, being unconcerned about her, hadn't asked. In some ways, he'd always been a fantasy person for her, existing only at the time of their meeting, then disappearing like Tinker Bell, as she walked out of the museum. And today the magic must be weaker, for he hadn't appeared at all.

Despairing of his arrival, she made her way along the beautiful Victorian hall to the Tea Room. She loved this place. The iron balustrades, the contrast of cream with green, the shimmering, delicate glass and ceramic of the exhibits were a haven of unchanging beauty in an ugly world. Tea, in contrast, was fairly standard, but a glass of water taken at those tables among the potted palms would have tasted like nectar. She didn't allow herself to linger over the cup, convinced she'd find Edmund waiting and fretting that she wasn't there. She almost ran back along the length of the hall. He would have gone. She was sure of it. It was then that she saw him standing below Leader's picture, clearly just about to leave. She stopped in her tracks, the pain in her chest suddenly severe, her breath coming in rapid gasps.

Charles arrived later than intended at the museum. The lunchtime meeting had run over and he'd almost forgotten the promise he'd made. He remembered with a jolt when he opened his briefcase and found the letter there. Very strange, really. The old man had never struck him as a secretive sort of person, but here was some aspect of his life which had been completely unknown to Charles. A bit like discovering a beneficiary in your parent's will to be someone whom you've never met. In fact, very like that because, after all, he didn't know what was in the letter. But he did know what was in the will, because it'd already been read a month earlier. There were no surprises there.

Charles was slightly out of breath from running the length of Colmore Row, so he paused to gather himself in the entrance hall before mounting the steps two at a time. There was no one there. Under Leader's picture, Dad had said. He knew the one, because when he was a boy his father had often pointed it out to him. What memories this place held. Through the long years of Mum's illness, he and Dad had managed a trip here two or three times a year. Just the two of them, wandering through the halls, then a tea and a Coke. As a small boy, his favourites were the dinosaurs, or possibly the Coke. Later, it was ancient Egypt, and later still, the art and ceramics. He couldn't say these visits had greatly influenced his choice of career, but the museum was a wonderful private enclave where he and Dad could be together, alone, just for an afternoon and forget the anxiety of Mum at home. It'd come as something of a shock to discover that the place was special to Dad for another reason as well.

Charles sat down under the picture and waited.

And twenty minutes later, a little regretfully, he rose and began to fasten his coat. No one was coming today. Never missed a year, Dad had said. Well, she was missing this one. And presumably the next, and the next. Shame. He would've liked to have met her. And there was the matter of the letter; he wasn't quite sure what to do with it now. Deposit it with the family solicitor, he supposed. Or maybe he should read it, in case there was any mention of a gift or bequest. True, the will had said nothing, but clearly Dad hadn't wanted the present matter to be public knowledge. Charles straightened his tie, and smoothed back his now-receding hair, in the way he'd often seen his father do. Then he turned to leave.

As he went, he heard a commotion behind him and turned to see the staff in the gift shop rushing to the assistance of someone who'd fallen on the floor. There were several staff, and he doubted that he'd be able to do much to help. Lawyers were good enough for the paperwork of death, but not much use for giving succour to the sick. Best clear the decks and make way for the paramedics. He descended the marble stairs, his father's letter in his hand.

As he went through the great doors, he noticed that it had finally stopped raining, and that touches of watery February sunshine were shimmering on the puddles round the Chamberlain Memorial. The old and the new. Never changing; always changing. His father was gone, and so it seemed was his love, but some things continued and some things never changed. Rather like the city really. For the moment he, Charles, was left to carry his father's standard, but one day he too would hand it on. What would his father have done with the letter, if he'd been here in his place and had kept that lonely vigil under the picture?

Charles walked over to the memorial and stood there distractedly for a while before slowly opening the letter. Unaccustomed tears filled his eyes as he read his father's tender words of farewell to the woman he'd never known. Anguish overwhelmed him and, unable to finish reading, he ripped the paper into tiny pieces and dropped them into the water of the memorial. He was still standing there when he heard the sound of the ambulance siren, at first distant, then closer and closer.

Denial

Mark Paffard

It had been such a long day at work: warm, sapping, over-familiar; full of appointments, meetings, discussions. Arguments, in fact.

When I arrived at the pub they were all out in the garden. I knew the place – one of my old haunts, wasn't sure it suited me now – and hoped our first evening out would be a great success, but mostly I felt relieved to be in safe company.

Julie held up her cheek to be kissed, and squeezed my hand when I sat down. Bob and Belinda smiled their welcome. Their hands were out on the table, relaxed, as though they were tending a flame.

It was a nice pub, after all, and a nice enough suburb of Birmingham: slightly bohemian, usually quiet. The garden was just a yard out back, at the end of a corridor, from which the doorway looked like a mouse hole. Perhaps we could go on somewhere for a balti later, slum it and enjoy ourselves?

Bob stood up to get me a drink, but something arrested his face and, as he sat himself back down, I realized that someone had put his hand on my shoulder. It was oddly light, like a piece of driftwood. I looked up into the stranger's face.

But, of course, he wasn't a stranger. He was looking down at me with a kind but faintly manic smile on his worn, grey-bearded face. One of his teeth was broken. Turning further to greet him, I could feel the touch of Julie's hip.

'I thought you'd forgotten me,' he said. His voice, stirring my memory, also broke the spell of his face. I had listened to him, once. But everything had changed.

'You don't come in here much now, do you?' He said this absently, as if he had other concerns. Then he lowered his voice: 'I don't suppose you'll be in here again?'

'I don't know,' I said. 'Why don't I call you – some time?'

'Have you still got the number?' he asked. 'Or shall I write it down?'

'No, no,' I said, 'I've got it. I'll call you, shall I – John?'

'Do that, if you wish! Goodnight.'

He turned away and bumped his head on a hanging basket, which spilled out a lemony scent of geranium. He raised a palm to it, his jacket hanging from his shoulders and his greying hair scalloped behind his ears. Then he took another step and was gone.

Bob stood up again to get me a drink. He stared at the hanging basket and paused.

'I remember him,' he said. 'He's the one who got himself arrested outside the Council House.'

'Arrested?' said Julie. 'What for?' She had her hand on my thigh.

'Oh,' said Bob, looking at me. 'Pete could tell you best. I was in the chamber, in that housing debate, and someone came in and told us there was a ruckus going on. Stupid, really, because there was only this chap and maybe a dozen others. So anyway, I came out and . . .'

'Drinks, Bob!' Belinda said crisply.

'Coming up!' he said, heaving his shorts clear of the bench. 'Anyway,' he added, 'Pete can tell you about it. You were with him, weren't you?'

'I was *there*,' I said.

'Right!' said Bob. 'We've all moved on. Two pints, then, and two halves . . .'

Belinda rolled her eyes. 'Never get Bob going about his council days, even though he's doing much better *now*. So, Pete, how's business with you?'

I put my own hands carefully out, and pointed my fingertips to spark at hers. There was always that spark with Belinda, the touch of panther behind her makeup, so I knew her question was loaded. She knew that what I did was less business than bureaucracy – impossibly compromised by the interest groups I served.

Life had at least been different in the days when I knew John. Simple, because I believed in something unambiguous. Yet if I gave it a name, like equality or freedom, of course I'd say that I still believed in it now. But now he was silvered by decay.

In the old days he'd been strong and certain. He never spoke much, but he could be relied upon always to be at our meetings, his Guinness squarely in front of him, and his eyes alive with the rightness of what we were doing. Even with the women comrades he was never diverted into private conversation, though I heard that he'd slept with one or two of them. Whatever his private affairs, he submerged them when we were together, and he kept us together.

On demonstrations, I liked to walk beside him. Half the trouble on demos comes from the fearful boredom. Dressed in a plain shirt and jeans and with his dark hair a little overgrown, John always kept rank, making light of the endless pauses and the gritty air. You felt that even the policemen admired him.

But that day at the Council House there were no police. Not at first. We'd acted spontaneously, partly at John's insistence, though some had urged its pointlessness, since the council tenants themselves were hardly likely to mobilize.

'They're being oppressed, though,' John had said, 'on our doorstep.' So we – most of us – had gone.

About twenty of us sat down on the steps until the police turned up. John had a placard. He always ended up with one, untroubled as to whether it advertised *Socialist Worker* or *Morning Star*.

After some debate among the dozen police officers, we were asked to move to the opposite side of the square and, making a show of reluctance, we moved. It was just a square, then – a barrack yard with a dingy statue and a sullen fountain. Hard to imagine the same protest in the fancy plaza it is now. I noticed that John wasn't with us. He'd stayed on the steps of the Council House; was sitting there as if he just hadn't heard.

An officer spoke to him, but John didn't move, and the officer went away and talked into his radio. John leaned his placard against a pillar and lit a cigarette. He looked preoccupied but, framed as he was by the building like a man in a photograph, no one could say exactly what he was thinking about. It seemed predictable, afterwards, the way four of them came up quickly and lifted him, almost chaired him, off to the waiting car. I took a step forwards, but someone held my arm, and then John caught my eye and shook his head firmly, *No*.

Characteristically, he came along to the next meeting as if nothing had happened, unless he seemed especially keen to talk about our next move.

And that was the difference tonight, I thought, five years after I gave it up, building my career instead, and now wanting to marry Julie. Not his expression, nor his age, but the fact that when he spoke to me he was looking *back*. He hadn't moved on like me. Instead, time seemed to have hollowed him out.

Anyway, he was gone, and Bob had returned with the drinks. As he sat down again he whispered something in Belinda's ear, and Julie took the chance to whisper in mine:

'Belinda doesn't like me very much.'

A shiver passed through me in the still, warm evening. I looked at the hanging basket hanging dead straight on its chains, and the soft lamplight falling on it. It seemed to me impossible that, having found the time to get together, we four should create anything but harmony. It would've been better, of course, if we'd gone to a restaurant, because at those conference lunches we'd got on like a house on fire. It had amused and touched us that we were the only couples among the delegates. Not only that, but we were the ones who actually came from Birmingham. In our limited free time we'd strolled proprietorially around Gas Street Basin, pleased to escape the air-conditioned glass and plastic savannahs of the hotel for the eye-jabbing springtime gusts up the canal. We'd even slipped, almost like naughty children, into a dark waterside pub and each downed a quick short.

In fact, we'd felt like conspirators, enjoying our liberation from small talk with strangers, and having to glance – but not stare – at name-badges pinned on chests. I couldn't remember which of us had suggested that we meet as friends, but I'd thought at once how useful we could be to each other. So Julie's whisper shocked me.

'Give it time,' I whispered back, and squeezed her hand.

I should've realized that Belinda and Julie were opposites, just as Bob and I were. I was the strategist while Bob, who gave the impression of having bluffed his way up the ladder, was still a leader of men. Even his beard and his shorts said so. And Julie, with her full figure that hit you in the face (her fine breasts that belonged to *me*, I thought in passing), surprised people with her sudden strength of mind. Belinda, on the other hand, gave it to you straight, and only afterwards did her sexuality hit you like the end of a whip. I couldn't afford to have them taking a dislike to each other.

Suddenly I knew what to do. I stole a kiss from Julie. Belinda turned away from Bob and looked at us with a knowing smile.

'Young love,' she said, kindly. As if it followed naturally, she asked Julie about her dress, and within a minute they were comparing notes.

Bob and I looked on. The hanging basket let down its scent and the lamplight spilled on their breasts. Bob gave me a quiet wink. I asked him how his grown-up daughter was doing. She was the apple of their eye. 'Was Debbie,' I asked (pleased I remembered her name!), 'home for the summer?' Bob slowly shook his head. 'She must be working hard?' I persisted. (Law, I remembered – second year.)

Belinda looked across. 'Actually, Pete, we're worried about her. She's in with a bad crowd.'

'Nutters,' Bob said. Looking harder at me, he added, 'Like that chap tonight. Your friend.'

'Oh no.' I shook my head. 'Besides,' I said, 'those people disbanded. They've gone.'

'But, Pete,' said Julie suddenly, 'weren't you and John *close* friends?'

'*No*,' I said. 'What made you think that?'

'Because you've been thinking about him.'

I looked at Julie. We all looked. She looked back at all of us. I looked away at the other tables.

'Don't you believe it,' Belinda said to me. 'Those people are still around. We don't know how they got to Debbie, but I can tell you it's – *tragic*. They even got her arrested –'

'Arson,' Bob said, gloomily. Julie and I looked at each other.

'That doesn't sound like her,' I said.

'Of course it's not,' he said angrily. 'She's been set up, and brainwashed. The bastards are hiding behind her.' He downed his pint in a gulp. A crack of thunder came from behind the pub.

'But,' said Julie thoughtfully, 'she must be in love with someone? And then, whatever she *did* – well, sometimes you just don't *hesitate*, do you?'

'Oh for God's sake!' said Belinda. 'Don't be so naïve. She's in love with a fucking *idea*.'

'You mean, like John?'

'John who?'

'Pete's friend.'

'Him?' Bob scowled at her. '*Him?*' But his face was vaguely ludicrous, like a hopeless position in chess.

Julie looked at him calmly. I noticed again the fullness and tautness of her breasts. Then a single drop of rain smacked onto them and darkened the fabric.

'Look,' said Belinda, 'I think we'll have to call it a night.' And as we dived into the warmth, and the rain fell like a sheet behind us, she suddenly burst into tears. Bob put his arm around her.

'All the best,' he said, over his shoulder. 'Another time. Be in touch.'

'I told you she didn't like me,' said Julie. 'Anyway, I wanted you to myself. Buy me a drink. I like pubs.'

Forty minutes later we were standing in the doorway. Julie was tucked behind me, and the rain was pouring down. Then John stumbled past and went off down the road. I hadn't seen him inside. In a second, his grey hair was plastered, dripping off his scalp. He bowed his head under the streetlamps and moved away terribly slowly, and darkly, like a slug.

Julie was looking the other way. 'Here's our taxi,' she said. '. . . Whatever are you *crying* for?'

Finding Rifka

Sidura Ludwig

The children in the Birmingham Central Synagogue know him as the man with the shakes. Their parents tell them he is to be respected, not just because of his age, but because he fought in Normandy during the war. And if it weren't for men like him, well, maybe there wouldn't be any Jews in England. The seven-year-old boys try to remember this when they run by his seat, maybe accidentally knocking a prayer book to the floor with a startling bang, which causes Mr Steinberg to jump in his seat, lose his composure, his hand shaking as he draws his finger to his lips to make the children settle down.

'It's shell shock,' they whisper, not really understanding what that means, but imagining the old man thrown from his bunker by a bomb blast. They giggle then, watching his finger shake violently in front of his face; Mr Steinberg barely able to hold his own prayer book in his other hand and so it too falls to the floor, gently. Inevitably, one of the fathers reaches over, picks up the book and then reminds the children that Mr Steinberg is a hero. They can only dream of being such a hero. So the seven-year-old boys stop giggling but still stare, wondering how he could possibly be a hero when he doesn't look anything like Superman.

Mr Steinberg's seat is by the eastern wall. It doesn't look any different from the other seats in the synagogue, but all the same, no one else sits in it, ever. When the men come to pray, they leave it empty and how it always is – Mr Steinberg's tallit hung over the back of the seat, his prayer book resting on the cushion. And if an unknowing visitor mistakes the seat as available, someone is bound to politely ask him to move places. This spot, they say, is taken.

Mr Steinberg is a regular shul goer. Lately, he hasn't always made it for morning minyan, especially as the weather has turned cold and his joints have taken to seizing up in the early morning. Sometimes he wakes at six a.m., before the sun, his knees throbbing, stiffening his legs with each pulse. He lies in bed, massaging his kneecaps, as if trying to melt them, hoping to thaw them enough to put his trousers on, and his shoes, and then make his way to Central so that he can be a part of the quorum. But as December rolls forwards and the sun sleeps in later and later, Mr Steinberg finds there's nothing he can do but lie in bed until his heating kicks in. All this means he does most of his morning prayers lying down.

Those old enough to understand think of Mr Steinberg as an upstanding citizen, a *machor*. Here is the man who organized the building of the synagogue after the war and who, twenty-five years ago, put up part of the money for the two walls of etched windows, the ones picturing the twelve tribes of Israel. Surely this is the synagogue's pride: these windows facing the car park and the pavement, which, on Friday evenings as the Sabbath is coming in, collect the setting sunlight and distribute it around the sanctuary, painting everything gold. Two windows were built in blessed memory of Mr Steinberg's wife, who died before her time. The women who sit in the synagogue balcony look at the windows and wonder if each one represents a child Mr Steinberg wishes he'd had.

Only a select few in the synagogue really understand Mr Steinberg – there's Mr and Mrs Herman, who came over to Birmingham from Poland just before the war; and Mr Silver, who used to live in London and still rations his sugar for fear a great war might come again. Congregants like these understand why Mr Steinberg insisted on etched windows not stained glass. The synagogue executive had wanted colourful art windows – like Chagall – but Mr Steinberg insisted otherwise. Those who understand him know that while he was busy in Normandy, his niece Rifka was supposed to be in hiding in Poland, waiting to come over to live by him. Only, after he'd finished fighting the Nazis, she'd disappeared. The people he wrote to responded that she'd never been there in the first place. He never did understand how a four-year-old girl with thick brown curls could just go missing when there had been a plan in place to keep her safe.

Those few congregants also have family who disappeared during the war. And so they all know that when Mr Steinberg made the windows, he made them so he could keep watching for his Rifka. There's always the chance that she will come walking by the shul. And he wants to make sure that she sees him when she does.

In the meantime, there is Eli who sits with her father behind Mr Steinberg and plays with her father's prayer-shawl tassels. She's a chatty three-year-old who, on Saturday mornings, can't stop herself from running up to the Torah to kiss it when it's time to bring it out of the Ark. She also has thick brown hair in curls piled on her little head and she wears dresses with wide skirts in navy blue and rose pink. Mr Steinberg keeps a bag of sweets beside his seat so that when she returns from greeting the Torah, he has a little something to give her. Once, she tried a sweet and promptly spat it out into her father's hand. The lemon drop was too sour for her young tongue. However, every time she comes back from the Torah she stops in front of Mr Steinberg, who puts a hard wrapper in her hand and then brushes his hand over her head.

'You are a good girl, Rifka,' he whispers to her, so quiet she barely hears him and has therefore never corrected him about her name. Somehow, Eli understands that this is the special name Mr Steinberg made up for her. Just like her father calls her 'sweetheart' and her mother calls her 'doll', Mr Steinberg calls her 'Rifka'. She believes her special name means 'the girl who receives sweets'.

Mr Steinberg knows better than to think Eli really *is* Rifka. It's just that his eyes and mind are at that stage when sometimes the past becomes the present. When he lies in bed during those cold December mornings, it isn't his dearly departed wife whom he thinks of, but his niece whose picture still sits protected in a copper frame, resting by the side of his bed, waiting for the day when maybe his memories will stop torturing him. He thinks, when he lies like this, of the letters he'd received from his sister over in Poland, and how the last one said Rifka had been sent to live with a nice Polish family until all this *tzuris* was over. He cringes his aching muscles remembering how his sister asked him to find Rifka after the war, in the event of the girl finding herself without immediate family. He reviews all his searching techniques, as if he's checking a map to determine whether he's missed a corner. And then, as the sun rises, he is always saddened to think he has tried everything and that maybe Rifka is still waiting, somewhere, to be found.

This week in December, he deliberately stays home from shul in the morning because he has business to get in order. A young woman, nice girl, not too loud, comes every morning to cook his meals and then washes up after him. She does his shopping too, takes him to Sainsbury's in Selly Oak where it's never too crowded on a Friday morning.

They have tea together in the little café by the vegetable section. The girl, Sian, has curly blond hair which she twists around her finger when he's talking to her.

'I found this one for you,' she tells him on Friday, as they sit drinking their tea, slowly because Mr Steinberg's hand shakes when he raises the cup to his lips. Sian reaches into her purse and pulls out a long, white Rackhams box.

'Eli's a bit young for it now, but it's something her parents could put away for her. Just like you said,' she tells him, as he lifts the cover. Inside is a dainty gold watch with a bangle strap. The clock face has Roman numerals, just as he'd wanted, with two tiny diamonds – one for the twelve and one for the six.

'Thank you,' he says, handing it back to her for safe-keeping. 'That's just fine.'

This week is the start of Chanukkah and Eli's family has invited Mr Steinberg for Shabbat dinner after services. He plans to walk home with Eli's father and the watch is a little something he'll give to the girl after the meal. He'll tell her mother to put it away for her until she grows old enough to wear it. He doesn't expect Eli to appreciate it now, but he does imagine her when she's older, maybe twelve, still with that lovely hair, slipping on the watch before shul, and looking grown-up despite her age. She will, he hopes, appreciate finer things once she gets a little older; a gift most young women these days don't possess, he laments. He fully anticipates that Eli will be different.

Later, at home, Sian helps him into his grey wool suit. He wants his grey waistcoat as well and his black fedora hat. He asks for his cane – and when she hands it to him, she asks if he wants her to accompany him to the synagogue.

'I'm well and fine enough to walk myself,' he tells her, maybe more harshly than he'd intended, but he hasn't, as yet, needed help walking to shul.

Mr Steinberg walks slowly out of Michael Court and

onto the Bristol Road where lights from passing cars whirl past him, people desperate to get home for the weekend. He uses his cane to steady himself along the pavement and waits by the kerb for a gap in the traffic so that he can cross over to Speedwell Road. The redbrick wall on the corner seems to flicker in the evening sun and Mr Steinberg catches himself thinking of fires and powerful heat strong enough to burn bricks. He moves quickly along the wall to Central, fearing, even in the cold, that the bricks are hot enough to burn him. And as he walks, his mind battles two sides: the side that knows such thoughts are irrational, and the side that thinks them anyway.

In the sanctuary, his mind quiets and he wills his cane to deliver him safely to his seat. The men around him seem to dance in their prayers, seem to sing out praises to the Almighty with more vigour than in the weeks before. Mr Steinberg, secure in his seat by the eastern wall, tries to join them, but finds that his mouth refuses. His tongue freezes and all he can do is watch the young rabbi lead the congregation in welcoming the Sabbath Bride, the Queen Day of Rest.

'*Bo'ee Kallah, bo'ee kallah . . .*'

Come here, my Bride, come here, my Bride, they beg aloud, a normally joyous melody that seems this week to scrape the inside of Mr Steinberg's ears. The joy is manic like a spinning top and the song of praise becomes pins pricking at his head. He shuts his eyes to stop all the clamour and then, just as he thinks he has himself settled, he opens them again only to see Rifka standing in front of him. She holds out her little hand for a sweet she won't eat and Mr Steinberg reaches to his side to fetch her a lemon drop.

It's then that he falls over, and it's Eli's father who first sees him fall. His sweets spill out around him and the watch, which he'd stuck in his pocket for Eli, bounces on the hardwood floor. He lies on his side, paralysed, while Eli's father speaks to his open eyes. *Doctor*, Mr Steinberg hears faintly; *help*, he hears as well. The room, which had once been spinning, is now still and very silent despite the commotion. All Mr Steinberg can think of, however, as he lies there, waiting, is of Rifka who'd been standing before him. He tries to speak but his lips won't move to allow his words through.

Eli is standing behind her father, her own dark eyes fixed on Mr Steinberg's frozen lips as if she knows he's trying to call her by her special name. They stare at each other until the ambulance comes. Eli wanting to ask for sweets. And Mr Steinberg trying to say, 'Rifka. For you I never stopped. Looking.'

I Was Told

David Hart

I was told clearly enough to change at Shrewsbury, but when I woke and asked the man opposite who was reading *Atonement*, he said we'd just left Wolverhampton. When we reached Birmingham the train was later than I wanted to know, and through the windows there'd long since been visible only the night lights. After wandering about the station not thinking at all clearly, I found myself in this alien city phoning the only person I knew.

I said, 'Is Richard there, please?'

'I'll fetch him. Who is it?'

'It's Mary. Mary, an old friend.'

Who was *she* then? Richard came to the phone. He said, 'Hello, who is it?'

'It's Mary.'

'Sorry?'

'You don't have to be sorry, you haven't done anything. Not recently, anyway. It's me, Mary. No?'

'Which Mary?'

'Oh for God's sake, Richard, it's me!'

There was silence; the penny had dropped.

It had been how many years now? – I didn't remember. Nor had I been caring. I hadn't been thinking about him. He was still in my little address book, battered though it was. And phoning him was obviously a big mistake. But if I'd simply put the receiver down – and it would have been such a simple thing to do – I knew I would have destroyed something that, although never quite secure, had been in some obscure way continuing, left unfinished.

He said, 'It's been a long time.'

'It has, and I'm sorry, I mean I'm sorry to be bothering you at this late hour. Or at all. But I'm stuck here at New Street Station, and –'

'Why?'

What sort of question was that? Did he want the story of the past however many years since we'd last seen each other? Did he want me to *explain*?

'Why?' he said again. 'Why are you stranded at the station?'

'I should be in Liverpool, that's why.'

'I don't understand.'

Had he always been this pedantic? I said, 'I fell asleep on the train and I'm now very tired, and –' And I stopped. Whatever had I imagined I was doing? I said, 'I'm sitting in a patch of bright sunlight on the beach at Ynyslas, there is no such thing as time, I shall eat my egg mayonnaise sandwich and go into a deep, deep sleep, for ever.'

He said, 'Mary, what do you want?'

'It's bloody obvious, isn't it?' Then immediately, as so often before, 'I'm sorry.'

'What?'

'What do you mean, "What?" I just need a bloody bed for the night.'

'Mary?'

What was this coming now? Oh, I remembered that so clearly, that 'Mary?', implying while not saying anything, running me into a corner, expecting me to be clear, CLEAR, for God's sake!

I began to say, 'Richard, listen –' till he interrupted me:

'I'm living with someone now, I mean someone who isn't you. You could go to a hotel, or a B&B.'

That 'someone who isn't you' wounded me: the sheer absurdity of his saying it. As if I didn't know she wasn't me. This was me, on the station concourse on the bloody phone, tired, hungry. And I'm not naturally a hotel or a B&B type.

'I could, yes. But I'm supposed to be in Liverpool.'

'What's that got to do with it?'

'It's got everything to do with it. I've a friend in Liverpool, called Josie, which is where I'd have been staying. Oh God, I haven't phoned her!'

'Mary?'

'Stop saying that.'

'I'm sorry.'

'Stop being bloody sorry!'

'Come here, Mary, if you really have nowhere else, but –'

The 'but' was huge, I knew it was. I left open the space anyway and he put his address in it. Not that I didn't know it: I'd half lived there for however long it was, seven or eight months, but the reminder of the address completed the invitation.

Outside the station, it wasn't the Birmingham I'd remembered.

The city had obviously been having fun knocking everything down and was now having fun building it up again. Open boxes into the sky, and St Martin's Church disappearing behind them. In this eerie, spotlit night, and the cranes lit and still. I admitted to myself, grudgingly, that there was something beautiful about it.

The taxi dropped me outside the house in Acocks Green. Richard opened the door a little, then a little more. He was nodding his head. He stood back and I went in.

He ushered me along the hallway and into the kitchen. A

woman was standing there in her nightie and dressing gown and slippers.

'This is Michelle. Mary.'

Our hands moved a little but were withdrawn again. I said, 'Hello.'

She said, 'I'm sorry you got lost.'

Richard said, 'You can use the spare room.'

'Thanks.'

'Coffee?'

I was starving hungry and coffee seemed at least a start, even as I was telling myself it didn't matter, I'd at least have a roof over my head and could get to Liverpool in the morning – and I hadn't phoned Josie. 'Can I phone my friend?'

Josie said the curry was still on the table, cold, so was the fruit salad, warm, so was the empty wine bottle, and that when the ten o'clock news had started she'd eaten her share.

I sat at the kitchen table with Richard and Michelle and drank the coffee. Such talk as there was came dragged on ropes along grit.

Michelle, after giving Richard a look, went upstairs to bed. He'd changed. Even at this time of night he was wearing a tie. And something had happened to his eyes, they were flatter.

'Any children?' I said.

He shook his head slowly.

'You've repainted.'

'The place needed it.'

'How's the work going?'

'Work? Oh, work. I'm in PR, at the ICC.'

I raised my eyebrows and he explained *ICC*. Conventions came and went, he said, call them conferences, assemblies, trade fairs, summits; he advised on Public Relations, shunted and honed the message, and gave it visual effect.

I said, 'Well, it's different.'

'Yes.'

'But creative.'

'It's just a job.'

'Not better than just a job?'

He shook his head slowly.

I said, 'What does Michelle do?'

'She's a writer.'

'Great!'

'Why?'

There'd been something askew in that 'She's a writer'. I looked at him through slit eyes. It was something I'd got into the habit of doing and he used to respond with wit, with fun. Now he looked away.

I didn't sleep well, but on and off drifted in and out of the shallower reaches of it and through some weird dreams. I woke early, left a thank you note and was out of the house and on a number 1 bus into town. I was at the top end of New Street, pedestrianized since I was last there, waiting outside what to me was the new café when it opened, nor had I seen the Iron Man. I touched him, and he told me to bugger off to Liverpool or back to Borth where I belong. I exaggerate, but not much.

It wasn't any use turning up at Josie's until late afternoon. She worked all day. The plan was: I'd spend a few nights with her, and while she was at work I'd go and look at what Richard Wright had been painting on the walls at the Tate and also I had a secret ambition to put something in that great well of a space in the Anglican Liverpool Cathedral. I was going to reconnoitre. So my plan now was to avoid the rush hour, spend a leisurely train journey to Liverpool asleep, then have a couple of hours in the gallery in the afternoon, before braving Josie.

The great stone woman at the head of the fountain reminded me I'd lost interest in losing weight. Queen Victoria told me to take Josie a gift a bit more munificent than the now-squashed herbs and mushrooms I was bringing from my little garden with its tiny greenhouse.

Josie is a picture restorer, we were friends at art college, I make collages and installations, am poor, she works at the Walker, has expertise and earns steady money.

I thought, buy her a book. But what book? And where?

But first of all, go to the Ikon, see what's on.

But before that, go to the new Waterhall.

But think again: this city was not where I'd intended to be; my time was limited; I was hungry – no, *very* hungry – and did I have the energy? No, I didn't. Did I care what was on where? Well, maybe I did, maybe I didn't.

In the Waterhall I was soon asking myself, 'Why did I give up painting?' And I was replying, 'I gave up painting, dear, because I'm a frustrated car mechanic.' But that wasn't quite true, I told myself, what I should have been was a *boat* mechanic. There wasn't much call for them these days, and anyway I was thirty-five at least before I named it. So I was kidding myself to think I could have been a painter – but to do it like Shani Rhys-James, wouldn't that have been something?

At the Ikon, Braco Dimitrijevic's serious fun with some great pictures made me laugh and cry. Here was the tiny painting I'd never seen in the flesh, Van Gogh's wonderful *Old Woman Digging Potatoes*, perched now in a cart loaded with them, and trails of real potatoes across the floor. And here was a drawing by Ferrari I'd never seen: the Madonna and child with Mary Magdalene and a bishop, whose name long gone, is poking his head between them: the draughtsmanship magical, and slap in front of it on a ledge, a soup urn and an onion. I was happy.

*

In Paradise Forum – a whimsy of a place if ever there was one, with classical statues made, I shouldn't wonder, of chewing gum – I bought a big filled baguette and ate it walking down New Street.

Into one Waterstone's, then the other: I felt like dancing. Borth doesn't have quite these kinds of bookshops, these theme parks of books, these book palaces. Aber has its bookshops, but they're just token gestures compared to these. So it was up and down in the lift, looking out to the great building site and along New Street, and then a determined movement towards Art on the fourth floor.

Books! Books! Books! There was a feast here and soon I forgot what I was trying to do: choose a book for Josie that I could afford. Then I remembered and chose Botticelli, then I forgot again and found myself browsing in Chagall. I sat with him on one of the easy chairs and was woken by someone dropping a large book near by, on purpose or not I wasn't sure. Had I been snoring? Probably.

The anticipated pleasure of handing over a really nice book to Josie returned; I found medieval tapestries and put Botticelli back. Then put the tapestries back when I found Piero Della Francesca, whispering his name to myself over and over, my voice then transposing into Josie's. She'd like it. So, regardless of expense, I took this one to the counter.

When I'd paid for it, I went down a floor and heard someone call out, 'Michelle?' I looked around. And there she was. The other assistant addressed her as she arrived from across the room: 'I'm trying to help this gentleman remember the name of the author of a book on the Holy Land.' Michelle took a deep breath then, and as she thought about it, she caught my eye. She said immediately to her colleague, 'No, I'm sorry, look it up under titles,' and turned away.

My first impulse was to turn away too, but something else running counter to that sent me towards her. I caught up with her when she stopped at a table and started tidying some books that didn't need tidying. I said, 'Nice place to work. Thanks for the hospitality. Sorry, I –'

'It's okay.'

'So you sell books.'

'Looks like it.'

I didn't know if I liked her or not. But we had Richard in common, she had that ache about her, and something made me say, 'Can we have coffee?'

'I'm working.'

I looked at my watch. 'Christ! I'm supposed to be on a train. It's worse than that, I should have been in Liverpool by now. Well –' I slowed down again '– so long as I get to Josie's for supper.'

'Well, have a good journey.' She hadn't even turned round.

'This is getting crazy. I'd like coffee.'

She turned round. 'I'm busy, really.'

'Don't you get breaks?'

She had words with her colleague and said to me, 'First floor.'

So we sat in Coffee Republic drinking flavoured espressos and we both really wanted to talk. About Richard.

By the time she went off sick at about five we'd still only skirted around whatever it was that we knew mattered and was there somewhere to be talked about. We'd agreed how sad it was that Richard had given up photography, on which he'd embarked as a promising professional; how sad it was they didn't have children ('He doesn't want them'); and then I said, 'Richard told me you're a writer.'

'You didn't detect the irony?'

'I did. But are you?'

'I'm a writer like a cow lays eggs.'

We were standing outside the Pavilions now, within

what for me was loudness beyond reason coming out of HMV. I'm used to waves breaking on the sand. I said, 'Where can we go?' We found a pub, but it had no quiet space, so we found another.

'What do you write? What do you want to write?'

'Stories: shorter ones, longer ones. The longer ones are hypothetical, so are most of the short ones. But they're there, waiting, they are, I know they are.'

'Richard doesn't approve?'

'They're not money-spinners.'

'Nor were my collages and installations, especially the ones that only cluttered up the lounge and the garden and never saw a gallery, and the ones I could only dream of making.'

'You left him?'

'He says that?'

'No. He says he gave you the push, but I've never felt it rang true.'

'His photos were starting to get noticed.'

'But photography wasn't safe enough.'

'We neither of us had any money.'

'Why did you leave?'

I looked at my watch. Josie at that very moment was probably just arriving at Church Street, expecting me to be there within, say, half an hour. 'I've got to go.'

'Not yet, don't go yet.'

'Michelle, one missed supper might be put down to mere folly, but to miss two.'

'I don't want to go home.'

It must have been ten o'clock when we rolled out into Birmingham's Christmas lights. She was saying, 'It's agreed then, Mary, I'll come and stay with you by the sea,' and I was saying, 'Michelle, I live in the smallest house, I'm a bastard to live with, I need my solitude,' and she was saying, 'I'll find a room,' and I was saying, 'Better you think about this sober,' and she was saying, 'Sober doesn't work for me.'

I phoned Josie from a box. She said, 'Supper has been on the table these three hours, three and a half. I opened the rosé and have drunk it, and I ate my share of the food an hour and a half ago. Do you exist or have I imagined you?'

We walked about the city centre, finding warmish doorways and such other spaces as gave us some degree of draught-free, standing-up sleep. One man tried to pick us up, till I blew a kiss at Michelle; another gave me fifty pence and wished us a *Happy Christmas*. We found a night bus and travelled the whole route both ways, and eventually a greyish sun showed itself and we went to the station and caught the first through-train.

I am writing this at my little table. Through the window I can see the great sweep of the sand. On the settee, Michelle is composing her letter to Richard. My card to Josie needs only a first class stamp. Mrs Roberts-Ellis, the retired lieder singer, just over the hill, will lend us a sofa bed if we can get it over here. Bryn at the beach shop has a van. Piero Della Francesca is open at his *Discovery and Proof of the True Cross*. I say, 'I'll put the kettle on.'

King of the Baltis

M. Idrees Kayani

'I feel like curry tonight, like curry tonight!' chanted Finsid Qyini, as he danced around the kitchen, one hand stuffed up a chicken, the other holding a wooden spoon-cum-microphone. His eyes closed, he glided across the grease-stained floor, imagining he was John Travolta strutting his stuff, except that this wasn't Saturday night, this wasn't Brooklyn, New York, but the Balti Paradise, Sparkhill, and he couldn't sing or dance to save his life.

Apart from these minor details, the only similarity between Finsid and his hero was that he owned a white polyester suit with flared trousers, bought for three hundred rupees (about seven pounds fifty) at a market stall in Lala Musa. A suit, he boasted, that Amitabh Bachchan had worn in his classic Bollywood films of the late seventies and one which he hoped would bring him luck in the prestigious Balti Chef of Birmingham contest, which was taking place the following night.

Finsid had been waiting for the contest all year, and he knew that the next twenty-four hours would change his life. He was faced with two simple outcomes: victory would mean a winner's prize of a hundred pounds and a ten per cent discount for a holiday to Pakistan, courtesy of Uncle Travels (as long as it was in the off-season); secure his promotion to Head Chef in any balti restaurant in town; give him a hefty pay rise (taking him up to the minimum wage); and the constant praise and recognition that comes with being the finest balti chef around.

Defeat in the contest would mean a quick trip back home to Jhelum, Pakistan, and marriage to Marvi, his mother's auntie's husband's niece, whom he'd jokingly promised his grandmother he would marry unless she had some hideous deformity. He now reflected on his rather cavalier attitude and wished he hadn't been so flippant. He was willing to marry her, but the fact that she was still only seventeen whereas he'd just turned thirty worried him. He wanted her to grow up a bit so that she'd be better equipped for life in a big, bustling city like Birmingham, which was a million miles away from Mona Pind, a sleepy farming village in the heart of the Punjab, where the highlight of the year was a festival where water buffalo were electrocuted up the rear to shock them into running around a well for two minutes, so as to determine which was the region's fastest buffalo.

As Finsid pondered his predicament, his arch-rival, Tariq Butt, a large, bearded man in a brown knitted jumper and sandals, waltzed into the kitchen with a tray full of pakoras and samosas singing, 'Everybody was Balti cookin, man, his curries were fried by lightnin, it was a little bit frightenin, yeah, everybody was Balti cookin . . .'

'Bloody hell, Tariq, put a sock in it. I'm trying to work here.'

'What you, Mr Qyini, laziest bugger in the whole world, are you telling me you're actually lifting one of your bony fingers to do some work instead of using it to scratch your behind? Please don't make me laugh, I might never recover.'

'Oh, Tariq, such wit for a man blessed with a face that could grate cheese, an arse wide enough to block the M6 and body odour that if left unchecked could wipe out all life as we know it. You just have to accept the fact that you really are a complete *uloo*. A fact which, come tomorrow night, the whole world will know when you receive a big fat loser's cheque and a one-way ticket to Loserville.'

'My foolish friend, such big dreams for someone so puny. I'll tell you once again that dreams alone can't buy you a house, a fancy car or provide for your family. Hard work, the kind that makes you sweat at the thought of it, only that can help you succeed in this country. I should know, I've been here over thirty years now, working all day and night while you were still crawling on your hands and knees and pissing into a potty.'

'Spare us the lecture, Granddad,' said Finsid. 'Just because you have less hair on your head than I have up my nostrils, doesn't grant you permission to do an Uncle Albert and bore us to death with your old war stories. The simple fact is that you had your chance and you blew it, so it's about time you made way for Finsid Qyini, the new Balti King. The King is dead, long live the King!'

And with that, Finsid leaped onto the cutting table in the corner of the kitchen, normally reserved for slicing up meat, and started flinging giblets and sheep entrails at Tariq, while shouting, 'The Balti King is dead, long live the Balti King! Finsid, the Finster, the *Bathshah*, the Balti Man, the Lord of the Baltis!'

Tariq responded by throwing his pakoras and samosas at him, but to no avail – he was being pelted by gall bladders and gizzards, which bounced off his head or exploded onto his body, staining his apron with bile and urine, soaking it with their pungent stench, which was extremely difficult to remove, even with Daz, Mr Muscle or Tipp-Ex.

'You bloody *pendu*! I'm going to report you to Mr Moghal and he'll sack you today. I can promise you that. He's from my village in Pakistan, he'll kick your bloody head in!'

Finsid knew that Tariq and the owner were indeed very close, and he decided that he'd better scarper and lie low for a while, in the hope that Tariq would eventually calm down and forget about blabbering off to Mr Moghal. He jumped off the meat table, threw his apron into the clothes basket and rushed out the back door directly onto the road where his Toyota Corolla was parked. He drove round to his best friend's house, turned off his mobile and jumped straight into bed, praying he hadn't blown his only chance of making something of his life.

Finsid turned out the light and dreamed about baltis and giblets, Tariq and samosas, Marvi and buffalo, his white suit . . .

'Wake up, you lazy boy! Wake up, *oot oot, jaldi jaldi*, get up quick!'

Finsid's eyes, stuck together with purified ghee as much as sleep juice, struggled to see who it was who was shouting at him. Scratching his face, he sat up and let out an almighty yawn, which at first lifted his body and roused his spirit, only for his aura to climb back in and seek comfort in the warmth of his Sleepezee bed.

'Get up, you bloody layabout! Can't sleep all day, time to get up and work. Don't you know you have the contest today? If you don't win, I pack your white suit into your bag, book your flight to Lahore and make sure you have lovely *shathee* with Marvi. Ha, that will teach you who is boss in this family!'

Finsid's dear mother had walked across the road to his friend's house, knowing full well that's where he hid whenever he was in trouble. She was there to pester and annoy him, ensuring the worst possible start to his day.

'Ammi-ji, please don't open the curtains. My head, it's really killing me, Mom.'

As Finsid begged, a ray of bright sunlight blasted its way

through the smoke-filled room, scattering tiny sunbeams along the dust trails as they danced across the haze.

'Don't give me that, up you get! I'm still your amma; I can spank your bottom anytime I want. I don't care how old you are, you stop being naughty boy and start behaving and listening to your amma and abbu.'

'Mum, what time is it? I've got the contest today. I need to get ready if that isn't too much to ask.'

'Time, you ask me the time? Where your *gurree* that I bought for you, where your new watch?'

'Look, Ammi-ji, we'll have this conversation later. Right at this moment I don't give a monkey's toss about anything but the contest.'

'What are you talking about, *munkies*? You make fun of me? Get out of bed or I give you a *thapur* across your face.'

Finsid saw his mother advance towards him, her hand held high, and he knew that she meant business. A mother of six, including three six-foot tall sons: no one could lay down the law quite like Ammi. As Finsid ran towards the bathroom, she smiled subtly, indicating her delight at how she could still scare the living daylights out of her son, despite being more than a foot shorter than him.

On his way to the contest venue, the Black Diamond Suite in Sparkbrook, Finsid glanced at the dashboard and saw that it was nearly two fifty. The contest began at three on the dot, and this year the judges had decided that if anyone was even a minute late they'd be immediately disqualified. This was because all the contestants were Asian men – generally regarded as the worst time-keepers in the world since records began (except for Asian women, that is) – and because of a fiasco last year when half the chefs turned up an hour late owing to extended play in the Test Match between England and Pakistan.

With this in mind, Finsid decided to dispense with the Highway Code (not that he had a licence, having been banned a month ago for having no MOT, tax or motor insurance), and to drive like a true taxi driver, swerving like a maniac with one hand on the steering wheel and the other hanging out the window. Knowing the back ways like he did, Finsid weaved in and out of identical streets lined with dilapidated terraces, before hitting the main road in fifth gear – taking his Toyota Corolla through the sound barrier in fast and furious, burning-rubber style. He handbrake-turned onto the Ladypool Road at two fifty-nine, parked the car directly in front of the entrance to the Black Diamond and scrambled inside, with his apron on back to front and a hole in his carrier bag, which was leaving a trail of Tilda basmati rice in his wake. He looked up and saw the clock strike three. Perfect, he thought.

'Ah, you must be Mr Tinsud Yqini. I do hope that I pronounced that right. You appear to be our final contestant. Last but not least!'

Finsid shook hands with the Lord Mayor of Birmingham, who had more ceremonial gold chains around his neck than Mr T. He looked around the vast room and caught sight of all the usual suspects. A motley crew of council officials, the same ones who shook hands with the restaurant owners today, but if the council coffers were running low, would send in the public health officials to inspect the restaurants, only to discover rat droppings in the very premises they'd praised earlier. They'd then either issue huge fines or take some of the back-handers that came with the territory when dealing with Indian restaurants, notorious for paying cash-in-hand, employing illegal immigrants and sidestepping details such as income tax and VAT.

Next to the councillors were upstanding members of the local Asian community, in their best suits and ties, trying hard to assimilate with their Anglo-Saxon counterparts, except that their kipper ties, striped socks, slip-on loafers and tight-fitting suits (designed by Georgie Armani, Johnny Versace and Guccy) could've been the same ones they'd been wearing when they arrived in England over thirty years ago. Their hairstyles – classic side-partings smeared down with Brylcreem and hair tonic – hadn't changed much either, apart from the obvious thinning on top and the liberal use of black hair dye. And the final bunch of cronies were those who attended events where they could freely scrounge whatever was going: in this instance, balti curries made by some of the finest chefs in the country.

Once Finsid had surveyed who, establishment-wise, was present, he made his way to the cooking tables, which had been lined up in two neat rows with five tables in each row. The nine other chefs looked at him and acknowledged his presence. He knew all of them. Some, like Kamal Boora, were old friends he'd worked with before. Kamal had studied with him at Birmingham College of Food, where they'd spent most of their time taking the piss out of English food and misleading fellow students as to the methodology behind creating the perfect curry. (The ideal balti dish does *not* consist of a whole clove of garlic, four pounds of butter, several green chilli peppers and a solitary leg of chicken!)

Finsid shook his fist towards Kam and shouted, '*Kiddah!* Kam's the man with the secret under his turban, his knife in his pocket and cooking genius in his fingertips! Good luck but remember, my boss can take your guru, anytime, anyplace!'

Kam smiled and jokingly withdrew his kirpan and put it to his neck, making out he was going to slice up Finsid, good and proper. This gesture provoked an angry response from one of the judges who shouted out from the back,

'There's simply no need for that kind of behaviour. I have to inform you that you must abide by the rules if you want to participate in this contest. This is a matter of utmost seriousness.'

'Hey, mate, what you talkin about? We just makin a curry, right, not going to sit a bloody exam or elect a new government. You *goreh lohg*, you have no sense of fun, know what I mean? Just keep your underpants on, man, take it easy and chill out,' said Ghulam Mustafa. Ghulam was probably the hardest chef in Birmingham: on several occasions he'd chopped drunken lager louts to bits with his trusty meat cleaver, Ali, which he polished every day and even took to bed with him on the off-chance that some of his victims would try to get him to return their hacked-off body parts. Which was highly unlikely because Ghulam had made a curry out of them all, which he'd then personally served to the West Midlands Police Force at their annual dinner dance!

Finsid arrived at his designated table and, to his dismay, found himself next to Tariq, who was fastidiously testing the gas burner and hot plates, ensuring that everything was in good working order. Finsid began whispering to himself, 'Two hours next to Butt Man . . . I'd rather take my pick from Thatcher, Stalin or Hitler, at least they'd talk instead of sing, although it's been said that old Stalin could belt out a decent Bolshevik tune when the mood took him. Anything would be better listening to Tariq, the old fart.'

While Finsid was mumbling to himself, the chief organizer of the contest, millionaire businessman Mr Raja Suleiman, stood up on stage and began his address.

'My dear lords, ladies and gentlemen, I am pleased to announce that the Tenth Balti Chef of Birmingham Contest is taking place today in the heart of Birmingham, a great and magnificent city that is the pride of Britain. This part of Birmingham has been coined "The Balti Belt", a belt which has been stretching and expanding several notches each year, no doubt due to all the wonderful restaurants that cater for all tastes and varieties. I'm convinced that it will burst quite soon, probably as a result of the many delicious curries that have been eaten by our punters over the years!'

Mr Suleiman stroked his moustache and grinned widely, waiting for his opening remarks to arouse some mirth among the audience. Alas, no one stirred; there wasn't even a chuckle, just a few silent nods of the head and a coughing fit from Mr Nazir, also known as 'Benny' on account of his sixty Benson & Hedges a day habit. Mr Suleiman shuffled nervously back and forth on the podium and wiped away beads of sweat with his handkerchief.

'Today, for the first time in its history, the contest will be judged not only on the quality of the chef's cooking, but also on their entertainment factor. In a world where chefs on television have become household names, we believe that it's time that we had a balti chef on television. Taking a leaf out of the Bollywood recipe book, we could have chefs who entertain the audience with a song and dance, as well as educating the public at home about South Asian culture and discussing how meal times are an essential part of Asian family life. This melting pot of ideas is designed to create the perfect atmosphere for making a curry.'

'What he bloody talking about? He makin no sense to me at all. I come here to cook curry, not listen to speech about Bollywood or other rubbish,' said Sultan Hijab, an experienced old-timer who was cooking curries when no one else even knew what they were.

It was clear to Finsid that simmering tensions were lying just beneath the surface, which threatened to spill over if the proceedings weren't conducted in the right manner. There were open hostilities, not just among the contestants, but also between the organizers and the judges, who'd had a blistering row before the event. The argument had centred on the individual requests of the chefs, who each wanted to perform some kind of special ceremony commemorating their respective beliefs.

The Hindu chef Vikram Patel wanted to bring in a statue of Hanuman, the monkey god, Ganesh and Lakshmi, as well as sprinkling holy urine from a sacred cow over his table. This was deemed unhygienic by the Public Health Inspector, and aroused strong opposition from the Muslim chefs, who said that if Mr Patel wanted to worship animals, then why didn't he just visit Dudley Zoo.

The five Pakistani chefs requested the ritual slaughter of a cow, a sheep, a goat and some chickens, to which the Public Health Inspector replied that it was illegal to perform that ritual on unlicensed premises and to which Mr Patel riposted that if the chefs wanted to slaughter animals, then why didn't they just visit a local farm. All this caused an absolute furore and sparked up a rowdy debate on Kashmir, with the various chefs being warned to calm down or risk elimination from the contest.

The two Sikh chefs, Kamal Boora and Jarnail Singh, each wanted to wear their full-length ceremonial swords, claiming it was their religious right to do so. This was taken up with the Chief Inspector, who ruled against the idea because of violence at past events of this kind. The smaller kirpan or dagger was permissible, as long as it didn't extend beyond a certain length, to be checked on entry into the hall.

The final two Bengali chefs insisted on cooking a special Bengali meal, for which the principal ingredients could only be found in a remote part of Bangladesh. They wanted the council to pay for their flights and this was agreed, because of the multicultural nature of the event, until it was discovered that all they required was fish and rice and that the remote area they wanted to visit just so happened to be their own villages. The council decided not to pursue a case of fraud against them, as long as they promised not to make such requests again.

Mr Suleiman continued his speech, despite the incessant background bickering. 'That just leaves me to say a few final words thanking the many benefactors that have contributed to the success of this event. As you know, the contest is being kindly sponsored by some of our city's finest companies.'

Finsid looked up at the banner hanging above the stage and read to himself the various messages:

'UNCLE TRAVELS: WHERE EAST MEETS WEST. ALL OUR PRICES IS THE BEST — SO IF YOU NEED GOOD REST TO GET SOME ZEST — CALL UNCLE TRAVELS — WE ARE BEST!'

'BATA FASHIONS —LATEST IMPORT GOODS DIRECT FROM INDIA & PAKISTAN. TOP QUALITY ITEMS AT VERY KINDLY PRICES — EVERYTHING FROM BATA CHAPPALS TO JINNAH HATS. WE FULLY EXCEPT INDIAN & PAKISTANI RUPEES'

'DJ POWERZ: THE FIERZEST DJ IN SOUTH BIRMINGHAM! TOP DEX AND SOUND SYSTEM — BHANGRA & RAGGA & HIP-HOP & SOUL & SWINGBEAT — ALL MUSIK STYLES. I KEEPZ IT REAL — PEACE OUT — DJ POWERZ'

'MALIK DEATH SERVICES — FOR SAD TIME WE TAKE CARE OF YOUR GRIEF AND PAIN. BURIALS ONLY: SORRY NO BURNING OF BODIES'

'ASALAAMOLAIKUM — NAMESTHE — SUSRIKAA. THANK YOU FROM THE CITY OF BIRMINGHAM COUNSELL'

Mr Raja Suleiman finished off his speech by cursing Brick Lane in the East End, Wilmslow Road in Manchester (known as 'The Golden Mile'), the whole of Bradford (especially Lumb Lane and Manningham), Ilford and Southall in London. He vehemently criticized all these places as substandard, lacking in class and sophistication, and being unable to fully satisfy the needs of the local community in providing a safe environment in which to go out for a curry.

'Yeah, right, Ladypool Road, the Las Vegas capital of curries! Ladypool Road, also known as "Laid-a-stool-in-road" for obvious reasons because of what a curry can do to your stomach. In fact, that's why they are called baltis – not because they're cooked in a bucket, but because you need one next to your bed in case you can't make it to the bog in time!'

A chorus of laughter erupted from all those present, to which Mazar Khan raised his hands and bowed in courtesy. Mazar, often known as 'Mad' Mazar, because he worked fifteen hours a day, six days a week, just so he could build an elaborate mansion in his hometown of Mirpur, a place that he hoped never to see again. The reason for constructing such a building was so his relatives could marvel at its size and comment on how well he was doing in England!

Seeing the judges make their way to his table, Finsid sensed that now was the moment of truth. He tried to psyche himself up, but no matter how hard he tried the same old sinking feeling in the pit of his stomach kept returning. He'd gone to the chemist's earlier and washed down Lemsip 'Max' tablets with a glass of Enos, but this hadn't had the desired effect. Deep down, he knew the cause of his anxiety was that he had more to lose than anyone else out there and that perhaps he wasn't cut out for this kind of contest. The image of himself in a small village, surrounded by buffalo dung, dressed in his white polyester suit and married to a teenage girl with nothing to offer her except a lowly income and some chicken jalfrezi kept whirring away, round and round inside his head. Finsid knew that he couldn't last another week with Tariq, especially after what had happened yesterday. No, Finsid was determined to give it his best shot and would put his heart and soul into his cooking and musical performance, even if it meant looking like a complete *kothah* in the process.

The contest was spread over two hours, with each chef individually judged for ten minutes. The chef had to do a musical number of his choice while cooking at the same time. Finsid had kept his choice top secret from everyone, even Kam, because all ties, bonds, friendships and even enmities were temporarily suspended during the contest.

As the judges had started with 'Mad' Mazar first, Finsid calculated that he'd be the penultimate chef to be judged on artistic merit and musical performance. Therefore, he decided to prepare as much as he could before it came to his turn to perform. His speciality was going to be numkeen chaval – brown rice; kofteh aloo – meatballs and potatoes; daal – lentil soup; sheesh kebab – minced and spiced meat; muchli tikka – flaked fishcakes; mutter keema – mince curry with peas; and tandoori chooza – chicken cooked in a tandoor with yoghurt and spices. For dessert there was gulab jaman – fried semolina balls in syrup, and kheer – rice pudding. He'd based this menu on a combination of his own favourite dishes and those that were thought of as standards, such as tandoori chooza and sheesh kebabs.

Finsid got cracking with his cooking while 'Mad' Mazar was living up to his moniker by doing Govinda dance routines, a hyperactive Bollywood actor renowned for hectic musical performances. While dancing was a fulltime job for Govinda, it most certainly wasn't for Mazar, who at fifty was way past his prime and an angina victim if there ever was one. He ended his set by collapsing onto the table, setting fire to his apron and rolling onto the floor, prompting the Lord Mayor to take off his robe to smother the flames!

Sorry, Mazar, old bean, but that's one down and only eight more to go, thought Finsid as he saw the palaver unfold. This kind of shambles was commonplace and one to which all those associated with the contest had become accustomed.

Next up was Kam Boora, wearing a bright green robe encrusted with imitation rubies, and bouncing to the rhythm of dhol and tabla drums blasting through the loudspeakers. He leaped onto his table and let out a thunderous '*Kiddah, teek ho meereh Baaioo!*'

Kam then started belting out numbers by the world's greatest Bhangra star, Daler Mehndi. Seeing Kam shimmying and raising his arms aloft was a sight that Finsid had seen many times before, but not in such surreal circumstances. All Finsid could hear was jumbled up Punjabi words: '*Tunak tunak tunak tunak tunak tunak tun tun tun*' and '*Dardi rab rab kardi rab rab!*'

Meanwhile, Tariq was cooking away, totally focused on the task in hand. Finsid was aware that Tariq had been practising his performance for months and that he could easily win over the judges with his greasy charm. Although he was normally a reasonable kind of guy, Finsid felt that Tariq didn't deserve to be awarded the title of Balti Chef of Birmingham because he wouldn't be a good ambassador for the culinary art and he didn't really require the hundred pounds because he never spent money on anything other than woollen sweaters and boxes of Indian sweets. Finsid decided that the best way to sabotage Tariq's effort was to pretend to run out of salt. Tariq would naturally ask for payment in return for some salt, but before returning the salt pot, Finsid would replace it with sugar. Tariq, thinking he was putting salt into his curry, would in fact be emptying in loads of sickly sugar, thus sweetening up his savouries and ruining his chances of winning.

With his plan set in motion, Finsid only had to wait for

the judges to listen to his performance of a selection of Amitabh Bachchan's legendary *ghazals*, especially the sublime 'Kabhi Kabhi', for him to sweep up and collect first prize. Changing into his white suit, he was overcome with emotion. Perhaps tonight was the night his dreams would come true. As Finsid clapped along to the music and raised his hands high in the air à la Amitabh, he could see the judges smile and jot down notes about his various dishes. While he was doing high kicks and flipping chapattis and naan bread into the air, he saw his mother come into the hall. She was greeted by the Lord Mayor's wife and escorted to a table close to the podium, where the prize ceremony would take place.

'Oh, what have I done to deserve this? I bet she's got a one-way ticket to Pakistan, leaving tonight, in her coat pocket and she can't wait to stick it up my nose when it's announced that I'm not the winner,' murmured Finsid, desperate to maintain his composure now his routine was finished.

Downhearted, he slumped into his chair and pretended he was anywhere but here, where a rotund, bald man was currently trying to convince the judges that he was indeed a disco king, with the voice of a nightingale, able to juggle onion bhajis, poppadoms and samosas without any of them breaking. These ridiculous surroundings further heightened Finsid's sense that he'd lost, to the point where he even considered leaving before the winner had been announced.

As the judges convened to make their decision, his mother frantically waved a white piece of paper in Finsid's direction. Then the chefs gathered themselves up onto the stage to await the final verdict, and Finsid looked up high into the ceiling vaults, almost as if for salvation, for one more chance: anything as long as it was good news. He glanced across at Tariq, who had a smug grin all over his oily face, but even the knowledge that he'd sabotaged his annoying colleague's chances of winning failed to raise his spirits.

The chief judge had just begun his speech when a piece of paper suddenly landed at Finsid's feet. He looked out into the audience to see where it'd come from and saw his mother, now sitting beside his family and friends, beaming proudly and pointing at him, urging him to read what it said. Slightly bemused by her request at such a critical juncture, he read the following message:

'Finsid Qyini: We think YOU are King of the Baltis!'

A warm glow filled him and he felt almost moved to tears. As the judge read out the name of the winner, Finsid stood numb and transfixed, unable to take in what was going on around him. He was absorbing the bombshell that it no longer mattered if he won or lost. All that was important was that he stayed true to himself and considered how fortunate he was to have such loving family and friends. Comforted by his ammi-ji's message, he put the note into his pocket and watched Kamraan Khan – 'the new Jamie Oliver of Asian cuisine' – receive the winner's trophy from a plump, moustachioed third-rate Asian celebrity. As Tariq squealed with disbelief at the result, Finsid looked up towards the ceiling and mouthed a silent 'thank you'. After all, he did deserve something to go his way!

The Magician's Scarf

Laura McFall

There are days when it's too grey to notice anything; days when the tops of buildings disappear into ambivalence; days when nature gives up trying. But that Friday wasn't just another winter day. Through the morning's musty blackness, the sun was rising in a surround of buttercup yellow, and the air was fresh and exhilarating. Rubel Rana didn't notice. He kept his head down and walked like an automaton towards the bus stop. He rarely had to wait long for the bus, but if he did, his shoulders would tighten and he'd chew the inside of his mouth while glowering at the road ahead.

Most mornings, the people at the bus stop were the same. There was a young man who always wore an orange jacket, even in the middle of summer. His hair was carefully combed and through his headphones you could hear the milky tones of a woman singing the faraway, lonesome blues. There was the old man with no hair or teeth. His legs were as thin as a bird's, but he never sat down. Even when there was a seat free on the bus shelter's plastic bench, he never sat down.

Sometimes there were other people: the woman with her empty pram who always seemed to be clutching a paper bag, the man whose face was masked with piercings, the young girl in a Superdrug uniform whose auburn hair was scraped back into a disciplined bun. And at the weekend there were others: carers going to visit patients; actors new to the city trying to find their way to an unheated church hall where they'd sip black coffee and rehearse for a seasonal show; old ladies going to get their hair washed and set, to fulfil a vision of themselves from the past. A whole library of worlds and stories gathered around him every morning. But Rubel never noticed them. He never noticed anything, except for the ugly and the mundane.

When the bus drew up, its windows were steamed to the top so it looked like a travelling Turkish bath. He climbed on board and showed his pass, picked up a copy of yesterday's *Metro* and turned through the pages, then threw it onto the seat beside him. He wiped the condensation from the bus window with his black woollen glove and sat half looking at the world outside.

Sparkbrook. The Stratford Road. To a visitor, an outsider, it enclosed an entire repertoire of paradox and atmosphere. The halal butchers, the deserted old shops boarded over and covered with political graffiti, the stretch of dead lawn on the corner of Erasmus Road, the Probation Office, the boxing club at St Agatha's Church, the cheap eateries serving Pakistani, Moroccan and Somali food. To a photographer it would be a playground. To Rubel, it was just another road. He shut his eyes to make the world disappear; only it didn't. It left its murky residue in the quiet surround of his mind.

He got to the marketplace just after eight o'clock. Most vendors already had their stalls in place. Some were just pulling up in vans and unpacking plantains and yams out of cardboard boxes. Soon the entire market would be thriving, all the produce unpacked and displayed, opening itself out like a pop-up book into a three-dimensional world of chaos and variety. The bells of St Martin's rang out. Their felicitous sound bouncing off the immense mass of Bull Ring rust, while a sky of cranes moved around it like a giant protective claw. There was a smell of fried onions and cheap coffee, and the wet ground was already spotted with newspaper and polystyrene. Rubel bought a puddle-coloured cup of tea from the burger van, something he did practically every morning of his life, then he walked through to the indoor area to erect his stall.

Fabric. He'd never had much time for it. Although he loved the way the word sounded. He liked playing with the word when people asked him what he sold. He thought it sounded comedic, almost absurd, but in reality he thought it was bulky stuff, awkward to manoeuvre and difficult to cut. He envied the other market traders who had simple nifty objects on their stalls like pixie boots, wigs and lipsticks.

Every morning he had to untie the various rolls from their blue tarpaulin covers and stack them into accessible piles on the front of his stall. He dumped the cheap rolls in old plastic bins. The expensive fabrics – the bridal silks and velvets – he pinned up so that people could see them as they wandered around the market. Apart from this, he had no grouping system. The cottons were jumbled up with the linings, taffetas and sequin sheets. There were other fabric vendors who made significantly greater efforts, and their stalls were far busier, but it didn't really bother Rubel. He had no drive to make lots of money. He had no drive for anything, getting through the day was a big enough challenge for him.

On the other side of the city, Nesta McEwan sat in her tutor's study without hearing a word he was saying. It was the penultimate term of her degree course and she was running out of steam, winding down like a battery toy after Christmas. Although diligent up to now, she no longer seemed bothered about it all: she was exhausted. She wanted to be part of a world that wasn't driven by passes, fails and marks for originality. She didn't feel like a student any more. She'd grown tired of her hectic house-share and longed to find a studio on the canalside and throw chunks of old bread at the ducks. She looked around the room. Her tutor was delivering a sermon on the influence of modern art in British fashion. He made no attempt to look her in the eye. He was more occupied with his cacti collection that lay beneath the window. She started to wonder about his mild obsession with the accumulation of objects. There was a tray of yo-yos on his desk, and on the shelf a shoebox full of old springs. That was far more intriguing to her: the mysteries of mind that can't be communicated or touched.

He sensed her distraction and then asked with sudden force: 'Your ideas on the final project, Miss McEwan. What are they?'

Nesta smirked, which was something she'd never ordinarily have done, but she was feeling fatalistic about everything now, and tired of playing student-in-awe-of-big-important-tutor games.

'They're non-existent,' she said with emphasis.

Duncan Goodwin slowly raised one of his apricot-coloured eyebrows. She returned his look, offering no retraction. Conscious of her thin neck rising out of her embroidered shirt, she felt like a new queen adjusting to the practice of power.

'Well, you'd better think of something pretty quickly, hadn't you? Ideas have to be submitted next week.'

She slapped her folder shut and stuffed it into her bag. At the door, she turned to him and said, 'Thank you for your time, Mr Goodwin. I'm sure it has been of benefit to us both.'

On the other side of the door she leaned back against it

and smiled. There was something pushing out of her that she didn't recognize, a sudden confidence, a certain voice. She imagined Goodwin's face on the other side of the door. Incredulous. Perhaps embarrassed, and almost certainly confused.

Later that day, Nesta walked to the Ikon to find some ideas for her final project. The assignment was simply to 'design a garment of your choice'. The freedom it allowed her left her imagination still and dark, like night consciousness. A January drizzle began to fall on Broad Street. Not heavy enough to warrant an umbrella, but not light enough to ignore. It fell softly into her face and stuck there like gluey porridge on the roof of a mouth. She lifted her head to the sky as if in search of its wetness and walked on, seemingly the only person walking in that direction. Everyone else was walking away from the town and away from the rain. She loved to drive against the general movement of things. Not for the sake of being different, but because it reminded her that she was mortal.

The immaculate gallery doors stood before her offering privacy and refuge. She went through them with the care that one uses when entering a place of worship, then she crept up the glass staircase and entered the exhibition room. The light dazzled her, but it was somehow comforting. It seemed to sharpen the shadows, creating the sort of perfection only found on a film set. The paintings hung in their cell of white silence like little offerings; remembered moments seized and recorded in a few simple brush strokes. The squeak of her trainers on the polished wooden floor was the only sound. Her eyes circled the room. A guard sat in the corner without moving, his hands placed neatly in his lap like a garden Buddha. The paintings presented a series of experiments with colour. Normally she'd have dismissed them as predictable and over-treated, but there was something about their honesty that made her feel differently today. She realized that she'd been part of the critical academic world for too long, and their playful lack of weight drew her out of herself and then out of the building with a flourish.

Nesta swept through Victoria Square as if being pushed along by a fierce wind. The water from the fountain rushed down the steps like a deluge, and people marched in the same direction as the flow, as if a new world awaited them in the valley below. The Council House was left standing behind them, its quiet pride sinking further into the background, its gold-dipped dome becoming foggy and abstract like a half-remembered dream.

New Street was strewn with buskers and teenagers perching on benches. Men in thick coats were selling cheap roses with a joke for everyone. There were balloons caught in trees, perhaps leftovers from New Year festivities. She walked on, past the Pallasades and down towards the market. With its forgotten pubs and vast car parks, it was a part of town that she normally tried to avoid. But today it had an alluring vitality that she wanted to explore.

Rubel had been watching the clock all day. It was four thirty-four. At five p.m. he'd pack up, count his money and catch the bus back home where he'd pull open a can of beer and turn on the television. In his mind he was already there. He was unaware of the vibrant clamour that encircled him. He wasn't aware of anything until an unexpected customer spoke.

'I'm collecting bits of scrap fabric for a project. I wondered if you had any lying around?'

Rubel was about to dismiss her but something in her voice stopped him. He looked up from his paper. She smiled, as if recognizing the slight incongruity of her request.

'It's just if you were going to throw them away.'

'Give me a few minutes. I'll see what I can do.'

The girl thanked him and moved off. He watched her wander from stall to stall without any sense of herself, as free as a Sunday morning. She picked up an old alarm clock from the stall next to his as if it were an object she didn't know, and she studied the detail of its face with a rare concentration. Then she put it down and strolled off, tapping a paper lantern along the way. He almost expected it to release a flutter of birds. There were worlds in her that he didn't recognize. He leaned over the front of the stall and watched her until she was out of sight. The stallholder opposite caught him watching and smiled. It was the first time he'd ever met her eye.

He reached for his scissors and started to cut irregular pieces from random rolls. He tore down the displays and ripped off lengths of summer muslin. He delved into bins, snipping at plastics, towelling and upholstery cloth. He tried to cut them so they looked like legitimate scraps: odd triangles of netting, strips of PVC and mustard corduroy. He felt fuelled by a sudden urge to break out of something that had been restraining him for years. As he worked at his new task, a colour, not seen before in Rubel, rose up through him and floated out onto his cheeks. When Nesta reappeared a little while later, five large plastic bags were spilling over for her on top of his stall.

'I hope that'll be enough. What are they for anyway?' he asked.

Nesta looked into his large, empty eyes. 'I'm not sure at the moment. I'll let you know if they turn into something.' She flashed him a smile and walked away.

At home in her bedroom, Nesta emptied out the bags until a mountain of colour stood on the floor before her. But all she saw was a heap of scrap. Her only instinct was that the pieces should be linked. Fashion has become a uniform, she thought, and she wanted to create something less restrictive, less dictated by code.

Her machine lay hidden under curling patterns and magazines. She cleared a space around it, then sat down and started to sew. She had no predetermined design. All she was aware of was the rotation of the cotton reel as the scraps were joined together.

A fragmented scarf began to emerge. It reminded her of the blankets her mother used to make out of old jumpers and dresses. She remembered sleeping under them on caravan holidays, comforted by the individual histories of each patch that had once served other purposes before keeping her warm. That was all she held in her head, the life of materials beyond fashionable transience. It seemed to her that what was happening was a return to the craft of making something without a big idea, of making something that could be used. She knew her tutors would scorn her, possibly fail her. How could such a simple accessory fetch a decent mark? But it didn't stop her from threading the material through the machine.

Nesta carried on sewing until her fingers could barely move.

In the fresh morning light she looked carefully at the scarf. It seemed basic and primitive, like a young child's collage. Nesta smiled as she swept it around her neck. It was finished.

At lunch that day she sat in a reverie in the café as her friends discussed their futures. Paul was going to the Royal College, Nicky to Italy on a Guggenheim Scholarship. Things she'd also wanted, until now. She made a brief excuse and collected her things. Her friends looked up at her with surprise. Nesta had changed and none of them knew why. She hardly knew herself. All she felt was a need to get down to the market.

*

Once there, noises met her at every turn. Conversations between shoppers, babies crying, and the reassuring sound of a football crowd cheering on a nearby radio. She couldn't take a step without looking around at the compression of lives, and hers now a part of it. She searched through the stalls for the fabric man, but every alley looked the same. She wanted to show him what she'd made. She wanted to show him what his scraps had become.

Rubel caught sight of the girl approaching, his dormant energy stirring as he waved to attract her attention.

Panting slightly, she arrived at his stall and said, 'I wanted to come down and show you this.'

Then from the top of her coat she pulled the scarf, like a magician unravelling a continuous line of colour.

'I never expected you to come back,' he said bashfully.

'I'm glad I did.'

The following Monday, Rubel was the first to arrive at the market. It was a sharp, icy day. He stood among the rusty stalls, looking around. He'd given himself time that morning to do this. There was no sound. Just that of his breath which passed out of him and into the endless space. He wandered through to the indoor area and peered up at the ceiling. It was made of glass and sloped into a peak at the top. On the far side, the café had been repainted and the market floor had been swept clean.

He wondered who by. Who else had shared this borrowed silence and heard their breath escape into it? He went over to where his stall stood and tugged at the plastic that covered it. It collapsed down into itself with a crackle, like autumn leaves falling into a comfortable pile. Then he started to arrange his fabric. The cottons he placed on the table in an ordered spectrum from violet to red. The synthetics he stacked in a row behind them. The samples of curtain fabric he hung over the frame of the stall, draping them in gathers and sweeps, while he positioned the bridal silk in carefully pleated fans on the display board above. He did all this slowly and lovingly, as if decorating a table for Christmas, working methodically through the hour until he was satisfied that his stall was complete.

Lunatic Logic

Eldon Davies

The year of our Lord, 1790, has been a most worrying one for me. Although I was credited with the discovery of dephlogisticated air nearly twenty years ago, this confounded Frenchman, Lavoisier, is doing his utmost to disprove the Phlogiston Theory, saying that when things burn, they combine with what he is pleased to call oxigene – what utter nonsense! Oh, by the way, I must introduce myself: I am Joseph Priestley, and I live here, in the Farm, Sparkbrook, near Birmingham, spending my time preaching in the Unitarian Chapel, and experimenting in my little laboratory. This is Michael, a close friend of the family.

'I have made some good friends since I arrived here from Yorkshire – such as William Murdock, James Watt and Matthew Boulton – who are all greatly taken by the new ideas in Science, just as I am. This town of ours, I feel, is destined to play an important role in the prosperity of our country in years to come.

'Tonight, the moon will be full, and, as usual, I will meet my friends at Matthew's house in Handsworth, a matter of a few miles from here. I should be honoured if you, Michael, would come with me. Matthew is doing very well for himself – his engineering establishment has more work than he can cope with, and his house in a good neighbourhood reflects his growing wealth. Time to wash and change, then we'll be off.

'Best foot forward, my dear fellow! I usually hire a chair to take me to Soho House, but funds are short at the moment – calx of mercury, which I use in my researches, is rather expensive, and I also need to eat, even if only moderately! There's a damp cold tonight, and the clouds are hurrying across the sky. And a strong smell of smoke in the air from the many chimneys of houses and furnaces in Nechells and Aston. The ground is very muddy underfoot, as last week's snowfalls have now melted, and the recent rain hasn't helped. "*Blast your eyes, sirrah!*" – I do beg your pardon, Michael. That carriage has spattered me with mud, but, as a man of the cloth, I should have been more moderate in my language. Watch your footing here, my friend, there's a deep puddle. Good thing the moon is out at present, or you would have got wet!

'Cast your eyes over to the right. You see those fires burning – that's our famous Bull Ring, a long-established market, where you can buy most things. They've had much trouble with footpads hereabouts – keep your stick handy. My flambeau will give us a modicum of light. That imposing edifice is St Martin's Church – it has been in existence since the fourteenth century, but is in rather poor repair at present. There's a most appetizing smell of roasting chestnuts, isn't there? At the top of this hill we'll find St Philip's Church, a fine sight, you'll agree. Lots of alehouses around here, so watch your step, the clientele are rather rough, and always impecunious! Over to your left are the junctions of this town's many canals. More canals than in Venice, my friends tell me, although I find that hard to believe. Some really rough characters work aboard the narrowboats, and that's a fact!

'Not too far to go, now. We pass St Paul's Church, then up the hill to Handsworth. I make this journey once every four weeks or so, round about the time of the full moon. Its brightness affords me some light, you see, as I pass through the darkened town. There *must* be a better way than flambeaux to light up these mean streets. Perhaps one of my scientific friends will put his mind to solving this problem.

'Excuse me if we pause for a moment, for the way is steep, is it not? Look at the poverty evident in this area, although some of the older parts of the town are worse. "Here, my child, take this penny home and give it to your mother. God bless you." Off we go again, Michael – last part of our journey now.

'At last – Soho House. A fine sight, such noble proportions; I trust Matthew is satisfied with his success. Ring the bell, dear fellow, and we'll get in from the cold . . . "Thank you, Mary." Give her your cloak and hat, and we'll go in and meet the company.

'Good evening, gentlemen. Forgive me, but I have taken the liberty of inviting my young friend Michael to join us in our discussions. He is interested in things scientific, as are we all, and is to commence employment in a London laboratory shortly. This, Michael, is the famous Mr James Watt, and here are Mr William Murdock and Mr Matthew Boulton. Are we to expect our other friends, Matthew? What of Dr Withering and Dr Darwin? I have not seen Mr Wedgwood for many a day . . . Thank you, Matthew, a glass of wine will be very welcome on a night such as this. Come, Michael, join our little circle around the fire.'

For a moment, the only sounds in the room were the ticking of the long-case clock, the hissing and crackling of logs on the fire, and the sucking noises of churchwarden pipes being lit. Michael looked around him; the room was furnished with an opulence he'd never experienced before. Priestley nudged him gently and whispered, 'Well, Michael, what a wealth of talent we find in this one small room!' Then, more loudly, he remarked, 'I think, gentlemen, we might make this evening's meeting even more interesting than usual if we were to indulge in a little of what is popularly referred to as crystal gazing! How do we see our fine town developing? Are any of our discoveries or inventions likely to influence our way of life in the distant future?'

The gathering was silent for a moment as those present collected their thoughts, and the smoke from their pipes spiralled upwards in the candlelight. Murdock broke the silence. 'My own research into the use of gas for lighting is a good starting point, I think.' Priestley nudged Michael delightedly, as if to say, 'See, already an answer to my earlier query!' Murdock went on, 'Gaslight is steadier and stronger than that of candles and suchlike, but a great deal of work will need to be done if we are to take gas from where it is made to where it is to be used.'

Boulton chipped in, 'True, William, but our factory will, no doubt, be able to produce the equipment needed, when you have perfected the prototypes.'

A buzz of agreement arose from the gathering, inter-rupted by Mary, who opened the door, bobbed a little curtsey, and announced, 'Captain Keir, sir.'

In strode James Keir, rubbing his hands briskly together. 'A cold evening, gentlemen,' he boomed, and was introduced to Michael. When he'd been told the purpose of the meeting, he remarked, 'There is talk, as you are well aware, Joseph, of a cleaner sort of energy, known as "electricity", which might be better, easier and more convenient than your stinking gas, William! Just think, if this mysterious force could be made in large quantities, as is not the case at present, perhaps by using your steam engine, James, as the primary mover in some way, we could use the electricity for all sorts of things – lighting, perhaps even heating for our homes, my furnaces – without the pall of smoke which is an inescapable product of our present methods.'

Boulton remarked, 'The amount of smoke our manufactories produce is bound to have a harmful effect on local people's health. Besides using their labours to increase our wealth, I have been thinking more and more of late that we fortunate few ought to consider our labourers and their dependents by providing medical treatment in a specially built sanatorium. I know you think along these lines, Joseph, as a man of the cloth, and our eminent medical friends will be keen to assist us with the practicalities of the scheme.'

Priestley nodded vigorously, and said that it was a disgrace that a town the size of Birmingham had to rely largely on the bumbling activities of ignorant, unsanitary nurses and downright charlatans. 'The day *must* dawn when a proper sanatorium serving the town and its environs will be opened, promoting expert and modern treatment for all. I foresee it will come in our lifetimes.'

Michael listened in amazement to this discussion. A vision of the future began to build before his eyes – a cleaner town, buildings and streets lit by some mysterious energy; comfortable, warm homes without the reek of smoke and sputtering candles; a place where the sick might go for expert medical care! What else would these remarkable men think of?

Keir spoke up next. 'All the goods we produce, my friends, have to be carried at a slow pace by barge, or lumbering wagons along muddy roads. It all takes time and, as we know, time is money. What I would dearly like to see is faster, more reliable transport. Surely, William, your work with James Watt could be harnessed – forgive the pun – to make some sort of cart, wagon, carriage or barge which would propel itself, without the need for horses to pull it at their slow pace. With all the expertise of working with metal in this town, I can think of nowhere better suited to the manufacture of these horseless means of transport.'

Murdock smiled in reply. 'Another pun, James: don't let's put the cart before the horse! What you are suggesting may, I admit, be possible, but have you any concept of the power needed to replace even four horses? Such horseless carriages as you propose would be quite enormous. And there's another matter to be considered. With large numbers of these speedy – ah – locomotives, let's call them, moving along our roads, the very roads themselves would need to be far better than our present dirt tracks to cope with the wear and tear. What is to be done about *that*, sir, pray?'

'It would be expensive, sir,' said Michael, emboldened into making his first contribution to the discussion, 'but could not stone blocks be laid close together to form a solid, hard-wearing surface to carry your locomotives?'

'Indeed, Michael,' smiled Murdock, 'that is certainly a possibility.'

'Another idea has struck me,' said Michael, his eyes shining with excitement. 'I have heard tell of things called "tramways" where carts are guided along iron rails; they are much used in the coal mines of South Wales, I am told. Would it be possible for your steam locomotives to run along rails such as these, drawing wagons at speed, filled with your manufactories' products, or even with people?'

'Our Dr Darwin might be inclined to say that people were never designed to be carried at high speeds!' chortled Priestley. 'Yet, I am sure that they would pay well for the privilege of being carried swiftly and in comfort. To journey from London to Edinburgh takes over a week by coach, and a locomotive could surely improve upon that, in terms of time and the wellbeing of the passengers.'

'I foresee danger in some of these suggestions,' said Keir, 'although there are great advantages in your ideas. A town such as this could have a building where all your tramways would meet, coming from all parts of the country. Mind you, I think the smell and smoke would make such a building a noxious place to visit! Far better, perhaps, if electricity were used to power these locomotives? Without the need for ventilation, the building might even be put underground.'

A heated argument broke out regarding the relative merits of steam power and the little-known electricity, although finally the consensus was that steam would probably be more of a practical proposition, at least in the foreseeable future.

Boulton changed the direction of the discussion at this point. ''Tis all very well to talk thus, gentlemen,' he remarked. 'We have not yet given proper thought to how these marvellous machines are to be constructed: a workforce capable of fine workmanship will be needed. Anybody can swing a hammer or dig a hole, but not one in a hundred can read a plan or carry out intricate work. Ask John Whitehouse, our clock-making friend, how difficult are such tasks as cutting gear-wheels and the like. No, gentlemen, we must turn our attention to the education of our workers, to make them capable of the tasks they will be called upon to accomplish. At present, men such as we, the rich and privileged, are able to read and write; our workers have no such benefit.

'We will have to set up places for *all* children to be introduced to the rudiments of learning, before they go into our manufactories to earn their living. Surely, if the breadwinner earns a reasonable wage, he will not begrudge paying a small sum for the education of his offspring. I am not talking of the learning of Latin, Greek, and all the other fields of knowledge taught in grammar schools, but those things which will help our workers achieve the tasks we set them. Basic subjects could be taught to all, and those capable of becoming foremen and overseers could be sent on to more advanced learning in other institutions.'

'Matthew, you are, as always, anxious to look to the wellbeing of your workers,' said James Watt. 'If we are to give them the chance to earn good wages, they will also need places to spend that money. Oh, I know that the present low alehouses will always take a substantial portion of workers' wages, but shops selling decent goods at affordable prices are needed. They could be grouped around our Bull Ring: clothes shops, shoe shops, bakers' shops, shops selling food of all descriptions, even shops selling books – because, mark you, there will be larger numbers of literate people to buy them.

'Even if people cannot afford to buy books, they should not be cut off from the opportunity of reading great literature. We have had a Circulating Library for over ten years, and this could be greatly increased in size from its present stock of about thirty thousand volumes. There is a suitable site in the region of Temple Row, and another at the top of New Street.'

'Amen to that,' said Priestley fervently, 'but to return to the question of shopping. The task of the housewife is not a very pleasant one in weather such as we have experienced recently. Twas but a day or two ago that I observed a woman trudging through the snow, laden with her meagre purchases, and soaked through, obviously very cold and miserable. Why, with all the power we have available, should there not be a great shelter over the shops and market area?'

'Yes, indeed,' said Keir. 'It could be made very light under this cover, were it to be constructed of glass on an iron framework. My factories could produce glass enough to furnish the project, I'll warrant. What a boon to those making their purchases if they could carry out their business under cover, and in pleasant surroundings. People would want to meet their friends as well as merely to shop.'

Watt chimed in again. 'The people will want entertainment, and I speak not of cruel activities such as cock-fighting and dog-fighting, but wholesome sports where a man might take his children without exposing them to evil influences or danger. Also, I foresee the building of theatres to rival those of London. Can't you envisage them: magnificent buildings, warm, well-lit, with comfortable seating for their audiences; none of that old-fashioned limelight or flares, but using gas, or your – er – electricity, perhaps, Keir?

'Then there's music. We all know how fond you are of music, Matthew, so what about a specially constructed hall for the performance of great works? I know that Christopher Wren called an organ a "damned kist o' whistles", but have you heard the organ of Lichfield Cathedral? Erasmus took me there last month, and it was magnificent; it is rumoured that the organist plays not only using his hands, but his feet also! We could have a great organ built in our hall, one grand enough for all who heard it to marvel at the forward-looking town of Birmingham! I see it now, rows of gleaming pipes of mathematical beauty, making sounds from the merest whisper to earth-shaking chords. I could, no doubt, design a pump which would supply all the air needed without the necessity of having people to keep its bellows filled.'

Michael joined in once again, not so shyly this time, as he'd begun to warm to this genial group. 'If Birmingham is to be as great a town as you envisage, my good sirs, then its products will doubtless be taken to the ends of the earth. Why should not some of the famous products of foreign lands be brought here, and stored in such a way as your townsfolk can look at them and marvel? Paintings and sculptures from the great Italian cities of Venice and Florence, the delicate porcelain of China and Japan, weapons, cloth and other wonders could be housed for the edification of the good people of Birmingham.'

'Well said, young Michael,' said Boulton, 'but why stop at manufactured articles? There are many plants which could be gathered in far-off lands and brought home here to be cultivated in a museum of living things. William Withering and Jonathan Stokes would be most interested in this idea, I daresay, as they are much inclined towards the study of botany.'

Keir added, 'And there's Science itself. Our little group of thinkers is fortunate indeed in being acquainted with the joys of discovery. Why should this same joy not be available to all? I suggest we could erect a building to house the wonderful discoveries of the age, and even provide those less knowledgeable with the opportunity to place their hands on equipment such as we are familiar with. One of your great steam engines, James, your apparatus for making dephlogisticated air, Joseph, and who knows what besides, would find places in this "Palace of Science". I foresee crowds would be drawn to it, like iron filings to a magnet!'

The talk then switched to the wealth of the region.

'Taylor and Lloyd have a good little banking business in Dale End,' said Watt. 'I hear talk that Lloyd is keen to spread his business into Wales and down to London. With the ideas we have expressed this evening, I foresee that manufactory owners will need loans to expand their businesses. The efforts you made about twenty years ago, Matthew, to ensure that Birmingham had its own Assay Office, can only magnify the region's importance as a financial centre.'

'And then there's this revolution taking place across the Channel,' added Keir. 'My friends tell me that our town supplies over seventy per cent of the British Army's muskets. We have enough brains in this part of the world to invent new weapons. After all, muskets and cannon are basically unaltered in four hundred years.

'News came from France some years ago of the Montgolfier brothers, and their journeys made through the air, suspended beneath their balloons of heated air. Surely there is room for a fertile mind to work on ways of transporting men and their weapons by flight from one place to another? Men travel by land and by sea; there can be no reason why they should not travel through the air also, particularly if your engines, James and William, can be used to provide the power. Can you not see these great flying machines leaving a suitable field on the outskirts of the town for far-off places, and returning with travellers with wonderful tales to tell?'

'We are in some danger of trying to run before we can walk, gentlemen,' muttered Boulton as he struggled to keep his pipe alight. 'Excuse me for a moment.' He rose from his chair and went to the fireplace, then pulled the bell cord. In answer to his summons, in came Mary. 'More wine, if you please, Mary,' he asked.

'At once, sir,' she replied, and left the room.

'Now, there's another thing,' said Boulton. 'Will there ever be a means of communicating with people out of earshot? Would it not be marvellous to be able to talk from this room to Erasmus in Lichfield, or even further afield?'

'Why just talk?' suggested Murdock. 'Why not try to send pictures to people far away? Oh, I know we could commission an artist to paint a picture of our gathering and send it by post to, say, the Royal Society in London, but what would be gained by that? Far better to be able to send pictures and speech rapidly between towns, cities, even countries. Our semaphore towers might somehow be adapted for the task, do you not think?'

'Bah!' growled Keir, 'you might as well try to put a man on the moon, sirrah! We get too fanciful by half!'

At this point, Mary returned with the wine, and the companions refilled their glasses.

'If these visions are ever to become reality, my friends, Birmingham will one day need its own equivalent of what Oxford, Cambridge and Durham enjoy – its own university, where the highest branches of learning can flourish, rooted in rich industrial soil,' Watt said with a faraway look in his eyes.

The wine that had been drunk that evening had certainly stimulated the brains of the gathering. Boulton proposed a toast: 'Gentlemen, raise a glass to His Majesty, King George the Third. May he, in his wisdom, raise this flourishing town to the status of a city, before too much time shall elapse!' The company shouted its approbation, and Priestley added, 'But remember, "Unless The Lord keep the city . . ."'

As the last glasses were drained, the companions began to make their preparations for departure. Keir clattered away on horseback, while Watt and Murdock climbed, somewhat unsteadily, into their carriages, leaving Priestley and Michael to shake hands with Boulton, and to wish him 'Goodnight'.

'Well, Michael, now you've met my friends, what d'you think of them, eh? A lively collection of thinkers, you'll agree. It gets colder by the minute, so the sooner we're back in Sparkbrook, the better. The smell of smoke is strong on the wind, so perhaps we *do* need to think of an alternative source of energy, rather than relying on coal. My "Lunatics of the Full Moon" (that's what I call them in private, although we are known hereabouts as the "Lunar

Society" on account of our full–moon meetings) are the most forward-looking people I know. Among our regular members, one may list at least seven Fellows of the Royal Society, so you may safely assume that they know what they are talking about.

'A noble vision they gave us this night of the Birmingham of the future, did they not? Of course, many of their predictions are nothing more than common sense; for instance, sanatoria for the cure, treatment and comfort of the sick, and rapid forms of transport for passengers and goods – these things will surely come, will they not?

'Other speculations are, I fear, just guesswork; merely our feeble groping in the darkness, hoping that God's light will be granted to His people. Will we *ever* manage to communicate with far-off places more rapidly than by post, beacon or semaphore? Maybe we shall, but I confess that I am quite unable to imagine how. However, time alone will tell.

'You ask me, Michael, when we can expect these marvels to become reality. Some of our predictions will become fact reasonably soon, no doubt, but this business of rapid transfer of speech and pictures – well! I cannot see it happening in less than, say, five hundred years, because the whole idea is so fantastic. Again, God will provide the answer in His own good time. Would it not be exciting to live in the Birmingham of the future? Our successors will indeed be fortunate people! Come along, Michael, best foot forward, home is calling!'

Face Like a Feyenoord Shirt

John Mulcreevy

Terence Goodman pressed a forefinger against the condensed windowpane and moved it in circles so his view changed from a dot to a fish bowl of the city centre beneath his office in the sky. The trick, he thought, is not to try to rule things like imperial Britain might've done; nor to try to own things like modern America. The trick was to simply manage things. He didn't need the sucker-uppers to name a street after him. A Goodman Street already existed in the middle of Birmingham. He didn't need a bronze statue plinthed within easy reach of bird shit and spray-paint – the price founding fathers paid for immortality. He was happy just to manage.

On clear days he could look right down New Street onto the new developments. There were girders and joists – some in concrete and glass, others still skeletal with workers' luminous yellow hard hats like strands of DNA whizzing around the steel bones. This is what Terence managed. He told the rulers, his superiors in local government, what they could and couldn't rule. He told the owners, the retail and leisure corporations, what they could and couldn't own.

It wasn't quite as crudely defined as that. In order to accommodate he'd give the impression of bending over so far backwards he could've pulled up his socks with his teeth. It was management. When the people got fed up with bad services and smug excuses, his superiors would be emptying their desks and drifting in limbo for the next four years. When the people decided to keep their money in their pockets, the corporations would shrink as quickly as their share dividends.

Not being a ruler and not being an owner made Terence fireproof. He wasn't exposed to the whims of the electorate so he wouldn't be unseated, and recessions were just another opportunity for lucrative consultancy. He grabbed his jacket from its hook and rifled the pockets for keys and cards. Before leaving for lunch he looked out of the fish bowl again. There were no balloons today. That ought to have reassured him – but didn't. He took the lift twenty floors down, automatically adopting a nod and smile to colleagues gliding in and out. At reception he leaned over and whispered to the security chief.

'The matter I mentioned, Emile.'

'Keeping an eye open, sir.'

Emile turned back to idly scanning his bank of screens and Terence strode out through revolving doors onto a different New Street to the one he'd known two weeks ago. There was a hesitancy to his step, an alertness to his gaze. Before it'd begun, crowds seemed to part in recognition of his straight-backed, confident stride. It was almost as if they sensed that here was the man who managed them while they shopped and studied and slaved. Now, any shape darting unexpectedly into vision caused a jolt in his shoulders. He walked into the trattoria and sat down in his usual place. It hadn't taken much to turn this city that he'd held on a leash like a prettified poodle into a rabid hound snapping at his throat.

That's what the past could do. It was why he'd taken Emile to one side a week before to ask if anyone matching the description had been in the foyer. His words fading into throat clearance as he spoke. 'Nothing to worry about, Emile, but if you could just, er, make sure you don't let in anyone who . . .'

Who was there when the car blew up on Jubilee Day? Ambrose was there, and little Mortiboys, Chico and his brother, Roller had said he'd be there but hadn't turned up, Murph, of course, Dung Beetle and Terry Zero.

It was boiling hot that Tuesday in June. Most of them met up at Terry Zero's around midday. Chico's brother arrived later having baulked at a day in front of the telly at Janet's mother's house.

Outside, noises breezed across the dreamland. The forced laughter of families who only ever meet on public holidays. Distinctions could be drawn from the sounds; the clucking of housewives, the growls of their husbands, the screams of children. Voices of a freed people – but freed only for a day. Off the dual carriageway and halfway down the crescent and up a side road they found the voices. Men with bushy sideburns and sweat-stained shirts guarding a barrel of beer perched on a creaking table, women in Sunday-best frocks or trouser suits weaving through the commotion with trays of sandwiches and drinks, children shaking stiff triangular flags rushing in front of exhausted grand-parents. All with faces and arms ripened by sun and euphoria. The group marched, Murph at the front, into the side road and the street party.

Terence prodded his pasta with a fork. He shouldn't have ordered something swimming in bubbling tomato sauce. It reminded him. He pushed the plate away, gulped down in one go the half glass of wine, then took out his digital organizer. The evening's work and play appeared on-screen. He'd committed to an address on regeneration at the Institute. That'd be easy – a home fixture. The panel about the housing stock sell-off wasn't as enticing. Usually he made it policy never to appear at forums where the people were liable to break into dissent. Being crucified by tenants' groups and the SWP, plus the attendant photo and report in the following day's paper wasn't good management. Let the triple-chinned, publicity-hungry councillors put their heads on the line of moral baseball bats. Fortunately, Terence had double-booked. A ploy he frequently used. So, tonight he'd present a cheque from the mosque to the help centre instead. He'd still have plenty of time to meet with the Bannions. They'd recommended he try the new Thai.

The *Dambusters* ringtone in his breast pocket interrupted him. Jacqueline sounded stressed. Nothing new in that – his wife rarely sounded anything else. Occasionally he'd tell her to relax; give up a committee or one of the gym memberships. To no avail, she was governed by aspiration and lifestyle supplements.

'What is it, Jac?'

'Some sod has only gone and fly-tipped in the front garden.'

'Done what! Bastards. Well, phone the environmental, they'll get someone out.'

'And how long will that take? Could you pop back and get rid of it? I said I'd pop round to see Ann about the fête. And, I don't want it there when I bring Daniel home. You know what he's like. He'll only want to play in it.'

'Play in it. What is it exactly, Jac?'

'Didn't I say? It's a kiddies' car. One of those big plastic buggies with a teddy bear in the front. God knows what's happened to it. Looks like it's been on a bonfire.'

'A car . . .'

'I'll leave it up to you then. Put it in a black bag or something. Are you still there, Terence?'

*

Murph looked around. Red, white and blue bunting snaked from lamppost to tree to drainpipe. Her face was sellotaped to windows and doors, printed on shining plates and laminated gold paper crowns. Just a woman whose ancestors knew how to win on battlefields and in courtrooms.

He led the group on past curling sandwiches and perspiring cucumber slices. Chico paused to scoop a cherry off an individual trifle; Murph mockingly waved a mini Union Jack and Dung Beetle spat through a gap in his teeth at the whooping monarchists.

'Give em a war or a queen and they're happy, eh, Murph,' grunted Ambrose.

'Over there,' said Murph. 'On the wall at the end.'

The disc jockey was about fifty. The sun reflected yellow spots onto his shining bald pate and shining polished shoes. Terry Zero sniffed contemptuously at the hi-fi. The deck hissed; the speakers crackled. It was nowhere near as good as the set-up he had at home.

Chico and his brother slid the record collection along the low garden wall, looking at the names: K-Tel party albums, a *Golden Hour* LP, recent singles by the Dead End Kids, Joe Tex and Brotherhood of Man. The DJ looked at the group, remarked how nice to see young fellows with short hair and asked if they were cadets. Murph pointed to the Jam and Damned badges on his T-shirt and just reeled him in.

'As a matter of fact we are, sir. This badge which reads J, A and M was awarded for Junior Army Manoeuvres and the other for starting a fire with two twigs.'

'Splendid,' said the DJ.

Dung Beetle poked Murph excitedly. 'Go on, Murph.'

'I was wondering,' smiled Murph, 'if you could possibly play "God Save the Queen" for us.'

'Do you know something, lads. I'd love to but I'm afraid I haven't got it on record.'

Murph unslung his rucksack and pulled out a seven-inch single. Chico's brother covered his mouth to conceal a laugh and snot shot down both nostrils.

'Actually, sir, I have a copy of it with me. I'll just put it on, shall I?' said Murph, affecting a voice far removed from his normal sandpapered larynx.

Murph took off 'Ain't Gonna Bump no more with no Big Fat Woman', put his record on the deck, pushed the volume up as far as it would go and lowered the stylus so the Sex Pistols' 'God Save the Queen' erupted all over the party.

Terence held the bin liner and its contents at arm's length and wondered whether to leave it out for collection or take it to the tip. He didn't want the thing lying around, so he put it in the boot. Pulling out of the tree-lined drive, he looked both ways – not for traffic or pedestrians – for the fly-tipper. The Grove was deserted, as it always was at two thirty on weekday afternoons.

From Sutton Coldfield he spun through green belt until coming to the built-up and then impatiently weaved in and out of Kingstanding junctions. Each time he braked into a red light, things raced around his head.

Things like Dale Mortiboys leaning on his handcart.

If Terence had seen him first he'd have avoided him. He was the only one of the old crowd he'd spoken to in decades. Mortiboys, not so little now, had been a puny runt two years below him at school. You'd have seen more fat on a chip. Today, between a silver and a golden jubilee, he'd grown to over six foot with face browned by outdoor jobs and a physique developed from manual work and an aversion to beer. He still looked younger, much, much younger than Terence.

'Doing all right, are you?'

'Oh, yes, Dale. I see you're still helping to keep the environment clean.'

112

'Yeah. Got a couple of months' worth of contract left. Money's shit though.'

'I know, I know. If it were up to me, I'd double your wages. It's an essential job you're doing. We'd be knee-deep in Big Macs and the rest of it if it wasn't for you. Anyway, must be cracking on.'

'Right ho, Terry. You've heard about Murph?'

'Murph?'

'Yeah. He's back.'

Terence crawled behind lorries and vans through Perry Barr, Newtown, to the tip, then back to his office. He sorted what he needed for the evening and punched a text for Jacqueline telling her not to wait up. He switched one mobile off and took his other, the one she didn't know about, from the bottom drawer of his desk. At reception he tossed the keys for the Rover to Emile with instructions to put it in the all-night car park, then asked for a taxi. In the late afternoon air he skipped back to the bin liner containing the burnt-up toy car and teddy vanishing in a swirl at the tip; and he thought about the balloons.

Chico's brother and Ambrose stood, arms folded, obstructing the DJ's path to the hi-fi. Murph and Terry Zero punched the air while Dung Beetle and Mortiboys pogoed on the garden wall. The crackling, distorted roar from the speakers had alerted others. Snouts were lifted out of polystyrene troughs and heads turned. The men, all greasy fringes and shirts open to the waist, stumbled over tables and chairs. Big-armed women put aside tales of summer sales to join the charge. There'd been just enough booze and sunshine consumed for a scrap – and in the dreamland they loved a scrap.

Chico gestured at the oncoming herd as they got closer, then stuck out a leg. One of them sailed over his extended Doc Martens into a speaker. Murph snatched his record back and ducked a swinging hairy arm. Dung Beetle tripped on a border collie licking up streams of spilt punch from the table Ambrose had kicked over to stop a big bloke from grabbing him.

Led by Terry Zero, they ran towards the gully halfway down the side road. Ambrose swerved to avoid a flailing fist but didn't see the tin jubilee tray that caught him square in the middle of his nose. His assailant, a tiny decrepit thing in a floral dress, squeaked triumphantly while another purple-rinse defender of the realm punched his backside repeatedly. Eventually he broke free and made for the gully. They looked back to check for any signs of pursuit but the only followers into the gully were a couple of small kids and a wobbly legged border collie. The gullies, like a topiary maze for urban under-eighteens, connected a few side roads to the dual carriageway. They came out of shadowed mud tracks and overgrown hedges into the glare of Kingstanding Island, bleached by the risen sun.

Dung Beetle first saw the Ford Anglia; off-cream with driver's door ajar and keys glinting. They piled in, Chico jerked the ignition and the car spluttered into life. He revved and wheelspun away from the kerb towards Kings Road. In the back seat Ambrose, Chico's brother, Dung Beetle, Terry Zero and little Mortiboys saw the car's owner emerging from a gully frantically tugging at his flies as he tried to give chase. They watched him get smaller and smaller in the rearview mirror until he vanished altogether.

Balloons. Dozens of them drifting up Temple Row in the direction of his office. Initially, Terence thought it some advertising gimmick; probably a new bar in Brindleyplace: 'This balloon admits two for free before ten p.m.' Zara brought one of them into the office.

'It's got a funny message on it,' she said.

'What is it?' inquired Terence, looking up from his desk.

'Erm, it says: Who made his mate's face look like a Fey-something shirt?' replied Zara, perplexed.

Terence took the balloon. 'Feyenoord. Who made his mate's face look like a Feyenoord shirt.'

'And what's that supposed to mean when it's at home?' Zara burst the balloon with a pin and dropped it into the litter basket.

The taxi door clicking open brought Terence back to the present. He took a receipt from the driver and walked up the steps to the Institute. In his pulpit, confident rhetoric replaced the nerves of the past fortnight. He was a practised public speaker, as were most of the audience. This, as everyone in the room knew, was less about the regeneration of the second city, that happens every few decades anyway – with or without invitation-only buffets. This was about being in the company of your own tribe; the captains and barons, senior partners and accountants, entrepreneurs and managers. If it weren't for suits and influence replacing animal skins and swords they'd have appeared no different to Celts or Saxons capturing and dividing up their little lumps of land.

After false bonhomie and a fruity Bordeaux, Terence booked a room for later and took a taxi to the mosque in Handsworth. A speech, a presentation, a few handshakes and then back into the city in Councillor Sadiq's Mercedes. The Bannions were waiting for them at the restaurant. There were five Bannion brothers; three were sitting at the best table. John, Tom and Phil, all under forty, all in Paul Smith. John and Phil had taken over the family builders in their mid-twenties and started buying their own plots to put bricks on. Now they had developments from Gloucester to Lincoln. Tom Bannion ran a different type of business. By the time the waitress arrived with coffee, tentative plans for Soho Road were in place.

The night had fetched down turning the city thorough-fare into a fluorescent kaleidoscope. Terence and Tom briefly discussed the new Thai. Tom took hotel room details and said he'd be along in an hour. It was a short walk to the hotel over a canal bridge and past the Convention Centre so Terence set off on foot.

'Murph wants to see you.'

Terence felt the familiar jolt in his shoulders. He spun round and there was Dale Mortiboys. 'D-Dale,' he stuttered.

'I was going to wait for you tomorrow at your pasta place. Bit of luck catching you here.'

'About Murph?' said Terence.

'No harm in having a word with him. Look, Terry, he says he just wants a chat. He's been through it a bit and you're doing all right.'

Terence thought quickly. It was money. The balloons and the toy car, just the preliminaries to an appearance with a begging bowl. He agreed the time and place with Dale and continued to the hotel; his head a jumble of stabbing thoughts bringing migraine and dizziness.

The Ford Anglia sat on the top of Barr Beacon; the hill between Birmingham and Walsall once used for rituals. As high as the Urals – 227 metres above sea level. Chico kicked in the front lights while the others looked down on the dreamland as a Jubilee Day soundtrack danced across the night; tunes, mostly unrecognizable, punctuated by revellers kissing and kicking their way home. Murph pointed down at the estates' flickering patterns as down-stairs lights went out and upstairs lights on.

'When we leave school we can end up just like that lot or we can do something better. Instead of all the royal bollocks we could have punk schools that wouldn't be going on about kings and queens, and they wouldn't be there just to teach the kids how to rot in factories.'

'And the coppers would all be punk, and the army and the politicians,' added Terry Zero.

'You'll never get politicians like that,' chided Ambrose.

'Course we will,' said Terry Zero, 'because if they don't they'll get shown a wall and a firing squad and told to go stand in between.'

Murph nodded. Chico was jumping on the roof of the car, percussive thumps echoing around the hill. The others wandered over. Terry Zero took out his lighter.

'Torch it,' goaded Chico. Dung Beetle seconded the suggestion. Terry Zero waved the flame at the battered, petrol-leaking Anglia; Murph eased himself into the front seat.

'Hang on a minute, my Pistols single's in there.'

After the explosion they ran and ran from a ball of burning metal and flesh. Down the hill and over grazing fields, down Doe Bank Lane and over Queslett Road. They outran the howls of disturbed dogs and didn't stop until they reached the gullies where they bent over double and gasped air back into their lungs.

Murph wasn't dead, but he might've been if Ambrose hadn't dialled 999 before they went home to lie awake under different ceilings filled with the same demons.

Having turned sixteen, after months in hospital, Murph returned to school. The blast had caught the right side of his face, neck and torso. Most of the skin had gone, leaving only crimson sinews wrapped around bone. It looked even worse because he was so pallid that now his unaffected left side seemed ghost-white. For a while all the school was nice to him, even the head who'd threatened him with expulsion at least once a term before. It didn't last.

He'd only been back in class a couple of weeks when the trouble started. Some younger kids had been at the frieze in the canteen. There was a wall of paintings of different footballers from around Europe. The Feyenoord player had a half-red, half-white shirt. On it were drawn eyes, nose and mouth and above it written: Martin Murphy.

Terence wolfed down tagliatelle and glanced at his watch. He didn't mind thinking about Murph today. He'd been a good kid back then in 1977. He'd kept quiet when the police tried to trick him into revealing everyone's names. It'd been funny when he let off the fire extinguisher in the canteen and a scream when he forced that cocky third-year to eat the football frieze. It stopped being funny when he started bringing the lighters and air rifle and dead rats and homemade flamethrower into school. Terence had stopped hanging around with Murph by then. There'd been exams and Georgina to keep him occupied. He emptied his glass and left.

It was nearly time for the rendezvous by the war memorial at the top of Barr Beacon. He hadn't been back there since running away from the detonated car, and he wasn't going there today. Some of the Bannions' less savoury associates would be, though. Murph would be forty now and a lot different to the youth released from school and put into mental care. Released from mental care and put into prison. Released from prison and put back into mental care. He probably wanted a couple of hundred quid to disappear again. Terence could've paid it; told him that's your lot and don't come back for at least another twenty-five years. It would've only been 'down the back of the sofa' money and he did kind of owe Murph for not grassing. But instead he'd called on the Bannions. Their associates had been instructed to offer a severe warning about any future pranks with balloons and toy cars.

Terence stepped out of the lift. He was too busy to spend time on yesterdays. He had new shiny empires to manage.

He afforded himself the first carefree smile in ages as he entered the office.

'Someone looks effing pleased with themself.'

In Terence Goodman's leather swivel chair sat a figure in tatty deerstalker hat with brim pulled down and off-black reefer coat with lapels pulled up.

'Shit!' said Terence.

'I'd say that was a fair description of what you're in at this precise moment,' said Murph.

'Barr Beacon?' coughed Terence.

'I thought Mohammed might not go to the mountain.'

Terence stood transfixed by the eyes, tiny turquoise globes peering out of shadow.

'It's good to see you again, Martin. Dale Mortiboys did mention . . . you need a bit of help.'

'Mortiboys, yeah. He's gone for a burger with your security bloke. They know each other from boxing. Close the door, eh, Ter-rence.'

That answered Terence's next question. The most advanced CCTV system in the city and the man operating it had gone to stuff his face.

'I think he said something about money. Is that it, Martin?' squeaked Terence, still standing awkwardly on the wrong side of his own desk.

'You always was plasticene. We all come out of the packet in bright colours, then you get mixed and end up like a lump of purple shit.'

At that moment Terence realized that Murph hadn't changed. He's here because he's just been released from somewhere and he's waiting to be put somewhere else, he thought. Under the hat was still the boy who could turn a six-month stretch into a fourteen-year sentence.

'I'm going to have to ask you to leave. I can lend, give you twenty or so. I am rather busy and my secretary . . .'

'She likes burgers too.'

'Can you just tell me what you want?'

Murph got up off the chair and moved to the big window behind the desk, momentarily revealing the mesmerizing red sinews.

'You had the brains you could've done something better instead of sitting up here like a pigeon getting ready to fly off and crap all over the city,' said Murph, his head moving from side to side to take in the bustling panorama below.

'Can you just please tell me what you want and then leave?' pleaded Terence.

'What have you done with the Bull Ring?'

'What?'

'The Bull Ring. Where are the old folks going to go? The ones who ain't got storecards and fancy white-collar wages.'

'You blame me for your face, don't you?' sighed Terence.

'The last place I was in, good place. Your lot shut it down. One of the social workers said she might lose her home because of it,' said Murph, still squinting out of the window.

'I'm sorry, about everything,' said Terence.

Murph turned to the shaking former punk-rocker turned middle-aged enterprise facilitator. 'Can't decide what to do about you, Terry Zero.'

Terence breathed long and hard until his diaphragm ached. On his desk, between the bubble-jet fax and dictation machine, propped against the scanner was something he hadn't seen since his schooldays. A paint-stripper modified into a flamethrower.

Lena

Ava Ming

The strains of the ballad floated down from an open window enveloping Herold in hazy memories. No one sang like Lena Horne. He closed his eyes, savouring the melody.

As the sound of Lena's voice filled her bedroom, Margaret yielded to indulgent reminiscence. Outside, Herold's rake scraped a steady rhythm against sun-bronzed earth. Inside, she was once again loved and cherished, just like many years before.

2

Two hours later, Herold slowly surveyed the garden as Margaret stood on the patio steps.

'There you go, pruned, trimmed and mown, just as you requested,' he announced.

With one hand shielding her eyes from the sun's glare, Margaret gazed at the tennis-striped lawn edged by a vista of flowerbeds and neat hedges that Herold had created over the past few weeks. 'Thank you, Mr Mackenzie. Now drink this lemonade before you burn up out here,' she urged.

Herold wiped away beads of sweat. As he took the proffered glass his hand brushed against hers, sparking a frisson of excitement. She looked away awkwardly as he tensed and cleared his throat. Savouring the cool liquid, he stole a sideways look at Margaret. Grey-green eyes, a figure still trim after all these years. An innate femininity that compelled you to open doors and pull out chairs for her. Lustrous black hair. Hips that swayed with the grace of a gazelle and finally that gently captivating, gorgeous smile. Much appreciated, but seldom seen.

Placing the empty glass on the patio table, Herold gathered his tools, happy that she liked his work. He always charged her far less than any of his other clients, while she insisted on paying a large and unnecessary tip.

'Well, Mr Mackenzie, how much do I owe you today?' Their closing conversation was the same every week.

'A cheque for the usual amount will be fine.'

'Are you sure? It seems like you worked extra long today and in this heat too!'

'I have no problems with the heat.'

'I'll just get my cheque book.'

After self-consciously avoiding direct eye contact with her during their conversation, Herold stared as she retreated into the house. He would gladly waive all fees in exchange for one hug, or a kiss from those cupid-bow lips. Perhaps it was time to recommend another gardener for Miss Margaret – this longing was killing him.

'Here you are, Mr Mackenzie. I've added a little extra, I hope you don't mind.'

'Oh, there's no need for that.'

'Well, buy a surprise gift for Mrs Mackenzie then.'

Herold looked at his feet, embarrassed. He thought she knew. There was no Mrs Mackenzie, never had been. Aware of the silence he began, 'Well, I'll be off –' just as she asked, 'Would you like to come to dinner after church on Sunday?' He faltered. She'd taken him by surprise. 'I mean, it would be nice to have you . . . for dinner . . .'

Margaret trailed off, feeling foolish. Her eyes widened, and her mouth opened and closed as if trying to retrieve the words she'd let loose between them. Herold would think she was throwing herself at him. As if reading her mind, he was about to reassure her: 'I would never think that. How could I ever think of you as anything but beautiful?'

'So, God willing, I'll see you same time next Tuesday then, Mr Mackenzie. Mr Mackenzie?' Margaret touched his arm, startling Herold into the realization that she was waiting for him to leave. She hadn't spoken those words, blushed in cute embarrassment or invited him to dinner after all.

Disappointment and emptiness: emotions held in check as he simply replied, 'Yes, Miss Margaret, God willing, I'll see you next week. Goodbye.'

Herold sang along softly as Lena Horne sang 'Stormy Weather' on his tape. Knotting his tie and brushing back his wavy hair with Dax Oil Sheen, he imagined crooning to Margaret, as they stood cheek to cheek. Patting on Old Spice, he slid his arm around her waist and held her dainty hand in his as they danced and twirled gently across his lino floor.

Herold put on his hat and eased into his comfortable shoes. It was going to be a long night. The fellas were waiting; he had scores to settle. Music ringing in his ears, he slipped the pack of ivory dominoes into his pocket and walked to the car. No six-love brush for him tonight.

The weekly domino meeting was a ten-minute drive away at the Cottage Community Centre, Kyrwicks Lane, Sparkbrook. Every Thursday evening the small hall came alive as men from the surrounding area sat down to taunt each other verbally while aiming to break their own triumphant records.

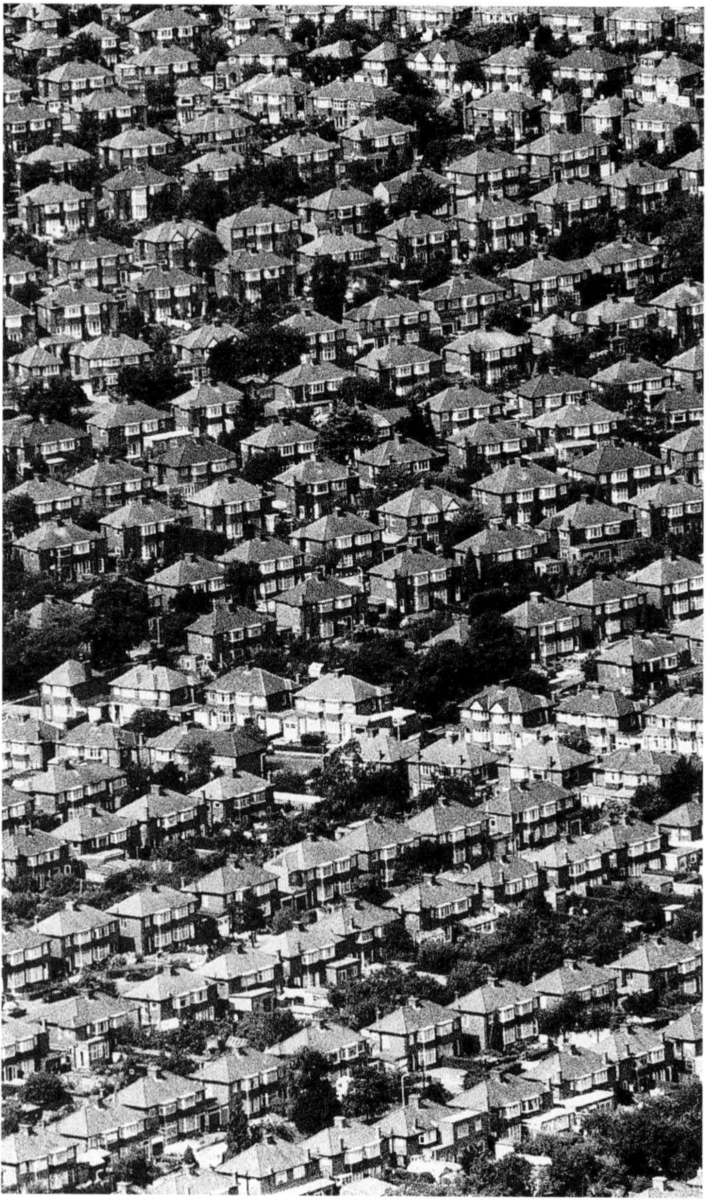

3

BAM! The trestle table shook as another player slammed his hand down. BAM! BAM! The quartet of men directed energy and strength into their game. The weekly domino tournament was serious business. Slamming sub-consciously subdued or enraged your opponents. BAM! If you couldn't slam then you weren't ready to play a man's game. BAM!

'You still aiming to wine and dine Miss Margaret, eh? Don't you think you aiming a bit high?' The bait came from Fyfield.

'Always minding other people's business, ain't you, Fyfield?' BAM! Herold slammed back.

'She keep she figure good for a woman she age.' This from Herold's partner, Albert. BAM! BAM!

'What I want to know is, how low you think you going to go, how far you think you can get, you wan see her panting, in a sweat!' A blow this time from Trini.

'Man, pay him no mind. He just jealous.' Herold was happy to let the men fight it out. 'You all gossip like old women. Turn up the music; Lord Kitchener calypso always does give me inspiration. Meanwhile I ready to give you all brush tonight.'

4

With a final glance in the mirror as she checked her immaculate hair, Margaret slipped on her heels, lifted the needle from yet another Lena classic, and headed outside.

From the porch she waved the taxi up onto the drive. The house was set well back from the pavement and taxi drivers often went straight past it although she described the wooden picket fence and black and white awnings quite clearly on the phone. She told them the house was right opposite the Friends Meeting House on Stratford Road, about one hundred and fifty yards from South

Birmingham College, but still they could never get it right.

Finally seated in the taxi, she ruminated about her gardener. She remembered his muscles glinting ebony black in the sunshine. Iron-grey hair softened by natural waves ending in wispy curls at the nape of his neck. He was about her age, but his West Indian features still turned heads. Margaret wondered just how many widows used Mr Mackenzie's gardening services while dreaming of using much more. She was reluctant to admit it, but every time he checked his watch, the thought of him leaving her hung heavy like a lead weight.

Margaret paid and thanked the driver as they pulled up to Hall Green Methodist Church. A distinctive cross illuminated in neon blue was set high at the front. Lower down, an oval-shaped plaque with gold lettering read:

The Millennium is
CHRIST'S 2000TH BIRTHDAY.
Worship Him here now.

5

'So, Miss Margaret, I hear you're back on the market for a man,' Jasmine began as the ladies sewed, sorted and ironed the white gowns for Sunday's baptism.

Margaret kept her head bowed over her needle, an enigmatic smile on her face.

'Some say Mr Mackenzie is a good catch, handy around the place, good with his hands, eh . . .?' Eulalie fished.

Margaret said nothing.

'Him short though. I like my men tall and broad.'

'What you mean "my men"? When was the last time you had a man?' Cherie piped up, unable to resist pointing out the obvious.

'Well, from what I hear, Mr Mackenzie little but him tallawa!' Laughter erupted as the ladies were reminded of the old Jamaican word for 'mighty'. Margaret laughed too, relinquishing her earlier resolve to remain detached.

'Miss Margaret, pay these women no mind, is just they jealous. Whatever going on with you and Mr Mackenzie is between you two.' Margaret glanced warmly at Desrene, then she addressed the room.

'I'm glad you all taking such an interest in my affairs. But I'm not getting married and I'm too old for babies, so don't go putting two and two together and making five, you hear? Now, how we getting on with these gowns?'

6

As Herold arrived at Margaret's the following Tuesday a sudden rain shower prompted him to shelter under the front arch before making his way around to the back. The sound of music caught his attention. He thought he'd left Lena at home, but here was Miss Margaret playing another one of her tunes. '*I don't know why but I'm feeling so sad.*' Did she know what that voice did for him? How Lena made him feel?

Turning towards the house, he rang the bell. High heels tapped across a wooden floor. Shapely hips outlined through frosted glass made his nature rise. He was no longer a mere labourer to Miss Margaret's upper-middle classness. The pull of lust rendered them equals.

'Come on through, Mr Mackenzie. I'm glad you could make it. How are you today?'

'I'm well, thank you. And how are you keeping?'

Polite small talk cushioned the air between them. She entered the lounge, he followed her lead. She posed upright on the settee. He sat stiffly in the armchair. She poured tea, offered rum cake. He sipped and commented on the garden. She murmured polite agreements until she felt his eyes on her. He held her gaze. Words ended, he desired and needed her. She smiled an invitation for him to lie beside her on the wide sofa. She stroked his cheek. He smoothed her beautiful hair. Somewhere in the background Lena sang.

A light rapping on the glass patio doors jerked Herold from soft fantasy to firm reality. He was three quarters of the way across the huge back garden. His afternoon's work would soon be over.

7

'Mr Mackenzie, I think you ought to call it a day, those dark clouds could mean another downpour.' As Margaret spoke, the heavens opened and a parched earth hungrily absorbed fat raindrops.

'Let me help you gather your things.' Margaret opened the door and moved towards Herold.

'No! I have it, Miss Margaret. Stay in out of the rain!' Herold snapped as he grabbed his tool bag. Slightly startled, Margaret faced him before moving closer, laying true feelings bare, all pretence washed away. Herold threw his bag to one side, eyes fixed on her beautiful face. He leaned forward to inhale her familiar musky scent. Masculine brown lips brushed against womanly softness. His arms encircled her waist, his strength held her close – afraid of discovering that this was just another illusion. Eventually Herold looked into her eyes. He had to see how she felt. Was he wrong, was this wrong? Taking his hand, Margaret led him towards the house.

In an upstairs room, Margaret and Herold finally acknowledged their love. He slowly removed layers of delicate, lavender-scented clothing from the body of the woman he yearned for. She responded to his kisses with a passion she thought existed only in the young. His caresses grew from tentative to searching as she willingly allowed him to discover her. Together they satiated their longing.

8

'You make me feel like a sensual teenage girl.'

'Miss Margaret, you are beautiful at any age. I've adored and desired you for so long. Too long. If only I could have told you.'

'Well, tell me now, Mr Mackenzie, show me now.'

When it was over, Herold held Margaret tightly as they slept. She was too precious to let go. They'd shared something ethereal, beyond thought, words or feeling.

Herold slowly opened his eyes and glanced at the bedside clock. Two hours had passed since they'd been in bed. Miss Margaret was still draped across him, her silken black hair spread over his chest. Remembering the love that had passed between them, Herold leaned down to kiss Margaret's forehead. She was cold. He felt the side of her face with his palm.

'Margaret. Margaret!'

He struggled from under her. Kneeling on the floor, he shook her shoulders. Her eyes stayed closed. Her body gave no resistance. Was his new love dead? Herold sobbed as he slumped to the floor.

Some time later Herold dressed.

There were no more tears, only deep sorrow and the raw pain of emptiness inside him. He lifted the needle of the old record player and put on one of Lena's 45s.

Herold searched through Margaret's bureau looking for a gown to dress her in before he called the doctor. As he slipped the lacy cotton over Margaret's arms and chest, a bundle of papers fell from its folds. After fixing the nightdress to make sure she was decent, Herold turned to the dropped papers.

He found a pile of sepia photos and letters, newspaper cuttings and a note addressed to him.

9

Dear Herold,

See how bold I am, calling you Herold, although I would never say that to your face. From my upstairs window I watch as you tend my garden every week in rain or sunshine. I often wish your strong hands were holding me instead of those tools. I want to tell you, never mind the lemonade, I am all you need to satisfy your thirst. I dream of lying here with you and often my longing for you is so strong I think you must be able to feel it. Or is my imagination just running away with me?

I heard you humming along to Lena while you worked. Her music has been the one constant in my life since I came to England. Would you believe it was a white lady who introduced me to her? When Lena sings, she sings my thoughts and my feelings. Did you guess that, my darling? You see, I understand that someone like you could never be with someone like me. We West Indians were brought up so strictly by our parents and grandparents. Back home you would just be the gardener and I would not be allowed to talk to you, much less offer you lemonade. Even here in England, I could not expose you to the shame of what has happened to me. My dear special Mr Mackenzie, you deserve the very best, no lies, no scandals, no skeletons in the closet. That's why I always played Lena. It was a small way of sharing my favourite thing with you.

I have just come back from seeing the doctor. The cancer has now spread through my lungs. I believe the hospital staff are being optimistically kind when they say I have six months to a year. I know I will only be here for a few more weeks.

When you find this letter, Herold, remember that I

wished many, many times that things could have been different between us. Play Lena often for me and be happy, look after our garden.

Love always, Margaret

10

Hot, salty tears flowed. Herold was also a product of Jamaica's class system, which taught that labourers like him should know their place. He cursed his shy, reserved nature. Why did he wait? They could have had more time together. But it was too late.

Now Herold understood why Margaret had seemed to be growing more and more frail over the last few weeks. He remembered how she'd tried to hide the fact that she was often breathless and in pain. Once he'd helped her to a seat when he'd seen her through the kitchen window, close to fainting. She always said it was nothing, that she was fine, but deep down Herold had known something was wrong.

But what did she mean by skeletons, and scandal? Turning over the wad of papers, Herold found the newspaper clippings. The first was dated 5 September 1952. There was a black and white photo of a young-looking Miss Margaret standing next to a pretty white lady. They looked unhappy, almost embarrassed. Unfolding the page, Herold began to read:

Jamaican immigrants have not only brought calypso music to England, but also shameful relationships. Miss Margaret Patterson, 23, formerly of Kingston, Jamaica, and Mrs Lena Delaware, 25, of Harrow Rd, London, were caught in flagrante by Mrs Delaware's hard-working husband Victor, 32, one evening. Heading upstairs, Mr Delaware discovered the two women in his bed:

'They were carrying on with disgusting acts. I felt sick when I saw it,' he stated. Mr Delaware added that Miss Patterson had been a tenant of theirs for six months.

11

Other letters wrapped in red silk ribbon caught Herold's eye.

3 June 1952

Dear Margaret,
Wasn't Lena Horne brilliant and beautiful at the Hammersmith Odeon? Victor's working late again tonight, come down about nine.
Love and kisses,
Lena xxx

4 July 1952

Dear Margaret,
Victor hates me talking to 'the lodgers'. 'When we've made our money off these negroes we'll kick em out and get our house back,' he says. Don't let him get to you, sweetheart. Come with me tonight, to see the new Lena Horne picture. Say yes, darling.
Lena xxx

10 August 1952

The bastard. I can barely lift my arm. God help me if he's broken it. Margaret, I need you, I really, really need you . . . Come downstairs tonight, I'll be waiting.
Lena xxx

12

Herold stopped. There were more, lots more. Love letters from Lena Delaware to Margaret, telling of a love which had sprung from mutual loneliness and the delight of Lena Horne's voice. Pages of despair describing how life with a sadistic, brutal husband had driven her to find love in the arms of a Jamaican woman. Once Victor had discovered his wife's secret he stayed long enough to crack Lena's jaw and rape Margaret before going to the press to make money from his story. Margaret's subsequent miscarriage and the vilification they suffered at the hands of eager reporters had driven her and Lena to a small bedsit on the outskirts of West Bromwich, where they lived together for five years until Lena emigrated to America. There were no letters telling why they'd broken up.

Herold sadly shook his head. The middle-class Jamaican immigrant and the battered cockney wife. Lesbian lovers. Now he knew why Miss Margaret had been such a loner. This must've destroyed her life. Had she ever opened up to anyone? She never mentioned a husband, or children. But now that he knew how much love she had to give, anger welled up as once again he realized that it was too late. She should've told him, she should've trusted him. Did she really think he would've walked away?

13

Ten days later the sun refused to shine at Kings Heath Cemetery as they lowered Margaret into the ground. Jasmine, Desrene, Cherie and the other churchwomen wept for the dignified, genteel lady whom they'd never really got to know. The men from the domino club stood back with doffed caps. The single red rose that Herold had tossed into the grave was joined by another. Herold looked up. A woman stood near him, cheeks wet with tears, face lined with age, blue eyes moist with memories of the woman who'd brightened both their lives.

'Can I give you a lift?' Herold offered. Lena Delaware looked into empathetic eyes as she nodded her acceptance.

The Tears of Trevor

Nick Jones

Somewhat surprisingly for a man who's so fervently anti-American, my father Stan has for years adopted a baseball-like, match-day policy of three strikes and you're out with his wardrobe.

He's always been ludicrously superstitious, to the extent that whenever he witnesses a defeat of his beloved football team, Birmingham City, he makes a cross with an indelible black marker on the inside of the clothes that he's wearing at the time. Conversely, my father is very partisan towards anything that's worn at the time of a Birmingham victory; such hallowed items then have a small circle religiously penned into the hem, marking them out for future reference as somehow 'lucky'. Only when crosses exceed circles by three does an item of clothing meet its Waterloo. Not that such garments are thrown away; that'd be just silly, as well as hugely expensive. No, 'three strikers', as Stan refers to them, are just relegated to the status of non-match-day wear.

It's a system of apparel-abuse which exasperated my mother throughout their years together. Six months into their marriage, having witnessed a whole series of perfectly good shirts graffitied by his superstition, she vowed never to purchase good quality clothing for my father again.

Stan, never the proudest or vainest of men, became from that day on a charity shop's walking mannequin.

It's almost as if my father believes, were he only to crack the Ensemble Enigma, then Birmingham players would need only to avert their gaze to Stan Jacobs in the Tilton Road End, see him standing there in his lucky garb, and through some magical neo-osmotic process, the league would be as good as won. Sadly, but not altogether astonishingly, despite decades of sartorial experimentation, my father has yet to concoct a combination of clothing which consistently does the trick.

Rough patterns within Stan's hypothesis emerged over time, as order – if one looks hard enough – can always be gleaned from chaos. Collared shirts seemed to be luckier than collarless; cotton outfits were more successful than acrylic. Light colours (particularly beige) were almost always more effective than dark, except in December and January when, for years, no matter how much Stan changed his game plan, Blues mysteriously kept losing. During such barren periods my father resorted to dark blue clothing which, he found, while seldom eliciting a victory, tended to evoke more one-point draws for his side.

My mother, of course, always yearned for a draw, as such circumstances meant that Stan's clothes would be left untainted by permanent ink and their wearable-in-public existence prolonged. To this day, my mother maintains that her sole success in eighteen years of life married to my father was to get him to agree that the three-strikes theory should only apply to league and cup fixtures; so giving his wardrobe brief respite in times of pre-season friendlies and testimonials.

When my father retired from the Post Office three years ago, he finally relinquished his Blues season ticket, citing four decades of frustration and a desire to save a few pennies as his reasons for turning his back on the Tilton.

However, some of his Villa-supporting colleagues, aware of Stan's eccentricity, joshed that he daren't face the prospect of walking through Small Heath in his birthday suit. Given Birmingham's gutsy but ultimately fruitless performances over the years and knowing my father's aversion to shopping, it's indeed a wonder that he now has any match-day clothes left to preserve his modesty.

It is Sunday 25 February 2001, a date which for weeks beforehand Stan has promulgated as a Bluenose Jubilee; a festival of celebration the likes of which Selly Oak hasn't witnessed since the sun-kissed, red, white and blue summer of 1977. Today, Trevor Francis, manager of Birmingham City, leads his team out to face the mighty Liverpool in the Worthington Cup Final at Cardiff's Millennium Stadium. For a rare moment in the club's miserably unrewarding 126 years of existence, the nation's footballing eyes will be focused on the team from Small Heath.

I guess my father had visions of impromptu street parties, families pulling together, galvanized by a common bond and a desire to return to old-fashioned values. In truth, though, any festivity based upon Birmingham City reaching the climax of a second-rate knockout tournament was always going to struggle to rival Sydney's millennium celebrations. And, as my father soon discovered, it would be hard to capture much popular support.

Stan's hopes for a council-funded Cup Final celebration were always slightly delusional and so in the fortnight running up to the Cardiff spectacle, my father took it upon himself to rouse local residents from their stupor and to muster them for some form of local revelry. With Scargill-esque verve, he fly-petitioned Tiverton Road and the adjoining streets in an attempt to champion his cause, but his efforts met with deafening apathy – just two shows of interest, one well-wishing note from the cornershop owner and a nightly barrage of abuse from suspected Villa-supporting teenagers in Dawlish Road.

Even a door-to-door canvas was hardly more successful. The people of Selly Oak were variously: already going to Cardiff, loathed Blues, were ambivalent about football or had been raised on a diet of Premier League football. It saddened my father to see so many toddlers sporting replica Manchester United and Liverpool shirts emblazoned with the names of vowel-deficient foreign megastars.

Stan ultimately decided to host his own private showing of the match and invite over his only son as well as interested friends and neighbours on the strict under-standing that those in attendance were favourably disposed to Trevor Francis's Blue and White Army. My father thus forsook a long-held hatred of all things associated with Rupert Murdoch by subscribing to the entire Sky Sports package in the week before the Final. Principles are one thing, but stubborn political grudges have to fall by the wayside when Birmingham City reach a major footballing final.

As I pull my car up to a brakes-need-servicing, screaming halt beside the terraced house which was my home for almost twenty years, it's apparent that even Stan's revised celebration plans have fallen some way short of expectation. Of the four blue and white balloons which he's tied to the front gate, three are now lifeless rubber skins thanks to a tussle with a rusty protrusion. The one blue balloon still bobbing looks sad and slightly deflated as if it too would shortly depart this cold, inflated world. Stuck inside the grimy bay window is a colour, double-page newspaper print of the heroic First Division side as it prepares to take on the mantle of David against the Goliath of Merseyside. Beneath this, a tatty blue and white scarf bearing the legend 'The Blues: Auto Windscreen

Champions 1995' clings to three strips of browning sellotape.

This well-intentioned but impotent Blues theme park is completed by a tape player fed through one of the smaller windows which plays a tinny acoustic version of the Blues anthem 'Keep Right on to the End of the Road' through pitifully inadequate speakers.

After a lengthy delay and a great deal of moaning and cursing from within, my father opens the door to me. His thick salt and pepper hair is more unkempt than usual; his gnarled fingers orange with nicotine stains. Although his tall, gangling physique is one which God never intended for public exhibition, I'm not altogether surprised to see that he's sporting nothing more than a pair of check boxer shorts and a grubby string vest. To my dismay, though, we're not alone; others are being subjected to the unseemly sight of his sun-starved, varicose-veined limbs. Judging by their apathy, it's not a composition with which his guests are unfamiliar.

Although I haven't seen Stan since Christmas, his frosty welcome is somewhat justified. Without moving his eyes from the TV screen where the match is already well under way, he growls that I'm typically late. Timing has never been a personal forte but only a footballing agnostic could be over an hour late for the start of 'his team's' first final of a major domestic competition in thirty-eight years.

Truth be told, in spite of my father's concerted efforts and fifteen years of glumly standing beside him in the Tilton, the magic that is watching Birmingham City script-lessly booting a football around never really infiltrated my psyche. As soon as I was old enough to summon up some strength to my convictions, I announced to my father that I no longer wished to make the bi-weekly trek to St Andrew's. His usually emotionless countenance was immediately contorted with rage and despair, imparting a sense of total betrayal and disgust at his son's heretic stance. Thereafter, our father–son relationship, never terribly warm nor deep, quickly revealed itself for what it was – a shallow acquaintance based flimsily on a one-sided love for an underperforming football team.

For this afternoon's proceedings the front room is playing host to Stan, Rhys Thomas from next door (a Wrexham fan by birth but an adopted Bluenose), my father's darts partner and lifelong Blues sufferer Frankie Dennis, Frankie's hyperactive five-year-old hooligan Robbie and Mrs Isanovic, an Eastern European octogenarian.

In all the years I've been acquainted with Mrs Isanovic I don't believe she's exchanged more than half a dozen words with me, and her failure to even acknowledge my presence by lifting her head from her furious knitting suggested that today was unlikely to see us move that sum into double figures.

Rhys, picking up on my look of surprise at the notorious sportsphobe in our midst explains, 'Her central heating's on the blink.' Clamping a bony but hirsute hand to my shoulder and simultaneously emphasizing every syllable in his familiar, just-plucked-from-the-Valleys lilt, he clarifies: 'Blues reaching the Cup Final has clearly softened your old man. The old dear came round earlier as she needed somewhere warm to shelter.'

I can only imagine that Mrs Isanovic conveyed this message through a series of intricately drawn cartoons as to my knowledge her grasp of English, or at least her willingness to use that knowledge, is frugal at the best of times. Looking at the sartorial monstrosity that she's rapidly weaving, it's easy to understand why Mrs Isanovic's relatives bear such solemn expressions and why they only ever visit her under duress. Coloured wools seemingly selected at random by a myopic and crazed individual entwine into what one might kindly describe as a 'throw'. The very idea that she believes someone might, of their own volition, choose to wear such a garment represents a weighty argument for involuntary euthanasia for all eighty-somethings. It makes me shudder to think of the Isanovic children bedecked from cradle to high school in woollen variations on a constantly ill-chosen theme; their sallow, horror-stricken faces the stuff of fundraising appeals.

Isanovic isn't her real surname, rather it's one which she and her husband adopted when they came to England in the fifties in the belief that it sounded more westernized than their original family name. She's never revealed the spelling, still less the pronunciation, of her true surname, but one can be fairly sure that it'd represent a powerful tool on the Scrabble board.

The room's uncomfortably warm and I'm not sure how far this is at the insistence of Mrs Isanovic or if it's to make my semi-naked father feel less conspicuous. The greying woodchip walls cry out for a lick of bright paint, the only break in their sombreness a cheaply framed monochrome photo. The photographic image captured is grainy and poorly configured: perhaps taken either with a cheap camera or by a woeful photographer.

None the less, it's clear to those who know me that swamped beneath an ill-fitting, woolly BCFC hat and scarf is a podgy, five-year-old Geoff Jacobs. Towering over me while shaking my hand is the lean, long-haired twenty-year-old footballing prodigy, Trevor Francis. Both of us are looking into the camera, my face as glum and listless as Trevor's trouser bottoms and tie are gaudy and wide. The prominent positioning of the snap could be misinterpreted as evidence of a proud and loving father but for the fact that this is the only photo of me in the house and that the focus of the composition is very much on 'Tricky Trev'.

Accepting a cheap can of lukewarm lager proffered by

Frankie, I lower myself to the vacant space on the faux sheepskin rug beside Robbie who's recreating the sound of dropping bombs as he hurls a tennis ball venomously at a platoon of helpless plastic soldiers.

Turning my eyes to the television, I note without surprise that Liverpool lead by a goal to nil; breaks in play are punctuated by replays of Birmingham's torture – a magical thirtieth-minute strike from outside the box by Robbie Fowler which leaves the Blues goalkeeper diving spectacularly but despairingly at air. The score aside, though, Birmingham now appear to be enjoying the better of the possession in the second half. While their passing and movement is more workmanlike than inspirational, the players' passion, commitment and raw desire are evident for all to see. Gradually, initial fears of a massacre recede and hopes grow that a Cup Final upset is more than just an impossible fantasy.

Oddly for individuals whose usual verbal exchanges rarely venture above the parapets of the crude and obscene, the observations emanating from Stan, Frankie and Rhys seem carefully considered and dignified. I find myself in the midst of footballing connoisseurs and the realization terrifies me. Over the course of many seasons, these men have experienced the entire spectrum of emotions as they've watched and carefully dissected the game of football. Indeed, but for a patent lack of fitness, dedication, sporting ability and foot–eye coordination in their earlier years, they might now themselves be occupying the TV commentary box, regaling viewers with their incisive yet effervescent views on strategy, team formation, players' strengths and career histories. Theirs is not the pagan chant of the terraces. Their assertions are perspicacious; an impression reinforced by the flat, matter-of-fact tone with which their comments are delivered, as if their content is beyond dispute to any sane earthling.

Naturally, the conversation is given ample piquancy by the addition of four-letter words, derogations and questions over individuals' parentage, but each comment takes my naïve knowledge of the game and its participants that little bit further.

It's a terribly intimidating environment for me. Ironically for someone who's spent so many years trying to step out of the shadow of my father and assert myself as an individual, I now yearn for the anonymity and community which people with shared passions and comprehensions enjoy.

For my own self-worth and for the sake of Robbie's perception of me, I feel an enormous pressure to make my own telling contribution to the debate, to say something groundbreakingly perceptive. Even as I think, I'm being demoted in the three other men's eyes to the emasculated status of a football ignoramus; if only I'd taken the time to learn some of the nuances of the game during my years as a season ticket holder.

I fear, though, that anything that comes from my mouth will cause the three wise men whom I hope to impress to momentarily divert their attention away from the TV screen to me and make that most childlike of schoolground put-downs: the tongue thrust over the teeth of the lower jaw, against the inside of the mouth while emitting a guttural 'Nnnuuuurr!' – 'The Spacca' as we used to call it. No, best not to risk that humiliation, Geoff. Just restrict yourself to cries of 'Come on . . .!' linked with the surname or, much better, the nickname of one of the four Birmingham players I actually recognize whenever they're in possession and – *Hey Presto!* – an inconsequential but eminently recyclable break in my self-imposed silence.

Sadly for me, one of my four bankers for peer-impressing recognition purposes, the strongly built Nigerian forward, Dele Adebola (or 'Delly, Delly, Delly, Delly A-dee-bola!' as the crowd feels obliged to chant during the rare moments when he's in control of the ball) has been substituted at half-time, thus curtailing the variety of my orations by twenty-five per cent. However, my other three are still on the field of play. The young, small-statured blond striker is definitely called 'AJ'; the bald midfield general and captain's name is Martin O'Connor and I'm fairly confident that the good-looking, floppy haired defender is Darren Purse. If only Blues restricted all their build-up play to these three I'd be able to contribute all the more fruitfully. In an effort to delay discovery of my ruse and consequent exposure as a fraud, I sometimes vary my proclamations when the play constipates in the centre of the pitch by shouting, 'Play it wide . . .!' if AJ, O'Connor or Purse are on the ball and then pretend to draw lengthily on my long-since-drained can of beer, satisfied with my soundbites and feeling adulthood pressures ebb away.

Gradually I start to feel that I'm accumulating some credibility among my room-mates. This is something which Robbie would pick up on if he could tear his attention away for a moment from the cross-examination and very painful torture of the Seventh Battalion of the Light Blue Plastic Infantry. The soldiers are clearly either ignorant or very slow learners as one after another they refuse to relinquish the desired information. This despite being surrounded by a swelling sea of decapitated plastic bodies and an enemy wielding a pair of paper scissors ten times their size.

Five minutes of the match to go.

Although I'm now operating within a restricted comfort zone, I feel stifled by constantly having to hide my true ignorance. Soon, though, I'll hear the sweet shrill of referee David Elleray's whistle and my torment will be over. I can console the three men around me, give one of those knowing 'If only the referee hadn't been a Scousesympathizing Nazi' shrugs and return to the peace of my own home.

Two minutes to go.

The Blues' pressure is almost relentless, but for all the team's possession an equalizing goal for the underdogs seems destined not to happen. Naturally, I'd love my childhood heroes-under-paternal-duress to win but they're not going to score twice now. Let's put them and myself out of our respective misery and move on. In any event, we'd have only been annihilated at the hands of some Italian giant in next season's UEFA Cup.

I note with relief that the ninety minutes are up. As injury time ticks over, discordant whistles wail out from the red half of the Millennium Stadium pleading Mr Elleray to call a halt to proceedings. And then . . .

The Blues skipper is brought down in Liverpool's penalty area by a tall French defender and the referee immediately points to the penalty spot. The whole room falls silent but for the *click-click-click* of Mrs Isanovic's needles; even Robbie calls a temporary ceasefire. Purse steps up to take the kick.

I suddenly realize that I don't know Darren's moniker but, eager to say something both sensible and familiar before the rush of rhetoric from the others, I take an ill-judged stab at his footballing nom de guerre.

'Stick it away, Dazzly!' I roar.

Unfortunately, it transpires that this is not Darren Purse's terrace nickname and that I've let my true form show. Despite the nail-biting climax unwrapping before us, three sets of adult eyes flick momentarily at me – two registering surprise; the third, fatherly shame. Robbie pulls a Spacca at me.

With admirable poise, Purse bullets the ball into the goal and, as the net bulges, half the stadium and this entire room (one Eastern European excepted) erupts in scenes of uncontained rapture. People jumping to their feet, arms punching the air for joy and everyone's grasp of the English language bizarrely contracting to Isanovic-like proportions, the one word universally roared – '*Yyyees!!*'

And it's magnificent. And I don't want the moment to end. Grown British men, so often afraid to display their true feelings for fear of appearing too much like a continental European, are suddenly hugging each other, somewhat awkwardly as you'd expect since two people's pogoing rarely coordinates. Staggeringly, Birmingham City might be just thirty minutes of extra time away from European competition next year.

'Good old Dazzly!' jibes Frankie and we all laugh at my expense, and for the first time today I don't care. I feel like one of the lads.

Birmingham's endeavour dominates extra time and suddenly shots are firing more hopefully at the Liverpool goal. And then a moment when the impossible seems within grasp. AJ latches onto a ball and charges at the Liverpool goal only to be upended within the penalty area. Again, the entire Birmingham City phalanx is up on its feet, dancing around, demanding what's rightfully theirs – a penalty, the Cup, a place in Europe and a notable chapter in the club's uneventful history. But no, David Elleray bravely decides that he never wants to pass safely through the blue half of England's second city again and waves play on, dismissing a barrage of player protests. The TV camera pans round to show a scarlet-faced Trevor Francis storming up and down the touchline in demented and ineffectual protest. Simultaneously, a resigned feeling that it's not destined to be Birmingham's day infuses our front room. Should we fail to win in extra time, Birmingham's pedigree in penalty shoot-out deciders gives little ground for optimism.

It goes as we all feared. Time is called on the extra half-hour and although Birmingham for once make a decent stab at the penalty shoot-out, ensuring a torturous finale, there's a sense of inevitability when our diminutive striker AJ fails to beat the Liverpool goalie, Sander Westerveld. The trophy is Liverpool-bound.

As ecstasy and despair erupt in equal portions around the Cardiff arena, a dumbfounded Trevor Francis staggers over to console AJ, his face awash with sadness and disappointment, tears streaming down his cheeks. There are no such demonstrations in our Selly Oak front room, just numbness and an overwhelming sense of anticlimax. Stan firmly adheres to the belief that real men don't cry at anything other than possibly onion-slicing. Trevor's tears strike him as somewhat effeminate, but he'll forgive his hero such sentimental outpourings: a legacy no doubt of Trevor's former playing days with Sampdoria where grown men weeping was probably de rigueur.

Showing admirable spirit, the Birmingham supporters clap and cheer their defeated warriors, and as the players walk round the Cardiff pitch acknowledging the applause, 'Keep Right On' rises to the heavens. The end of the match marks the abrupt end of my own self-conscious torture, but for the second time that day I feel at one with this group of frustrated fans, and I have a sense of pride at their show of unity in the depths of such familiar adversity. Pointlessly racking my brain for suitable words of solace, I place a consolatory arm around Stan's shoulders – his body deflated and limp; his eyes staring at his grubby bare feet – 'Next year, eh Dad? Next year.'

Nobody really feels up for sitting through Sky's post-match analysis and so, following an awkward silence, the room rapidly disbands and everyone goes their separate ways.

Tiverton Road itself is strangely silent. As yet there are

no blue and white supporters pouring out of the local pubs, arms draped disconsolately over one another's shoulders, eyes glazed with disillusion. The lack of a public outpouring of grief seems to exacerbate my father's sense of isolation and despair. As I leave his home, I clumsily embrace my modestly attired father on the doorstep and hope that his hurt will only be short-lived. I secretly wonder whether I will ever see the Blues – Birmingham's eternal underachievers – in a major final again. I have my doubts, but as I drive away I make a mental note that in the event of such a phenomenon I'll ensure that my father's wardrobe is better stocked with sartorial alternatives.

Extinct

Rachel Taylor

It had been five years since Sarah had seen Richard. His parents had taken him away and moved to Cumbria when it had become clear that he'd been mixing with the 'wrong sort' – namely Sarah. But she'd kept in touch with him and finally managed to persuade him to come and see her. She had to keep reminding him that they weren't fifteen any more and could do what they liked now. And he was the only one who could know what she felt.

She wasn't sure what to expect from Richard. Recently, he'd been more reluctant to speak to her when she called and he'd stopped sending photographs. She used to like the photographs and had arranged them on her kitchen noticeboard. He always seemed to be standing at the bottom of hills, great swathes of countryside looming up behind him as if the land might swallow him whole. 'That's what it's like up here,' he'd say. 'Hilly.' And she'd say, 'But surely it'd be better to get a picture of yourself when you're at the *top* of the hill? More impressive.' But Richard didn't agree; he said that when you got to the top, you just wanted pictures of the view.

In truth, Sarah suspected that he never actually walked up the hills at all. But he obviously felt more at ease outdoors without any crowds or buildings, and she wondered what he'd make of her life here, back in the city.

As teenagers, they always used to meet in Chamberlain Square, on the sloping, circular steps by the fountain. It wasn't exactly *Roman Holiday* and Sarah knew she was no Audrey Hepburn, but she had a bit of a thing for fountains. Although it didn't make any sense to meet there, she couldn't help herself. She guessed that she should've arranged to meet him at the station or somewhere 'nicer'. There were enough coffee bars around. She cursed herself for always succumbing to tacky ideas of romance and nostalgia. But today was perfect for colouring in the blush of her rosy view. It was sunny. She could sit on the steps and look out towards the end of New Street and watch for him to come. Yes, she thought, this is just how it used to be. Then she shook her head and tutted – *stop being such a sap.*

She looked up again and saw him. But as he got closer, she thought she'd made a mistake. The man approaching didn't seem tall enough to be Richard. Then she realized that he must've done all his growing before he left, while she'd managed several significant growth spurts since he'd been gone. Richard looked short and wiry like a marathon runner. People had told Sarah she was 'willowy', but most of the time she just felt gangly and awkward. As he got closer and Sarah walked down the steps to greet him, they both became aware of the physical mismatch they would form. When it happened – it was brutal. Sarah placed her hand on Richard's shoulder and immediately felt like a Sunday School teacher with her pet pupil. His rucksack looked full and heavy. *Was he planning to stay?*

'Hi, Rich. It's good to see you.' She leaned forward, offering her cheek for him to kiss. He backed off and tortoise-necked into his shoulders. Sarah did likewise and lifted her hand away.

'Yeah. You too.'

Richard looked up at Sarah and tried to keep the two

parts of his jaw hanging together – the lower part looked like it'd been hooked to a falling brick. He turned away from her and seemed to decide to keep the conversation on safe ground for now.

'You told me I wouldn't recognize the place. Everything looks the same.' Richard gestured at the buildings surrounding them. He waved his hand and shrugged a shoulder – dismissive and unimpressed.

Sarah followed his gaze and looked around her at the library, the museum, the Town Hall and the fountain.

'Well, yeah, I suppose this bit's the same. But there are loads of other places. New shops . . . that sort of thing.' She floundered, upset by the clumsiness of their meeting.

'Right.' Richard jumped up a couple of steps, reassessed his height against hers and yawned.

'I suppose shops aren't your thing?'

'Not really.'

Sarah felt her enthusiasm ebbing away from her. Richard remained petulant. Disappointment stilled and silenced her as she tried to think of a way out. Sarah was praying for something to remove the awkwardness, but she'd never have imagined the form the answer to her plea would take. A set of double doors opened at the museum. Two men emerged carrying a life-size model of a dinosaur's head. One man was clutching at the ragged broken neck end and the other held onto a lethal-looking row of fibreglass teeth. Richard pointed.

'Oh my God. Remember that thing – the T-Rex. You used to be scared of that.' He smiled.

At last, thought Sarah. She played back off his amusement. 'Yeah, when we were about five. Anyway, you can hardly blame me. You'd go upstairs and there were all these dark corridors and cabinets filled with creepy skulls and stuff. Then suddenly, you went through a door and had that thing glaring down at you. Do you remember?'

'I remember that you cried.' He pointed at her, accusing.

'It was the shock! It looked like it was about to bite my head off.'

'You said you could hear it breathing. You were convinced. *And* totally hysterical.'

'All right, just cos you're into scaling mountains these days. But you're not so tough really.'

He looked away and they both watched as the men loaded the dinosaur's head into the back of a van. They wondered where the rest of its body was. Sarah pictured it being chopped up into van-sized pieces somewhere inside the building. The thought made her shudder. But she was grateful for the dinosaur's demise. It had provided a timely distraction after such a lousy start. She hoped the rest of the day would be easier, but she knew she couldn't count on a dismantled dinosaur cropping up again.

'Shall we head back to mine? You can dump your . . . stuff.' She peered over his shoulder at the rucksack and referred to the mental itinerary she'd constructed in spite of herself. 'I'll make us some lunch.'

'Mmm. Dunno. Why don't we eat in town? I'm all right carrying this. I'm used to it.'

She wondered if he was trying to prove how strong he was or whether he was just being obstructive.

'Well, it's just I bought some things in specially. But if you really don't want to . . .'

'No. Okay. Whatever.'

Richard gazed around him again. Sarah wasn't sure what his answer meant, but she decided to lead the way to the bus stop and head home as she'd originally planned.

The mood that'd lifted from Richard when they saw the dinosaur immediately dropped back onto his shoulders. As they walked through the city centre, he slumped along looking fazed by it all. He didn't seem able to hold a conversation with Sarah, his eyes were everywhere but he wasn't looking where he was going and kept bumping into people. He'd apologize to them as if they were aliens who might not understand him. Sarah found it hard to believe that he could've forgotten what the city was like or that living in Cumbria could've made him so incapable of dealing with crowds.

While they waited for the bus, Sarah pointed out the bar she worked in. She told him how manic it was on Friday and Saturday nights. He nodded along with whatever she said, though he didn't seem to engage with any of it. This was the city they'd loved in. Sarah could remember walking these streets holding Richard's hand. They'd kissed at this very bus stop so many times. *Had he forgotten? Didn't he care?*

Eventually the bus turned up and stopped with the usual reluctant scream of brakes. Sarah got on first and went up top. She sat down in a window seat. Richard was slow to appear at the top of the stairs. The rucksack had jammed in the stairwell halfway up. He sat in the seat in front of Sarah and placed the heavy bag next to him. The sight of the back of his head, so still and so dumb, made her want to hit him. What the hell's wrong with him? she thought. But she was still hoping for an unspoilt day, so she kept quiet and people-watched.

They edged and jerked along the Bristol Road out of town. They went through Selly Oak and into leafy, God-fearing Bournville. Eventually Sarah stood up and tapped Richard on the shoulder.

'Come on. This is us.'

He got up slowly. Sarah had been watching him during the journey as he stared out of the window – he'd kept sighing and shaking his head. He was restless, tired and dull all at the same time. Could it be that he was feeling nostalgic after all? Sarah wondered. These streets and the bus journey awakening more of the familiarity she wanted to share with him – like the dinosaur. They walked across the edge of the park and through some of the university accommodation to get to Sarah's flat. Students were wandering about. Richard looked like he would fit in, with his rucksack and his slightly nerdish springy hair. Sarah always felt self-conscious when she passed them, and even though she was the same age as most of them, she felt older somehow. She could see posters on bedroom walls through the rows of windows; tattered notices stuck to the doors advertised club nights and live bands. She turned to Richard.

'I always thought you'd go to uni. I was really surprised when you didn't even apply.'

He shrugged. 'I considered it . . . but it wasn't the right time.'

'Oh. Why not?'

'Family stuff.'

'Oh.'

She didn't pry any further. Sarah knew Richard's mum had had some nervous problem that she assumed had been blamed on her and what she'd put their precious son through. She waited for Richard to ask her about why *she* hadn't applied for uni. He remained silent, so she decided to tell him anyway.

'Well, it wasn't an option for me either. Nobody to support me. Obviously my crap exam results didn't help. So I had to get a job. Which is going really well by the way. I know being a barmaid isn't very credible, but it's good fun and I get enough to keep the flat on. So I'm okay. Happy – most of the time.'

'Great.'

She caught a look from him – he didn't believe her. And she couldn't blame him. She didn't really believe it either.

When they arrived back at the flat, she made lunch. Richard ate quickly while she pushed rubbery curls of pasta around her plate. She chatted and watched him. Afterwards, Sarah washed up and when she went back into the lounge, Richard was sprawled out, fast asleep on the sofa.

She sat down in the chair opposite. She looked at him and tried to remember the fifteen-year-old she'd been in love with. His bare feet hung over the arm of the sofa. Small but manly feet with hairy toes. She didn't remember him having hairy toes before. The smooth pink skin on the sole confirmed her suspicion that he didn't do as much walking as he claimed. The bottom edges of his jeans were neat and it looked like his mother had ironed a crease down the front. Sarah looked at her own jeans, frayed at the bottom, and her long bony feet poking out. Old purple varnish speckled her toenails like mould.

She looked back at Richard, hugging himself loosely, stubby fingers resting on his shoulder. His lips stuck out in a sleepy pout and his long eyelashes slumbered on his cheek. For all his faults, he was still beautiful. Not a word often used for men, but Sarah felt it to be the right one for Richard. He had a delicacy, an innocence that made it possible to call him beautiful – a beautiful boy. She'd long ago lost any such qualities herself, which made them even more desirable to her. She unfurled herself from the chair and stood over him. Then hesitated, wondering just for a second if she really had the nerve to do it. But then she thought about how they'd done it before so easily, so happily. And even though he'd been quiet all morning, she knew that sometimes when he was nervous he could be like that. She crouched down, cupped his cheek and kissed him.

Richard opened his eyes. She backed off, but held her hand where it rested on his face.

'Sarah, what are you doing?' Richard pushed her hand away and gawped at her.

Sarah moved away from him and caught sight of herself

in the mirror above the sofa. It was a shock when she realized how needy she looked. She was smiling – but it was a pleading smile – her face showing a last desperate attempt at happiness before crumbling into despair. And it all hinged on this man who was still so much like a boy. She looked back at Richard. He scowled up at her – a scolded child.

'Oh come on, Rich. It was just a kiss. Stupid maybe – but not exactly a crime. You looked relaxed . . . sweet . . . and I thought . . .'

'Relaxed! God no. I just don't know what to say to you. I *can't* face talking to you. I had to get you to shut up for five minutes.'

He stood up and paced round the room.

'Why do you always have to be such a wimp?' Sarah shouted.

He stopped pacing. Sarah actually felt something break inside her head. Her vision and her dreams spilled out from the crack. She could almost see them, pouring away from her and evaporating around Richard as he shook his head at her.

'You don't understand. You don't have any parents.'

'Oh yeah. Thanks for the reminder.'

'Don't be sarcastic.'

It was a stand-off. Richard was hoping to get away unscathed, wishing he hadn't bothered to come at all. But he had to wait. He couldn't help being curious to see if she'd go that one step further, and Sarah could tell. She could see his confusion in the way he ran his index finger along his bottom lip as he stared at her. And that confusion was irresistible to her, like picking at a scab or letting a match burn close to your fingers. Without her delusions to sustain her, Sarah felt glad of her anger. So she went for it.

'She'll have started school now. Don't you *ever* think about her?'

She watched and waited for her words to hit him like a fist in the face. But he just sighed like a bad actor in a hammy soap.

'No. I don't.'

'You *can't* mean that.'

'You agreed to the adoption. There's no point to all this.'

'I only agreed because I wasn't given a choice.' She stood up and began to pace. The crack in her voice brought her closer to tears. 'I had all these people advising me, no, *telling* me what do with *our* baby. Of course I didn't want her to be adopted. Look at what happened to *me* – kids' homes, foster homes. And whenever things improved even a bit I'd get moved on and . . .'

'I know, Sarah. You've told me all this in your letters, on the phone. I want you to get over it.'

'So why did you come here?'

'You *need* to get over it, Sarah. I'm engaged. I'm going to get married next year. I didn't really want to come. I didn't want to meet on the steps like that . . . like we used to. But you forced this by not accepting that what's happened is in the past.'

'Who is she?'

'You don't need to know.'

Sarah nodded. He was right. She meant nothing to Richard's family or to Richard. She walked over to the window and watched three students throwing a Frisbee around. It seemed hard to believe now – that she'd given up her child because his family thought she wasn't good enough. 'At least you'll have the freedom to do what you want,' other people had told her. They all conspired behind her back and no one told her the truth. She didn't have any freedom. She just about got by and made the best of things. Sarah felt his hand resting lightly on her shoulder.

'I didn't mean to tell you like that. I'm sorry. But it's for the best.'

She turned and looked at him; she'd forgotten until now how he blinked too much.

'I think you should go home, Rich. I'll see you off.'

He nodded, sat back down on the sofa and picked up his boots. Sarah noticed that they, like his feet, were clean and smooth. She wondered whether to ask him if he really walked up all those hills but she already knew the answer.

They moved along in silence once more. As they walked down New Street towards the station, Richard looked dazed again. The sky was just darkening and the lights from the shops threw multicoloured glows across their faces as if trying to find one to reflect their varying moods. They finally got to the station and stood on the concourse. Richard bent down and rooted through his rucksack, trying to find his ticket. A man in his twenties stood near by, holding a bunch of red roses. Sarah smiled to herself. But how unoriginal, she thought, remembering how she wanted to be – how she *would* be from now on.

'Shame about that old dinosaur, isn't it? I wonder where they'll put him,' she said to the top of Richard's head, still buried in the opening of his bag.

'Mmm,' came the muffled reply.

'What have you got in there anyway? Let *me* look for it.'

She pulled the bag away from him and started to delve in before he had chance to stop her. As her hand went down, she felt a bundle of papers. She pulled them out slowly, conscious of Richard watching for her reaction. A pile of letters in pastel envelopes addressed to him in her handwriting. She reached in again and pulled out the photos she'd sent and a couple of Mike Gayle novels that she'd hoped would somehow turn him into the sensitive type. She dropped onto her knees and felt the cold hardness of the floor strike her bones.

'Rich?'

He shuffled from one foot to the other. A schoolboy again – meek and shallow.

'I'm sorry. I was going to give all this stuff back to you. I wanted a clean break. I thought you might not accept things and I'd have to make it clear to you that there was to be no more letters or presents or . . . anything else.'

'I see.'

Sarah looked down at the debris of her bitterness. Each letter had been slashed neatly across the top with a paper knife and for a moment she wondered if his mother had been opening them. The paperbacks were smooth-spined and unread. A train ticket poked out from the inside cover of one of them. Sarah lifted it out and handed it to Richard.

'Oh yeah. I put it there so I'd remember where it was.'

He gave her a stupid puppy-dog smile that said: *how could anyone as useless as me be so cruel?* She bought into it. Or at least pretended she did.

'You better go, Rich. There's a train due in.'

'What about . . .?' He gestured at the mess on the floor.

'Don't worry, I'll take it. Just like you wanted. A clean break.'

He nodded, almost went to say he was sorry but held back in a rare moment of understanding. They said good-bye without touching and with few words. Richard walked away and didn't look back. If he had, he would've seen Sarah stopping one of the cleaners, a man carting round a yellow bin on wheels. He would've seen her piling handfuls of letters, photographs and a couple of paperbacks into the bin.

Sarah walked back through town. It'd all been too much for Richard – the crowds, the memories, the insistent *thud-thud* of it all reminding him that there's no peace. But Sarah took it for granted most of the time. And she was glad she hadn't escaped. *A place becomes a part of you whether you like it or not. It's what happens there that's important.* And Sarah wasn't ready to forget – not yet.

There'd been an accident and Sarah had a long wait for the bus home. An old couple stood in front of her and she watched them. The wife wore sensible shoes, which bulged out around her bunions beneath the soft leather. He wore a new coat, anorak style, made from modern material that he clearly found uncomfortable and which his wife didn't like. She fussed at his collar, moaned that it wouldn't stay down and finally proclaimed the coat to be useless. He batted away her hand and told her to leave it alone, just for once. *Part of the pattern of caring.* It did happen and it wasn't always perfect. Useless coats and lost children – different measures on the same scale.

Sarah wondered if she'd stand a better chance of coming to terms with it all without Richard around to disappoint her. But she was certain that if she couldn't accept things here, where it'd all happened, then she couldn't accept them anywhere. And there were possibilities here in the city, some special things. The fact that Richard couldn't cope with it all, only made it truer.

When she finally got home, she looked at the student flats again and began to wonder if there might just be something she hadn't thought of, or even known about – something that might get her there after all. Tomorrow was Sunday. She'd spend it wallowing, playing maudlin music with too much acoustic guitar and plaintive female wailing. She'd be lazy and not brush her hair and let her long limbs stretch out unashamedly. But Monday? Monday might be a different sort of day altogether.

The Visit

Julie Nugent

Donal stole another glance at his watch, holding it up to his newly trimmed ear to check it hadn't stopped. Still ticking. Still showing the same time as the digital clock that sat squat among the arrival displays.

The inward flight from Dublin had landed fifteen minutes ago, but there was still no sign of him. He looked around to see if anyone else seemed concerned. Not really. Still, it was definitely this flight. He'd phoned to check this morning, catching him at five thirty just as he was leaving for Dublin. The flight was at eight fifteen, and it was now twenty-nine minutes past nine. He hadn't phoned to say he'd missed it; should he ring home to check? He looked at the mobile in his hand. They'd have phoned to say if there'd been a change of plan. A new wave of passengers started to trickle forward. This must be the lot. Oh yes, he could tell straight away that this lot were Irish.

It was so different from the first time he'd arrived in Birmingham. Jesus, he could remember it as clear as yesterday, though it was thirty years ago next month. A bundle of fear and excitement, his homesick sadness masked by bravado as he jumped into this new world. He'd missed Jonjo then, but. His best buddy, blood brother, number one pal, head honcho. He hadn't been

there to share it all. Hadn't been there to take over and find
them lodgings, use a contact to get them both the start on a
job, lend him the money for a pint until pay day. No, he'd
had to do all that on his own, first time ever really. He
could laugh about his ineptitude now, but at the time it'd
terrified him.

Coming from a small rural town, he'd been amazed by
Birmingham to begin with. The sights and sounds that
previously he'd only ever encountered in the *News of the
World*. He thought he knew what a city would be like; he'd
been in Dublin enough times, but nothing had prepared
him for this. Of all cities, this place had always seemed so
human, so man-made. No hills or mountains for miles, not
a smell of the sea, not even a real river to speak of.

At first he thought he'd never get used to it; the greyness
replacing the green and the need to walk for miles to find a
drop of fresh air. He hadn't known the city then. Hadn't
known how the people had accepted the challenge of
adversity and made something of it. They'd created
waterways in the canals and moulded a landscape out of
roads and buildings. In doing so, they'd crafted a synthetic
permanence that was more real than any he had known.

It'd been a harder place then, though. Behind the scenes,
the tattooed muscles of the fairground workers ached as
they oiled the machinery. The big hair and bright makeup
of the party girls faded as they walked to the factory in the
morning. The pale light filtered through to the spent
cigarettes and discarded candyfloss that lay underfoot.
Gruff rather than unfriendly, its industrial heritage had
seeped into the environment and the people. Things were
hard but solid, uncompromising but dependable.
Weathered by storms and changing tides and times, they
carried on. He had no choice then either; he had to carry
on too.

Jonjo, or John as he preferred to be called now, had

chosen to stay behind. No surprise really. The eldest son of the town's auctioneer, it was just accepted that he'd step into the old man's shoes. Done well, they said, invested wisely, diversified into property, doubled the business in no time. He'd built a huge mansion of a place on the road in from Dublin, married a girl from Galway, a teacher. They had two children, who were both doing grand by all accounts. That was the reason for the visit, his first visit, to Birmingham. Noel, the youngest lad, had just started at college here, the College of Food, was it?

Donal stood there waiting, searching the faces of the incoming passengers. Dressed casually, purposefully, he had on his new Aran cardigan. It was a thin one for the summer, with a neatly sewn row of large wooden buttons that he plucked at nervously. Beige trousers slung low beneath a large stomach that nestled in the mossy green cotton of his open-necked shirt. His hair stood short and fine, fluffier around the balding crown. Speckled salt and pepper, it sprouted like a chick's downy fuzz. His face was rounded, crinkly about the eyes and mouth with a spreading warmth across his cheeks that ripened as he aged. You only had to look at him to know that this was a man who laughed a lot, yet the creases in his face had been watered by tears before now. A man's man all the same. He could hold an audience, tell a joke, break up a fight and start one if the mood took him. Funny, though, in the vast airport terminal he looked smaller than usual. A little lost.

Suddenly Donal's face broke out into smiles. His arms flapped frantically as he shouted over to Jonjo, 'Hey, over here!'

Passers-by watched on in amusement. The man he was calling looked around to make sure it was him who was causing the fuss. He hurried over quickly, his free hand extended in automatic greeting. Donal grabbed it and pulled him close into a smothering hug.

'Ah Jeez Jonjo, it's great to see you, fantastic. Here let me get a look at you.'

He gripped his arms as he examined him closely. John 'Jonjo' Callaghan had the walnut veneer of a man who stayed tanned all year round. Taller and slimmer than Donal, he was also more expensively dressed in dark grey slacks and a black Armani T-shirt. They were the same age, but you'd never tell. Jonjo's hair was much thinner, silvery white; his leathery skin rippled and stretched. Donal grabbed the sports holdall and suit carrier from his shoulder, simultaneously steering him out of the doorway.

'Come on, come on. Let's get you home. The car's only a couple of minutes away. I'll give Eileen a ring now, get her to put the pan down.'

By the time they got to the car, plans had changed. Trying to conceal his disappointment, Donal whistled to himself as he put the bags in the boot. He could understand why Jonjo would want to go to the college halls first; course he could. He hadn't seen his son for nearly a month; of course he'd want to go straight out to him.

Donal drove quickly and smoothly through the outlying city. They spoke easily but with polite distance, casual questions and answers, courteous enquiries about health and families. Falling quiet now, as the purr of the car's engine blurred with the dull hum of remote lawnmowers. *If he hadn't left, if he'd come too, where would they be now?* Both of them seemed lost to memory as, nearing the city centre, the years seemed to fall away.

The roads were getting bumpier now, the houses closer to the road and one another. Shops spilled across onto pavements, exotic fruits sweltering as hands pulled and squeezed at them. Sweat trickled and voices were raised as drivers, seared by the sun, struggled to get parked. Jonjo fiddled with the air conditioning. As he did so, Donal expertly manoeuvred his way through the traffic, beeping his horn in recognition rather than annoyance. He turned to his passenger, smiling.

'This is Sparkhill. You must remember me telling you about this place. The first place I ever came to in Birmingham. First digs I was ever in were here. My God, some of the stories I could tell you; some of the places we stayed. There was this one place; me and Mickey Brennan were only in it the one night. Let me tell you now.'

He settled back, relaxing into his role as storyteller. Jonjo smiled, recognizing this aspect from old.

'There was this one place, not too far from here actually. That garage we just passed back there, well it was down a road off that side street there. Anyway, we'd only stopped the one night and we went down to breakfast in the morning, eating away, no bother on us like, tucking into the bacon and eggs and that. Only Mickey gets up to fetch a glass of milk and wasn't there a stack of unwashed pans on the side; they must have been left from the night before. And he let out a scream that would've woken the whole house if they hadn't already gone out to work. Jesus, I must've jumped five foot in the air. "What the f'ing hell was that for?" I said, looking around, but I couldn't see anything. Well Mickey was speechless; he just stood there pointing, so I went over.'

Donal pulled a theatrical expression of disgust. 'Well, my God, if you couldn't see the tracks of mice in the dirty pans. Little footprints right there in the grease. Oh Jesus, it was disgusting. Well, the pair of us must've broken the world record the way we rushed to be sick, the whole lot, bacons and eggs coming right back up again. And then rushing to get out of the place. Oh God!'

He wiped his eyes as he chuckled at the picture. 'We told the landlady we'd an urgent job come up in Leeds and we had to leave straight away. The poor woman didn't have a clue. I don't think we even paid her for the night we stayed.'

He shook his head at the memory, laughing to himself, unaware at first that his passenger was looking on in distaste.

'Oh but there were some holes around then.' He spoke softly, almost to himself. 'There was another one there. Now that was supposed to be a rough house. They reckoned you had to sleep with a knife under your pillow to fight off the rats.'

They'd stopped at the traffic lights now and Jonjo, following the direction of Donal's nod, feigned interest. A large ramshackle building sprawled onto the pavement. Portly pigeons, stuffed to excess on junk food from the nearby halal takeaways, cautiously picked their way along the crumbling façade. The walls were coated with a scabby, peeling paint that revealed layer upon layer underneath; etched with individual histories, narratives of the migrant peoples that came and went.

As they watched, a couple of slender, dark-skinned men emerged from the boarding house.

'Refugees probably,' said Donal. 'Afghans maybe.'

Jonjo snorted. 'I know what you mean. You'd never believe the trouble we get at home these days, what with the bloody refugees and the immigrants and the Christ knows what.'

'What?'

'Oh yeah, Kosovans, Nigerians, Slovakians; the lot of them. The whole town's in uproar; there's fights nearly every weekend now. And the worst thing is there doesn't seem to be an end to them either, more and more coming in each month.' He was animated now.

'Well, you can hardly say anything, can you?' Donal interjected. His tone was apologetic almost, seeking approval, trying to be reasonable.

'What? Why can't I?' Jonjo looked at him in irritated amazement.

'You know. I mean the Irish have probably been the worst for that, you know, emigrating to other countries and that. We can hardly complain about immigrants, can we?'

Jonjo paused before he responded, fixing him with a lingering stare before abruptly turning away. 'I can.'

Those words closed the conversation and he settled back into his seat, whistling softly as he tuned the radio into his favourite sports station. Donal carried on driving. He said nothing; could think of nothing to come back with. Later he'd lie awake replaying the conversation, turning up the volume of insinuations. Then he'd think of the clever justifications, the logical arguments that would convince Jonjo.

As they drove to the address that Noel had given, Donal pointed out the church where he and Eileen were married, then the small pub where they'd had the reception. After that it was the hotel that Rosa Flanagan, Tom's eldest, got married in last week.

'I'd say you'd have known a few at that wedding,' Donal confided. 'Jeez, there were people there from home who I hadn't seen for nearly thirty years. It was a fantastic wedding mind, the food was amazing.'

'What's the husband like?' Jonjo had seen Tom not long ago when he was home for the holidays, driving a brand-new, top-of-the-range Mercedes.

'Oh a lovely lad. Irish, well, second-generation. His mother's from Cork, the father's Donegal, Frank McCarron. I worked with him for years, building some of the flats out Great Barr way. They're a lovely family.'

As they meandered through the city's roadways Donal reflected that he'd probably met more Irish here, like from the different counties and that, than he'd have ever met back in Ireland. The networks they'd built here were so much stronger, the fabric that connected them like a huge safety net that secured them in their new homes. He pointed out the newly refurbished Irish Centre to Jonjo.

'Did you hear that one about the fella over for a wedding in Ireland?'

'What's that?'

'He goes up to the DJ and asks if he could play a bit of Irish music like, so he can have a bit of a dance. And the DJ looks at him in disgust and says, "If you want Irish music, you'd better f. off back to England!"'

Jonjo smiled. He'd heard that one before.

When they arrived at the halls, they rang the bell several times before anyone answered. Eventually, a young girl with studs in her nose and eyebrows came out; she looked like she was still half asleep.

'What?' She squinted up at them, flicking dirty blond dreadlocks back from her face.

'Ahh hello, is Noel around at all; Noel Callaghan?' Donal was polite.

'No,' she said, abstractly picking at her nose, 'sorry he's not in.'

'What do you mean he's not in?' Jonjo's voice was curt, but she looked at him as if he was a little slow in understanding.

'He's not in, he's gone out.' Words of no more than one syllable.

'He must be in. He's expecting me, I'm his father. I've just flown over from Ireland this morning.'

'Ahh right.' Realization dawned on the girl's rather pretty face.

Jonjo moved forward as if to enter. She blocked his way, smiling now, though.

'He's had to go out, Mr Callaghan.' She was respectful but firmer this time. 'He, ehm, he needed to go to the library; he, er, he had an assignment to finish. He said to say he was really sorry but you can leave the parcel with me and he'll give you a call at Donal's as soon as he gets back.' She looked at Donal enquiringly, and he smiled back nervously.

'What do you think, Jonjo?' He looked over at his friend, whose crumpled face betrayed his irresolution.

'Well, I don't know, will he be long like? Can I wait maybe?' His tone was almost a plea.

'I'm sorry, Mr Callaghan.' Her voice soft, as if seeking to soothe and comfort him. 'He said not to wait, that he didn't know how long he'd be. But don't worry, about leaving the parcel like. Noel said that you might not trust me so he said to say that . . .' She whispered something into Jonjo's ear and he nodded gravely.

'Okay, okay, whatever you say.' Suddenly he sounded older, wearier.

It was approaching midday and the traffic was getting heavier. Donal cursed under his breath as he realized he'd missed his turning.

'Sorry about this,' he apologized as they joined a long and stationary queue. 'Not the best move I've ever made!'

Pedestrians weaved in and out of the cars flickering in the sunlight. A new crop of designer stores and restaurants had opened up recently and there was a fresh buzz about the city, a liveliness that reminded Donal of the first time he'd encountered it. People were moving back in rather than out of Birmingham. At least that's what his kids told him. And when you looked at the prices they were charging for some of the apartments in the town, you knew someone must be doing something right.

The city had changed a lot in the last few years. Remembering the awkwardness of its bumpy adolescence, he marvelled at the transformation he'd witnessed but had never really noticed before.

He felt strange, proud perhaps and a little subdued in the face of the city's assured confidence. It was still a friendly place, though – he smiled as a man thanked him for letting him pass in front. It hadn't forgotten where it'd come from, but it hadn't let that hinder its progress either.

'D'ya see that pub over there?' Donal pointed to a network of bars lining the canal. The sunlight reflecting off the water glanced back and forth from the chrome tables and chairs.

'That's where Mr Bill Clinton went in for a pint and a plate of fish and chips,' he announced gleefully. 'Did y'ever hear that story?'

Jonjo shook his head, smiling in spite of himself.

'It was the time of the G8 conference or whatever you call it. Y'know, when all the bigwigs got together over here. Anyway, Bill just strolled in there one of the days, walked up to the bar, no bother on him like, and cool as a cucumber asked for a pint of beer and a plate of fish and chips. Jeez, can y'imagine that? Clinton walking in when you're having a quick pint with your dinner. Sure, I bet they were falling off their chairs. And he was dead friendly too, you know. Oh God aye, chatted away like he was just another man off the street. They reckon his bodyguards weren't too impressed, though.'

'I'd say they wouldn't be.' Jonjo laughed at the image that Donal had conjured.

'And do you know what they did when he'd finished? They smashed the pint glass; smashed it into smithereens!'

'Jesus, why was that?'

'Fingerprints I'd say. Y'know, so that no one would be able to get the fingerprints from it. I'd say it was some sort of a safety precaution or whatever. Imagine that, though!'

The pair of them shook their heads at the thought. 'It'd save on the washing-up mind!' They chuckled.

*

The two men drove back in a more companionable silence; the heat of the afternoon sun inducing a relaxed and hazy lull. Now and again Donal would point or comment as they cruised past the places he'd helped to build. Pointing out the distant towerblocks, remembering the old bastard of a foreman on this job, the laugh they had with the two Welsh blokes on that one.

Gradually, the roads began to widen, stretching to accommodate the trees and bushes that guarded and scented the long sweeping driveways branching off.

'Did your two never think of moving away then?' Jonjo asked, breaking the silence. 'Y'know like, away from Birmingham?'

'My two? I suppose they did; well they were away at university like, but they both came back. I suppose this is their home, where their friends are.'

'And the jobs?'

'Oh yeah, they've both done well for themselves. Angie's working on the local paper and Jimmy's a quantity surveyor for a big German firm. They've been lucky like that, mind, there's others have had to move for the work.'

'Mmm.' Jonjo was thoughtful. 'It's the same with my two. Nancy's working up at a hospital in Dundalk now, did I tell you that? It's not too bad I suppose, we probably see her every month or so. It could be a lot worse I know. And as for Noel, I'm not sure what that fellow'll do, whether he'll ever come back or not. There's not that many big hotels at home, y'know!'

Donal tried to imagine it: his own two forced to leave. Their proximity had so long been assumed that the sudden twist in his stomach surprised him. He'd never really thought about the wrench his parents must've undergone when they left, one by one. In all, five out of the six of them had gone. Three to England, one to Dublin and one had flown further still: to New York. You went where the work was. That's what they'd always said. But had it been more than that? He remembered the excitement at the time. Coming to England, to Birmingham, the big city, the big break. It hadn't worked out for all of them, God, he knew that only too well. But he'd done good, better than he could've ever dreamed. And yet sometimes, he still felt that his going had been a failure; the fact that he'd never returned an admission of his guilt.

Back at the house, Eileen welcomed Jonjo warmly before shooing them both out of the kitchen so she could finish the fry-up she'd been waiting to cook all day.

They strolled down the garden, Donal swelling like a tick as he surveyed his land. Like many of his compatriots, he cultivated his garden with a passion that animated their conversations. The best way to eliminate club root, how to foil slugs and pigeons; whether or not the market was the cheapest place for seeds. Small strips of land were coaxed and nurtured into harvests that seemed to defy natural logic. He'd been looking forward to showing Jonjo the garden; spent the last two weekends tidying it up for his inspection.

Jonjo was polite but indifferent. 'I can't believe you still bother with all this stuff.' He shook his head. 'Jesus, it must take you ages to grow all this!'

'I suppose so.' Donal was confused. 'Still, it tastes so much better, y'know. No chemicals or that; sure you can't get better than the stuff you grow yourself.'

'You must be able to get organic veg around here, though,' Jonjo cut in. 'O'Briens now, in town, they started a whole new line in that a couple of years ago. He reckons it's been a fantastic success, says there's a huge profit margin on it for him as well.'

They strolled on to the end of the rows of cabbages. Jonjo searched for something to say, feeling that he'd disappointed him somehow. He tried to apologize. 'Sure, none of the ones around home can be bothered with any of that now.'

They walked back up the garden in silence.

And yet, as he remembered, he thought of all the times he'd paused, leaning on a shovel, the sweat running down his aching back. He'd look from his garden all the way up to his house and smile almost in disbelief. Or the kids running around when they were smaller, screaming at the worms he'd pretend to throw at them, helping him out with the spades they'd saved from their last time at Weston-super-Mare. The tennis matches they'd played with shrieking friends and cousins; the paddling pool that always sprang a leak. More lately, it was the barbecues that were all the rage; their grown-up children would come with friends to linger over warm beers and Sunday afternoons.

Many's the chat he'd had with his neighbours, past and present, sharing a drink as the summer sun faded. The smells and noises of the past lingered. He'd brought the old ways with him, they all had. But they'd created something else with them, something new, something which was Ireland and Birmingham; something which was theirs. He put his arm around Jonjo's shoulders, a sudden wave of emotion flooding him.

'You must be dying of thirst, John. Come on into the house out of this heat and I'll rustle up a cup of tea while we're waiting.'

The Girl with Blue-black Hair
Richard Lutz

I've always seen it plainly. The world. Dark and light.
Dark as a night's rain. Light as ice.

I was in Gap on Saturday and someone had put the
checked shirts with the long-sleeve, single-colour polo-
necks. Now, that's bad news. You just can't have it. Can't
have it. I restacked them and put the checked shirts back
on their pile and realigned the polos. A black kid – dreads,
Gap outfit, a worm of a moustache and one of those daft
earpieces like he's in the CIA or something – gave me a
glance, sharp as a laser beam. I shrugged. He smiled and
slowly shook his head. I finished restacking.

Another time. I was in the pub, the Crown, during the
lunch break. Pal of mine said: 'T, your round.' T is what
they call me. Just T. Nothing else. 'T,' he said, 'mine's a
pint.' But it wasn't my round. It was clear as day. It wasn't
my round.

'Jimmy,' I said, 'I got the first.' Jimmy shot Ray a look
like a bullet and Ray fiddled with his glass. I shrugged. It
wasn't my round. If it were, I would've jumped to the bar.

'T, you saying it isn't yours?' Jimmy tapped a beer mat on
the table.

'No. It's Andy's.' I wanted to make that plain.

'Andy left twenty minutes ago.'

'Still his round.' I offered Jimmy a fag. He lit his own, an angry flare.

That's the way I play it. If it's mine, I pay. If it isn't, what the hell. I've got to be straight. Or else things go wrong. You'll see. You'll understand.

The night of the Crown and Jimmy and me, I was still irked about having to lay down the law over whose round it was. To calm myself, I nipped down to the hospital. It always soothed rough edges inside me. Gave me some peace. Go see the kid. An Asian lad called Iftikhar.

I first saw him on the end of New Street right where they fixed up Victoria Square and all the kids hang out, smoking, right near the asylum seekers in those cheapjack leather jackets, hanging out near the fountain and in the empty doorways of the TSB offices. It was dusk on a Friday night and I was on my way to see Helen – she'd been drinking too much Spanish brandy alone in that seventh-floor flat. She needed a hand. I'll always give Helen a hand. She needs it.

But I stopped right there in Victoria Square. Six or seven lads, real big lads, were really giving this Iftikhar a kicking. Right under the Tin Man thing. He was bouncing off that metal man like a ball off a wall. I can still hear the hollow, soft sound when the boy smashed off that statue; that statue stuck there tilted and silent, staring into space, ignoring the fight at his feet.

What fight? Six or seven animals giving a single guy a kicking. I mean, we're talking black and white here, not colour, but black and white as in clear and simple. I did karate for a while up in Erdington, so I gave it a go. Actually it was the first time I'd used it for real. You couldn't walk past. Felt someone's stomach cave in like a soft pillow, felt the sweep of an arm as it waved crazily in the air, heard something prang against the Tin Man: maybe a knife, maybe bones. Then they ran.

I was there alone with the kid, crumpled against the statue, his head rolling as if a spring had busted in his neck. His face, brown as a penny, was a map of bruises. He was looking up, but he didn't see a thing. His eyes were emptying. I laid him flat and all I could hear was my own breathing. People started looping around us in a deformed circle. Two or three hit their mobiles and when the ambulance wheeled up I knew I wasn't needed. Just doing what was right. Black as rain. White as ice. Went off to see how Helen was.

The next night, I read about the attack in the *Mail*. Something about gang warfare up and down New Street. Wasn't. Just some lads. They named Iffy and for the next two weeks I headed over to the hospital at Selly Oak to see him.

On this particular night, when I'd finished the shift at the call centre, my neck was an iron band from seven hours on the phones. I didn't want to go to the Crown to see anyone. Didn't want to, not with that thing about whose stupid round it was. I walked out of work, had a cigarette and started heading towards Five Ways. I always liked that walk through the city centre, into the cavern of the ICC, over the canal that snakes like a rope through the city and into Brindleyplace and past all those bars and cafés and new buildings, the people behind stacked office windows. I liked the way the shadows were straight and hard as they crawled across the plazas and offices. I liked it. It felt clean and open. I felt clean and open.

I got to the ward as light ebbed from the city. Dusk, a jaundice yellow, melted into the sky – the same sky as when Iftikhar was beaten up. His head was still bashed around. He smiled and put his hand out for the football magazines I'd brought in. His parents were there. So was his sister with that penny-brown skin, sharp daggers for fingernails and hair so black it was almost blue.

His parents rose when I came up to the bed. His sister stayed seated and snapped gum. 'Tony, always so good to see you,' his father said. They called me Tony. Never T. Definitely not T. Iftikhar still couldn't speak because of the head injuries. But he kept on smiling and looking at me. Once in a while he'd grab a peek at the magazines, flip through articles on Beckham, Beckham, more Beckham. His family did the talking.

'Iftikhar starts physio next week. That's a good sign,' his father said. He was the type of guy who was always polite. I like that. He was still holding my hand in his own warm, soft hand; a hand of fleshy, meaty fingers. His face spoke of hope. His wife said little. The daughter, nothing. He offered me a chair next to the bed as if it were a throne. I knew it was best to accept the chair, a chipped plastic one the same colour as the ward's faded pink walls, a chair that had seen better days, better nights, better times in its long, chipped past. But it didn't matter. It might as well have been a throne. The ward hummed with dozens of bedside chats, including our own. Sitting there with them was like falling into a big, deep bed. It swallowed me up as the sky dripped to darkness.

'When my son leaves hospital, I want to bring you over to the house to see some real hospitality. It is the least we can do for a friend like you,' his father said. The sister, Tejinder, was checking her nails, but looked up suddenly. She'd never spoken before. 'Dad's right. Come round. Smethwick's a scream on a Saturday night.'

'I bet it is.'

'Tej is always kidding,' the father said. 'She always goes to town of a weekend. Her and her friends.'

'I bet she does.' I turned my head to Tejinder. 'Where do you end up?'

'Brindleyplace. Broad Street. Clubs.'

'I bet you do.'

'I bet I do too.' Tejinder kept absently smoothing the white sheets of her brother's hospital bed with one elegant hand. Her hair was long and straight, and with the other hand she quietly entangled thin fingers around her brother's small, squarish hand. The father smiled and then opened his hand to offer me a cracked cup of hospital tea as if I was already in his front room. The open hand was a blessing on me. But I only cared about the kid. I mean, it was right to feel that way, feel that you had to see the lad, this Iftikhar, through to when you saw him with some friends and not even thinking about that crazy fight any more. There was an obligation almost. His family didn't understand. I think they figured I was some kind of mercy freak. But no, it was just right to see the kid through.

The next night, I was down the call centre doing a late shift when Bobby got in touch. I was annoyed because a couple of the college kids were claiming phone calls they never took and picking up the cash for it. It wasn't fair. I talked to Joanne the supervisor, and she asked for proof. I didn't need proof. I saw some of the Matthew Boulton girls steal the call from this lady on Team B. It was robbery. Joanne didn't want to know: things worked just fine as they were.

So, I was mulling over what to do next. Someone once told me I was a great tunnel visionary. That's on the button, that is. I know what's right and wrong and don't get too wobbly about the side issues. I was going to blow the whistle on those kids. I wasn't caring about who would get in trouble or what people would think of me. I was annoyed. You don't steal incoming calls. Straight up: you don't nick calls. And that's when Bobby phoned. He was annoyed too. But for something else.

'You still seeing that Asian kid?' His voice was tight, sound of a hardened cough. That's the way Bobby spoke.

'Yeah.'

181

'Stop.'

'C'mon, Bobby, it's just a kid. He's hurt. He can't even speak.'

'I said stop.'

This was another of those right or wrong things. I save a kid from having his head rammed into the Tin Man and check him out, bring him some magazines. That's the right thing to do. Then Bobby says stop. So I have a choice of right and wrong. See the kid and not listen to Bobby. Listen to Bobby and not see the kid. Bobby was right. I stopped.

The night after that, Bobby and I were in the garage with the Astra we'd picked up in Oldbury. The R reg. We whipped out the CD player. It was good quality sound. Stripped it right out and gave it to one of my nephews who likes grunge stuff. I was hoovering up the back seat of the car. A car has to be clean. Can't work with a car that's not clean. Bobby was reading the paper and slowly shaking his head like a disgruntled father. He was tapping his fingers on his lips and shaking that head of his: a huge head, the shape of a big bull.

'Bad news,' he said to himself. 'Bad news.'

I knew I was in for one of those lectures. Sometimes people call him Bobby Doc because he sounds like a professor. Bobby's famous for his lectures.

Bobby tapped his lips again and folded the paper so he could read easier. 'It's not good.' Bobby squinted, even with his glasses, to read the small print. 'You see, these things like these two missing little kids . . .' He let the words drift like smoke, waiting for me to respond. I know Bobby well. I've worked with him for a while now. He patiently waits until you answer. Like a professor, I suppose.

'Which kids? I got no idea what you're getting at, Bobby.'

'These boys. These two cousins that are missing up in Derby. It's bad news. Bad news.'

'Yeah,' I said. 'Tough stuff. Real bad for the families. Real bad.'

'No, T, real bad for us.'

'Us?' I changed the nozzle and tried to stretch my back. 'Why us?'

'People start worrying about these kids, their parents, about the maniac who's taken them, maybe attacked them, and they come together. Despair together. And when people get like that – sentimental and emotional – they start thinking. It's a rallying point. It hits critical mass. And that's bad news. Bad news. It builds into something we really don't want.'

Bobby looked over the glasses pushed down his nose, bent over and slapped me over the head with the paper he was reading, the *Telegraph*. 'You know what I'm saying? Bad news. Anything like this is bad news. Even good news is bad news. England ever win the World Cup, I'm laying real low for a while. Real low.'

I stopped for a second, still holding the Hoover nozzle. 'Win the World Cup? No one's ever gonna win anything.'

'Win or lose, it doesn't matter. The country comes together, reacts as a nation. It makes people think of themselves as an Us. It's a wave of opinion and that isn't good right now. Especially now.'

I didn't say a word. Bobby Doc was sometimes way ahead of me. He gave me a look. 'Whatcha think there, T? Agree? Disagree? Finger on the buzzer? What?'

It was lecture time again.

'Dunno.' I went back to my hoovering.

'You don't know.' He smiled. 'That's the problem with you, Anthony: you do know. But you don't want to think about it. Think it through, partner, and things make more sense. More and more sense.'

'Things make sense now. I've thought things through.' My back was aching from bending down and cleaning.

Bobby wasn't finished. 'The more people in this country think about things like missing kids, football – even the royals, for God's sake – the more problems I got and the more problems you got. It's plain as . . . I don't know. Plain as . . .'

'Things.' I put down the Hoover. I'm not big on analysing stuff. I mean that's clear cut, white as ice. I changed the cleaner nozzle again to get into the crevices between doors and seats.

Bobby squinted to look at the paper, snapped back the financial pages and pored over company news. Bobby would read anything, he'd gobble down the *Sun* and then the next minute pick up the *Times* or the *Telegraph*. He was always hungry for reading. Me, I got on with cleaning the R reg. My body was humped over the back seat and I was leaning on my right elbow for leverage into the-hard-to-reach places. But I could sense something else besides the present psychology of the British public was on Bobby's mind. Finally, he put the paper down and peered over the top of his specs. 'You know that kid in the hospital.'

I was still leaning over the rear seat. 'The kid with the head?'

'Yeah, the kid with the head.'

'What about him?'

'It's impossible, you know that, don't you?'

'Bobby.' Again, I laid the Hoover extension to one side. My elbow was dead from resting too hard on it. 'You tell me "no". I don't do it.'

'It was a nice gesture.'

'It was more than that, Bobby.'

'Closure.'

'No, nothing's being closed here, Bobby. The kid liked my visits. His family liked it. I mean, it made sense.'

Bobby kept peering over his reading glasses and over the

edge of the paper. 'Time to stop, T. You saw the kid. That's it.'

'Yeah, I know. But I don't agree.'

'Agreeing doesn't come into it.'

He was right. Agreeing didn't come into it.

The next night – the night I wasn't rostered on a late shift – I walked over to see Bobby rather than take a cab. It was better that way. Cleaner. The weather had dipped. But that's okay with me – I like the streets when they're cold. I like walking over a canal chopped with shards of cold light. I like the way a dark, freezing city envelops me. Some people – like Helen – love the way a warm sun touches them on a beach. That's the way I feel about the cold. A big freeze embraces me. I once saw one of those nature films on cable about winter in one of those American states, I think it was North Dakota. It was too cold even to snow there. So, I was thinking, seriously thinking, that when this is all over – the Bobby thing and the plans and Birmingham – of heading for one of those places, maybe even North Dakota, where I can live alone and cold and happy.

But on this night I kept on walking with the dry, freezing air around me all the way out of the city centre, down the Pershore Road to Cotteridge. I got to Bobby's and he knew I'd been walking rather than taking a taxi or a bus. We took the Astra out. It had a dicky exhaust and that didn't make Bobby too happy. He kept slowly shaking his head as the exhaust belched. It didn't help things because no matter how many times I've thought one of those issues through, no matter how many times I've organized the technical side, I still have a rat's claw scratching at my stomach. It doesn't get easier. It just gets worse.

We drove behind Broad Street. I used to know all the old streets because Uncle Baz's workshop used to be at the back of the old Bingley Hall. But now that's gone. So has the workshop. And Baz for that matter. Those streets vanished and now these new ones carve their way through new buildings. Things change fast. So I was smart enough to bring the *A–Z* that I'd bought after that fiasco in Manchester when we just kept driving round and round in that van and it was getting late.

Bobby thought I was nuts. 'Wait a minute, T,' he said. 'You telling me you been in this city for, Jesus, what? Years and years and you still need a map?'

'Just hold on.' I was right. We almost got lost in a twist and a turn near a block of offices surrounded by scaffolding. Night does that to you. There were bollards by a cobbled entrance, a security guard near a restaurant, a car park I'd never seen before despite all the times I've been there checking it out. Took out the *A–Z* and the torch and there we were, right on the map.

Bobby had to laugh. Just had to laugh. And I tell you, it wasn't much of a time for laughs either. It was a time for doing things right. Like having a street atlas. And a torch.

We parked the Astra, that R reg that could've been a million other cars because it was so ordinary, right off a corner where there was no CCTV. All around us were those new glass buildings. Some hadn't even been fully let yet. We didn't run or hurry things. Bobby even made sure he zipped up his jacket after opening the boot. He put on his glasses, frowned slightly with concentration, squinted, rechecked the HMTD blasting cap and the base charge, and then he closed the boot very quietly.

He threw me a last look over the rim of his glasses, just like he did when he was reading the paper, and we walked in opposite directions. I would make the call with the coded word to tell them where the explosives were. That's the way an operation is handled. No chat, just a location and a word that rings bells into the night. I mean, when you know how things should be, you make cold clear decisions. It's the tunnel visionary in me. Like always having an *A–Z*. Like parking the car in the right place. Like seeing the Asian kid in Selly Oak. Like never seeing the kid again.

But I wonder, sometimes, if that poor, broken kid will ever walk. Or even talk again. And I was wondering, as I walked away, wouldn't it be nice to bump into his sister with the blue-black hair in one of these bars here in Brindleyplace. I'd buy her a drink and she'd have a cigarette hanging from her long hands, and she'd crane her head upwards like a tropical bird and blow the smoke hard and fast, and she'd laugh and tell me about work. That's what I was wondering about as I walked away, past all those bars and cafés and clubs. That's what I was thinking about as I kept on walking.

The cold wrapped around me, took me all the way up Broad Street to the phone I would use. It was so cold and clear it could've been North Dakota. Now there's a place I'd like to go. North Dakota.

Countdown to Carnival
Pauline E. Dungate

Ten . . . Monday

Tasha was halfway up the hill from Snow Hill Station when her mobile started chirruping in the bottom of her bag. She ducked into a doorway to grovel in the depths, cursing the rain, her mother and mismanagers of the railway system.

It wasn't her mother this time; it was her boss in the Schools Liaison Department of the Art Gallery.

'Are you in the classroom?' Jayne asked.

'Not yet. I'm in Edmund Street. The train was late. Part of the line's flooded outside Dudley.'

'Can you come straight down to the office when you arrive?'

Tasha wondered briefly what she had done wrong before remembering that Jayne always gave out reprimands in private. More likely to be a school group cancelling or an urgent meeting with the Museum's Art Department.

Tasha enjoyed her job as the resident art teacher in the Museum and Art Gallery, but was frustrated when new exhibitions and committees' demand for new resource materials took her away from what she regarded as her real job – teaching children about artists and their techniques. She'd rather persuade them to see what was in a picture than have them wandering around with worksheets, looking for paintings that had probably been moved to another gallery.

Jayne was seated at the round table in the Education Office with Luke Davis from events and Penny Williams, the Education Coordinator of the Ikon.

'Get yourself a coffee if you need one, and come and join us,' Jayne said.

Intrigued, Tasha shed her coat and joined them.

'Next Saturday,' Penny explained, 'is the Birmingham Carnival to celebrate the opening of the new Bullring. The Ikon, the School of Music and Dance Xchange were supposed to be working with three schools on a project to construct costumes for the parade.'

Tasha waited while Penny paused for breath, wanting to know what the problem was, and wondering how she was going to be involved.

'When I arrived this morning, I found staff mopping up,' Penny said. 'Last night's wind lifted a section of the gallery roof and water came pouring into the offices. Unfortunately, the only place to put the stuff they rescued is in the gallery space we were going to use to make the costumes. Dance Xchange hasn't got a space big enough, so my director, rang your director . . .'

Tasha got an inkling of what was coming.

'The director has agreed to hold back the preparations for the next exhibition in the Gas Hall for a week,' Luke said. 'We can transfer all the preparations here.'

'But,' Jayne said, 'he insists that one of our department supervises them.'

'What about my classes?' Tasha asked. She could picture his reasoning. Without one of the Art Gallery staff involved, he'd miss out on any kudos that arose, and since children were involved, it had to be someone from Schools Liaison.

189

'I've already spoken to most of the teachers bringing your groups this week. With one exception, they're prepared to do their own thing. The secondary school wants to rearrange the visit.'

Tasha allowed herself a small scowl. Why was it always assumed that she'd make no objection? 'What needs to be done?' she asked.

'I've already arranged for the materials to be brought over,' Penny said.

'Luke will get the technicians to bring down tables and chairs,' Jayne said.

'There's another problem,' Penny said. 'Paul Bartley from *mac* has done the preliminary artwork with the schools but he's gone down with a flu bug and is unlikely to make it this week.'

Great, Tasha thought. I might teach about textiles, but I don't often have to actually work with them.

Nine . . .

Tasha was impressed by the amount of materials that had been gathered for the project. It looked as though almost every fabric shop in Birmingham had donated something. The best, she was told, had come from some of the Asian shops in Handsworth and Sparkbrook. There were also canes and wire and string; sewing thread, ribbons, beads and paint; card, plywood, perspex, plastic and acetate sheets. In one box were fairy lights and batteries.

'I'm assigning one of the technicians to you this week,' Luke said. 'In case you need help cutting any of the materials.'

The children arrived soon after one o'clock.

There were forty in all, mostly girls, belonging to the Year 10 GCSE group from a secondary school in Handsworth. All were studying textile design, but some were also ICT students. The twenty-six from a primary school in

Sparkbrook redressed the balance – two thirds of them were boys. The ten children from the special school arrived late. The disabled parking bays adjacent to the Art Gallery were clogged with cars not showing the special blue badges, and they'd had to plead to be allowed across the pedestrian area to park behind the library. Four of these were in wheelchairs, two were profoundly deaf, three were partially sighted and the last boy suffered from Downs Syndrome. He, in particular, remembered Tasha from previous visits. He marched up to her and stuck out his hand. 'Too big to cuddle,' he said. 'Shake hand.'

'Hello, Anthony,' Tasha said. In the past, he'd affectionately hugged all those people he liked. Now he and his classmates were eleven and twelve year olds in Year 7.

All the young people would be taking part in Saturday's parade, if they were ready in time. Tasha knew that in New Orleans and Notting Hill participants took months building their costumes. These now had less than a week. Fortunately, Pat Bowen, the textile teacher from Handsworth, had brought the design portfolios and her pupils had worked out the materials and specs of what they needed. Looking at them laid out along the tables, Tasha was impressed by the detail that had already gone into them. She could see her role as merely supervisory, with only a few hints and tips thrown in.

As the children knew each other, they quickly re-acquainted themselves with their working groups. The boxes of materials had been placed in the centre of the hall. Apparent chaos erupted as they scrabbled to find what they thought they would need and marked out their territories around the outskirts of the space.

'We'll need an area for painting, and an area for gluing,' Penny said. 'So we need something to protect the floor.'

'Are there any power sockets for the sewing machines?' Pat asked.

Tasha hunted down Andy, the technician assigned to them. He was outside the hall talking to the receptionists and clearly uncomfortable with the swarm milling around inside. He was happy to be sent off looking for suitable dustsheets, while Tasha showed Pat where the sockets were set in the floor.

'Where are the sewing machines coming from?' Tasha asked.

'I'll bring them out in the minibus tomorrow morning. Most of my pupils will be told to make their own way here. Can they come in at nine?'

'I'll arrange it. They'll have to use the lift up to the second floor and be escorted down.'

Pat smiled. 'No problem.'

Eight . . . Tuesday

The lift broke down. Three of the Handsworth girls were in it at the time. They were stuck for fifteen minutes and Sonja was nearly hysterical by the time they were released. She was fine with lifts as long as they moved up and down and let her out quickly. She couldn't cope with being in a small space for a long time. If she could have got out of the building she would have legged it home, but at nine thirty all the other entrances to the building were still locked. She sat in the centre of the Gas Hall, all the walls as far from her as possible, staring up at the dome's glass roof, watching the clouds and crying. Until a pigeon landed on the curve and slowly slid down. With a lot of wing-flapping, it hoisted itself up to the ridge again and glided to the bottom. Sonja smiled, laughed, and went to wash her face before rejoining her group.

John, Lizzie, Davinder and Conroy posed a different problem. To get into the building they had to motor their wheelchairs around to the service yard and use the goods lift. Luckily, it ejected them straight into the corner of the

Gas Hall and they raced off in different directions to join their groups and catch up with their tasks. Fortunately, there were disabled toilets off the Gas Hall so it didn't worry them that they were trapped there until the engineers arrived at midday to fix the main lift.

The day before, most of the groups had cut out paper templates of the designs they intended to construct. 'Environment' was the theme of the carnival, so they'd settled on an insect life motif. Tasha watched one of the blind children, Rasul, caressing the shimmering fabrics before declaring, 'This one.' He couldn't see the colours properly, but the material felt right.

Andy set up a station with a drill and jigsaw and was kept busy following the instructions of those who wanted shapes cut from more rigid materials. Pat, Tasha and Mark Cohen, the primary school teacher, pushed some of the tables together to make a large enough surface to cut the fabrics.

By lunchtime, sawdust and scraps of discarded cloth mingled in the spaces between the groups.

Seven . . .

Tasha noticed that her advice was needed mostly for minor matters, such as resolving disputes about colour clashes, or could she hold this bit while Amina stapled it round the edge. She noticed Jayne walk through between the office and a meeting, a horrified look passing across her face as Anthony staggered over to greet her, a pair of scissors he'd forgotten he was holding extended towards her.

'Anthony, change hands!' Ruth Wiltshire, his class teacher, yelled across at him.

Anthony halted, looked from hand to hand, then stuck out the other one. 'Hello, I'm Anthony,' he said.

'Pleased to meet you, Anthony,' Jayne said, and hurried onwards.

Tasha heard him mutter, 'Funny lady,' before returning to cutting out shapes from metallic paper.

Some of the boys were constructing what looked like scaffolding around John's wheelchair. Tasha watched them for a while, then asked, 'How high is it going to be?'

'Two metres. Then the dragonfly goes on the top.'

Tasha looked at the half-built shape of wire and plastic on the floor behind them. 'Is it going to fit through the door? And into the lift?'

The boys looked at each other. 'Tape measure,' Liam yelled.

Year 5 Asif dashed over to their worktable, grabbed the measure and brought it back. Liam loped off. He came back shaking his head. John leaned back in the chair and looked up at the tower. 'Make it in parts,' he said. 'We can assemble it outside.'

There was a few minutes of muttering, measuring and arguing. 'All the towers will have to be the same,' Liam said.

Asif and Arshad were sent to fetch the other team leaders and after a few minutes' huddled discussion, they went back to work, the problem resolved. Tasha was impressed by their teamwork.

Six . . . Wednesday

Three of the Handsworth boys, Colm, Samir and Devon, had spent the first two days of the week over at the School of Music, laying down the music for their section of the parade. It was their own composition and had a good, heavy beat. With the help of Simon Walgrave, their mentor, and the school's computer suite, they had produced a CD that could be played repeatedly. The CD player was to be mounted on the back of Lizzie's chair. Tasha doubted the wisdom of having the speakers turned up loud so close to one person.

'Don't worry,' Lizzie said. 'I'll just turn off my hearing aids.'

'Right,' Tasha said. She hadn't realized that Lizzie was also profoundly deaf.

Work stopped while the whole group settled in the centre of the floor to listen to the music. There was a round of spontaneous applause when the track finished.

'I can dance to that,' Lianne said. 'It's great.'

'It's not finished,' Samir said. 'We need live musicians too.'

Simon and Monica had brought a box of percussion instruments across from the School of Music – maracas, tambourines, hand drums. 'It's rehearsal time for the orchestra,' Simon said.

Fifteen of the Year 5s and ten of the Handsworth girls disappeared into the AV room in the corner of the Gas Hall and closed the door. For the rest of the morning, the stop-start music of an orchestra learning a new piece could be heard faintly. Everyone else got on with stitching, gluing and painting.

Five . . .

At one point in the afternoon, Tasha glanced towards the revolving door of the Gas Hall. The Art Gallery director stood just inside the space, watching. Normally externally calm, Tasha thought she could see signs of the director's growing panic at the state of the place, particularly as Anthony chose that moment to cross from one side to the other carrying a loaded paintbrush.

'Anthony, you're dripping,' Ruth shouted at him.

'Oops, sorry,' he said and wiped his mouth with the back of the hand holding the brush, smearing royal blue across his forehead and into his hair.

'Dripping, not dribbling,' Ruth said. 'On the floor.'

Anthony looked down at the trail of blue splashes.

'Oops, sorry.'

'Here, I'll carry it,' Tasha said, rescuing brush and paint pot. 'Where do you want to take it?'

'Over here,' Anthony said. 'Don't worry, it's washable.'

The director, Tasha noticed, had disappeared.

Andy produced cleaning materials. 'Don't fret,' he said. 'The floor's been scheduled for sanding before the next exhibition opens.'

Shortly before four, the musicians gave a performance. It sounded a little rough around the edges, but they seemed pleased with their progress. The simple, repetitive pattern of sound to accompany the main melody was easy to remember and play on the move.

Four . . . Thursday

The leotards arrived at the same time as the coach bringing the children from Sparkhill. Some of the people Penny had approached for sponsorship had given money rather than goods. She'd bought white, sleeveless leotards for the girls to wear under their costumes. The boys had plain white T-shirts and, those that could be persuaded, footless tights. The first part of the morning was spent trying to match right-sized clothing to children and then putting the costumes so far over the top. That way, it was easier to see where adjustments needed to be made.

Isabel Sullivan arrived from Dance Xchange during the chaos. 'Keep the costumes on for the moment,' she said when Penny wanted them to hurry and change back into work clothes.

Isabel gathered the participants into the centre of the space. 'And you four,' she added, catching sight of John, Lizzie, Davinder and Conroy trying to wheel off unnoticed.

'Right,' she said. 'You will have to move in these costumes. So we are going to do a few warm-up exercises. Notice if anything is too tight, too loose, or stops you moving. Those are the things that will need fixing if you are to feel comfortable on Saturday.'

Tasha and the other adults watched the children carefully for major problems. Isabel was good. Not only did she show the children the movements, but she described them as well. Rasul and Heemat were able to follow, even though they were a few seconds behind. Anthony, too, had delayed reactions, but made up for it with his enthusiasm.

While the costumiers got on with the adjustments, the musicians again disappeared into the AV room to rehearse. This time Isabel was with them. During a calm moment, Tasha looked in: Isabel was adding dance to the music. They would have to move and play at the same time.

Three . . .

There wasn't enough space in the Gas Hall for all the participants to perform at the same time. Isabel had the musicians demonstrate the steps they had learned in the morning, then took the others in small groups to teach them their parts.

The four in wheelchairs needed to manipulate the wings of the insects perched on top of the towers as if they were flying in time with the music.

'I can't steer and move both wings,' Davinder complained.

'Puppets,' Tasha suggested to their design group who were looking at Davinder in perplexity.

'Yes!' Suzanne caught on quickly. 'One bar with both cords attached. The angle you hold it at alters the wings. Then Davinder has one hand free to steer.'

'We all need that,' John said.

'Easy,' Suzanne said, heading for the materials heap.

That fixed, the four had to practise steering in formation, not easy when they had to watch where they were going and manipulate the models at the same time. 'And the road will be rough,' Conroy said, just before he came to a dead halt. 'I've run out of battery,' he added sheepishly. 'Anyone got a power lead?'

'I have,' Lizzie said.

Tasha pushed Conroy over to a power point so he could recharge, while Isabel called the next group together to learn their steps.

'You make sure you get properly charged, Friday night,' Davinder told Conroy. 'We won't be waiting for you Saturday if you break down.'

'Yes, miss,' he said.

Rasul and Heemat were paired with two of the older girls to act as guides. Their costumes were designed with plenty of streamers, some of which linked them with their partners. Their problem was not only learning the steps, but devising a system of signals which kept them on the right road and stopped them falling over things. In the first couple of tries, Heemat and her partner ended up trussed like twin maypoles and giggling hysterically. Slowly, they sorted it out.

Two . . . Friday

The Art Gallery didn't open until ten thirty on a Friday. Isabel got everyone up to the second floor, where the run from the Buddha outside the Tea Room to the reception desk in the Round Room was longer than that available in the Gas Hall. She wanted the opportunity to put them in parade order and move through the space as if it were the real thing.

Tasha and Andy moved as many obstacles out of the way as possible. There was length, but not width. Dancers kept bumping into each other. Some were getting frustrated and the music was becoming ragged before Isabel gave up and Penny insisted that they had to use the morning for finishing the costumes.

Pauline E. Dungate

One . . .

Final rehearsal. Final adjustments. Final instructions. Penny took off a group who would be arriving on their own to show them the assembly point.

A final testing of the batteries and lights that would brighten some costumes with fireflies.

Tasha stood among the heaps of materials once everyone had gone. They didn't look much different from those they had started with four days ago.

Lift Off . . . Saturday

Tasha didn't have to come. She could quite legitimately have stayed at home, but she was curious to see the children in action. She'd borrowed the department's camcorder and arrived early. Some of the parents had come to help and they were already moving the towers outside. Someone had thought to bring sheets of plastic to cover them as a morning of drizzle was forecast. So far, the air was just damp. Inside, Conroy had plugged himself into the mains. 'Just to be sure,' he explained.

Security had opened the Gas Hall entrance to make it easier to get things outside. Some of the costumes would have struggled in the lift.

The assembly point was Fleet Street, a short walk away. Their meeting point was halfway down, behind the brewery wagon, and before the College of Food.

'I hope that horse behaves,' Anthony said. 'I don't want to walk in horse poo.'

The parade was due to begin at midday and the first display moved off five minutes afterwards with a burst of sound. Penny and Isabel fussed along the line, making sure everyone was in place.

'Ready, Anthony?' Ruth called from the side.

The boy looked at her and grinned. He gave a thumbs-up. 'Ready.'

Penny signalled. Lizzie turned on the beat. The musicians joined in a little raggedly. Penny gave the brewery wagon time to move ahead, then gave the signal. They made their first steps as individuals, but before they turned the corner at the top of the road, they were a shimmering swarm of glittering insects, moving and dancing together.

The parade moved down Great Charles Street, up Newhall Street and turned into Edmund Street. There they encountered the first crowds, carefully contained behind the barriers. They danced and fluttered through Chamberlain Square and along New Street. Gossamer butterfly wings and iridescent dragonflies swooped down High Street, around the city centre and back again.

In the centre, a caterpillar called Anthony bobbed and wove, picking up coins thrown at the parade, putting them in his specially made pouch. His painted face was grinning with pleasure.

And back at the Gas Hall, Penny had organized a picnic. Conroy glided to a stop in front of a plate of sausage rolls. 'Out of battery,' he said happily.

Checking Out

Simon Broadley

'A valet? Yessir, I'll send him right up.' Harold turns to me; there's a suit on the bed in 77 needs pressing.

But I'm about to knock off, got a girlfriend on the go and plans for Broad Street.

And I'm not even the valet – he's in Portugal with his boyfriend – I'm the hall porter: I drag luggage twice my own body weight breathlessly around the hotel for loose change; open doors with an agreeable smile; athletically hail taxis in the street when the doorman's on his break; replace soiled hand towels in the gentlemen's luxury restroom; take coats at the cloakroom; deliver flowers, letters, late-night condoms, even on one occasion a box of laxatives – and boy did he look like he needed them!

But I do *not* do suits.

Harold looks at me, unimpressed. This small man with his antiquated manners, grand gestures and silly moustache.

And anyway, I can't be late tonight. Not again. Helen will kill me. Or worse, just walk away, her saintly patience finally shot.

'Harold, please . . .?'

'Could've been and done it in the time you've been stood here arguing with me,' he says, matter-of-fact, the novelty of his limited powers undimmed.

Harold, as he says himself, was never young.

So, lips pursed, I stomp up the stairs to 77, snatch the suit off the bed and go down to the first-floor service.

It's more like a cupboard than a room, this little space that Clarence disappears to with other people's clothes. Clarence with his big moon face is always genuinely pleased to be of service.

How *does* he do it?

I slip the hook of the hanger through the chain suspended from the ceiling so the suit hangs in front of me like a headless but fashionable ghost, and I soften the expensive fabric by passing the steaming iron under and around it without actually touching the cloth, like I've seen Clarence do a hundred times.

When it's soft and warm, I float it down onto the ironing board, perform a few quick swipes and turns, slip it into a polythene cover embossed with the hotel's coat of arms and very soon I'm done and stalking back along the corridor to the service lift – pink tissue charge-slip fluttering – to whack it in the room.

These Italian designer business suits, they cost the moon but weigh practically nothing.

Creaking up the back passage of the hotel in the coffin-sized service lift, I contemplate the tedious minutes that contribute to hours spent and probably miles travelled in this bloody box. I wonder how many? And we're here.

As I drag the metal gate back I see it: a thin, fracturing crease, starting at the cuff and creeping up the sleeve. Oh, fuck it. I *could* leave it; he probably wouldn't even notice.

Poor, lonely Helen. She's tapping her watch once again and thinking *Typical!* and surely this is now the end, but nagging somewhere is the 'job well done' thing (how did *that* happen?), so I decide and with Dad patting me on the back I go back down to first-floor service where the iron's still warm.

I'll flatten this little crease . . .

I'm bent at the board with the steam condensing on my forehead and *lah de dah* like Mum used to in those heady days when *my* laundry was *her* problem. I don't really mind this. Not really. Because it's my hope/belief/conviction that one day I'll swap my paltry wage for a salary; this two-bit job for a career; that one day someone will press *my* suits.

And as I indulged this free thought, it must've happened.

I lift the iron and *smack* there it is. Size of a fat thumbprint and still smoldering – a dark brown burn on the cuff. *No*. It can't be. I've burnt this suit, this suit that costs more than I'll earn this month, before tax, before I'm certainly sacked.

Visions of the formidable General Manager, towering like some predatory dinosaur, thump inside my head. I could cry.

There's an honourable thing to do and there's a less honourable, downright cowardly, wholly practical thing to do . . .

I'll slip it into the room to hang and hope against hope that when he notices he'll blame some other evening, some other hotel, perhaps some other country: London – New York – Paris – Munich. Executive Class. Living on planes and in hotel lounges. It *could* happen. Might not be back in Brum for months . . .

I could throw up as I walk back to his room.

I stand outside the door, staring into the thick gloss paintwork, imagining the likely outcome of the next few minutes before I finally knock. There's no answer. He's not in. But suddenly, as I reach for my pass-key, the door swings open and our man, 77, is here with a mobile phone at his chin like a minute violin. He looks tired. Stressed. Looks like I feel. I look him straight in the eye and hand over the suit; this suit that I have skilfully ruined.

He thrusts his hand into his trouser pocket and chases awkwardly around before producing a pound coin for my trouble (oh, if only he knew!), gives me a sharp nod and turns back into the room, pulling the door closed behind him. I flee down the corridor, expecting with every fleeing step for the door to open with a roar.

I blow Helen out. *Who cares what happens now?*

Sitting in the kitchen, chain-smoking in the early hours of the morning, I practise the visibility of the burn on my dressing-gown sleeve. Could he? *Would* he? Somehow all my hopes, my half-baked plans for the future depend on this charred signature.

The next day I'm standing against the pillar in the lobby, smart and alert, but I can't bring myself to joke with Robert the doorman, toss coins with Big Lee on the front step or flirt with the beguiling cotton blouses juggling behind reception. I'm quiet and withdrawn as the small brown burn superimposes itself over my day, burns into my retina.

Every foot that appears on the landing to descend the stairs to the lobby prompts a palpitating fear; each chirping telephone call to the concierge's desk the same.

After a few hours languishing in the lobby, I'm sent upstairs with a clutch of light bulbs (we get through a lot of light bulbs). As I slink back down the stairs I glance to his room. The door is open . . . *closer* . . . he's gone. The room is empty and Laura, my favourite chambermaid, is bent scrubbing at the bath. He's gone! The relief exhausts me. I push Laura onto the bed for a laugh and skip out of the room swinging my pass-key.

Back in the lobby I'm bobbing about opening doors and pulling strings as per normal with all the usual pass-the-day nonsense for the guests. Once again, I feel quite priceless.

The girls on reception are bored and want to play. They've done their billing and filing and fax confirmations and now these well-bred young women with their fresh white blouses and tight black dresses, long silky legs and high heels are full of mischief, naughtiness, youth, fun and sexiness. Lucy, Vicky and the magnificently proportioned Karen lean at the counter and entertain my increasingly improper suggestions with arching eyebrows and flashing smiles. The combined attention of these three beauties is intoxicating, head spinning, wonderful.

Of course, they're completely insincere. But who cares?

After an hour or so of intense flirting, I slip into the cloakroom to count those crucial tax-free tips and knock back a can of pop. Among the baggage awaiting collection, a label catches my eye: 77 – three pieces to collect.

He'll be back, back to collect his luggage! I unzip the hanging bag: two suits, but mine isn't among them. He's *wearing* my suit, he's wearing my suit with the burn on the cuff and when he's noticed it and his temper is high he'll come back for me!

All afternoon there's a bomb in the cloakroom; primed and set. I can do nothing but wait.

Six with two to go. Their day done, the receptionists clack off together across the marble to be replaced by the single burly harridan who checks their work. It's dark outside and guests are gathering in the lobby to be stroked by the dapper duty managers as the taxis line up in anticipation of fares to the city's theatres, bars and restaurants.

The General Manager emerges with a stoop from his office under the main staircase. He moves effortlessly among the guests, in immaculate black tie, his all-seeing eyes swivelling in his giant head like a roving in-store CCTV system.

He remembers your name. He knows your business. He

nods sagely, throws back his head and laughs with a bellow at your feeble jokes. He's entertained by you and you're flattered that you (little you!) have captured the attention of this tall, intimidating man with his elegant manners. It's the personal touch that the guests appreciate, though in truth there's nothing remotely *personal* about it.

Harold strokes his moustache lovingly and wanders off in search of dinner, and I assume temporary control of the front desk: taking keys, giving directions, selling the city and its attractions with all the zeal of a low-budget Albert Bore: the up-market restaurants and bars of Brindleyplace, the remodelled Hippodrome, the ICC, NIA, *mac* and UGC. 'The *Post*? Certainly, sir.' 'Well, it *is* the Rep, madam.' When I was a kid there was bugger all here. Now even Walsall has a lottery-funded international art gallery.

Suddenly 77 is here. Staring at me across the desk. He looks rough. I catch my breath. '*You* again?' he says.

'No rest for the wicked,' I quip desperately, not daring to look down at his sleeve.

'I wonder if you could do some copies of these for me, they're terribly important,' he says, without so much as a smile.

I do my 'Yessir, rightaway, sir' routine and escape to the mother of all photocopiers in the management office.

As the guts of the photocopier churn, my eyes drift around the shelves of black Niceday box files that document in organized inventory the chaotic comings and goings of the hotel and its inhabitants. I'm in there somewhere . . .

With a buzz and a passing beam the photocopies are born spanking onto the catch-tray. I finger through them. Another bold new building project for the city. Scrupulous designs in pen and ink by someone with extremely fine handwriting: percentages of this, so many units of that; lines and numbers and fiscal, statistical talk with accompanying graphs that stagger like a frenzied cardiograph. I pick the copies hot from the tray, knock them true and head for the Garden Lounge.

There's a commotion in the lobby. A crowd is gathered in the middle of the floor. Someone is flat on his back on the marble tiles. Through the thicket of arms and legs, I recognize an outstretched arm.

'Looks like a stroke,' diagnoses a passing Quincy. The General Manager pulls the shirt open at the neck and shifts the collapsed 77 into what's regarded as a good breathing position. 77 is gasping for air, really gasping. His eyes are rolling around helplessly; his tongue lolling on his chin.

The ambulance crew is here now and they have him on a stretcher, strapped into a harness, wrapped in a red blanket, his arms tight by his sides and he looks quite a different creature as he's wheeled gnashing out of the door, past bewildered guests and into the ambulance in the street.

As I stand there, his photocopies still warm under my arm, I see that he is indeed wearing the suit with the burn on the cuff. But it doesn't matter now.

77 has checked out.

Future Laughter

Jan Stevens

The middle-aged waitress in regulation black waits at the table with her notepad. She is forty-seven but looks older, for the black surprised eyebrows and young pink lipstick with which she has drawn her face harshly emphasize tired eyes and a fret-worked skin, white against her regulation black uniform.

It is Shrove Tuesday and Pattison's Restaurant is quiet today. It's not yet one o'clock and the lunchtime workers are still restless at their desks, slyly glancing at clocks, willing time to move on.

The quiet murmur of the restaurant is suddenly fractured by an infectious burst of laughter which comes from the window table. Hearing youth and hope and gaiety in the sound, elderly diners turn towards the two in the window and even the middle-aged waitress sends them a smile.

Strong spring light pours through the high, arched window and disguises the young figures sitting at that table into two black shapes, both eating pancakes.

In shadows pooled beneath the spindly legs of their chairs, carelessly heaped duffel coats tangle with college scarves. These are yellow and grey, though their colours cannot be distinguished in the darkness under the table. To the curious, these scarves reveal much about their owners.

They say: School of Architecture, a place where women are rarely accepted. They speak of academic excellence and point to high standards. This, then, is the reason for the couple's merriment: they are young, confident – they are the future.

Closer inspection of the starched tablecloth, made brilliant white by the sunlight, reveals two sketchbooks displayed between sugar-crusted plates. One open page is alive with pencil marks, scribbled words, scrawled symbols, faint washes of colour. Two pairs of black mascaraed eyes – one pair brown, one pair blue – scrutinize these designs intently. The brown-eyed student leans forward, pushing a thick strand of hair behind her ear, and taps the page. They are her drawings.

'This stairway sweeps to a huge wide area and this is where I've put bars, little cafés, places to eat and meet.' She looks through a fall of dark hair and points a sugared fork to the complex pattern of pencilled shorthand.

'Is this an idea for your final piece?' Jennifer asks her friend (also called Jennifer). The two Jens, as they are known in college. The silver fork stabs the page again.

'I want to create space with focus, a dynamic combination of art, music, theatre, restaurants – with vast areas of light,' she adds, looking up. The other Jennifer's finger describes air pictures over the designs.

'All this wall could be window, it's above street level anyway. What a panorama, people eating and drinking while watching what's below them.'

Involuntarily they both look out of the restaurant window. Opposite them, on the thronging pavements, lunchtime shoppers scurry into the big C&A department store. Heavy traffic judders beneath them as buses, cars and lorries grind along Corporation Street.

For five years, the two Jennifers – the only two female architectural students in their year – have lived and worked in the city, dodging through its traffic-locked streets, searching its shops, exploring its grimy canals, breathing its fumy breath. They've calculated the perspective of narrow alleyways, blackened stations, empty and echoing churches. They've studied space in the noisy markets, smoke-filled coffee bars and hushed Art Gallery. They've drawn fine Victorian buildings and examined measurements and proportions. They work in the heart of Birmingham.

Pancake Day has become their ritual. Every year (on a different date according to the complexities of the Church calendar), they abandon the fug of the college canteen, the tea-slopped red tables at Lyons, the dimly lit Kardomah for the 'great aunt' atmosphere of Pattison's, with its starched white cloths and silver cutlery. And here they order pancakes. Every year.

The first year of college, Pancake Day was a toast to a recently formed friendship, a spontaneous celebration of their achievements, of heady days away from home, of the start of something just beginning. In the staid and secluded surroundings of this restaurant they have their big discussions, away from drawing boards and the constant teasing of male colleagues.

The conversation over the table on the second Pancake Day celebration was wholly devoted to deadline dates, work schedules, presentations and the relentless approach of their first serious set of examinations. The tone was muted and apprehensive. Jennifer left half her pancake and drank her coffee black. The ashtray was full and there was a smudge on the white tablecloth like charcoal.

The third year proved difficult as both students were on work experience. Brown-haired Jennifer had been placed at an architect's studio on Kings Norton Green and she'd taken the train in a real rush to arrive at the restaurant in time for pancakes.

Blue-eyed Jennifer, her hair now in a French pleat, carried a leather shoulder bag she'd bought on impulse in Rackhams sale. It was full of Valentine's cards: Shrove Tuesday was very early that year, the fourteenth of February. Their conversation veered from their new experience of 'real work' to the possible identities of the card senders. Jennifer walked back with her friend to New Street Station – its wrought-iron splendour obscured by pigeons and wreaths of smoke.

They talked so much on their fourth Pancake Day that it was two fifteen before they even left the window table. They continued a running conversation in breathless bursts all the way up New Street and round into Margaret Street, where they were late for a lecture. Seated at the back of the darkened theatre lit only by the slide projector's filtered light, they continued to whisper and nod and smile. For at Christmas, a sparkling blue-eyed Jennifer had become engaged and their conversations revolved endlessly around bridesmaids' dresses, flower arrangements, honeymoons and married life. For their new home, Jennifer and her fiancé had looked at some plans of a proposed housing estate in Northfield. Momentarily this reminded both Jens of their chosen careers before they returned once again to the topic of marriage.

This Pancake Day is their fifth and final year. The future beckons. For the one, marriage and, though she doesn't know it yet, a new life in Canada; and for the other, a meteoric career in the city. Dark-haired Jennifer has ambition. She likes this dirty, bustling city with its friendly people, its wealth of architecture, its undiscovered promise. This is where she wants to work: she wants to use the city as her backdrop – design streets for people, wide art-filled areas, vast shopping centres, towering office blocks – and preserve the best while changing the skyline. Blue-eyed Jennifer opens a battered purse and pokes among the pennies for a half crown. Their next lecture is at two, but she wants to make a flying visit to the Art Gallery first.

Burrowing into their scarves against a frisky wind, they people-dodge and stride in their pointy boots up New Street, past Hudsons, Woolworths, Lyons and into Victoria Square, where traffic circles and stops and fumes under Queen Victoria's disapproving gaze. Racing noisily up the mosaic-patterned stairs of the Art Gallery, they shatter stillness and faded dust. In the Round Room Jennifer halts beneath *February Fill Dyke*, scribbles rapid notes and draws urgent sketches in her book. This gallery is a familiar place to them both, but it's to this painting that Jennifer returns again and again. She likes the brooding, rain-dark clouds, the sky caught in the puddles, the gaunt trees, the hint of light. As her pencil darts rapidly over the page of her sketchbook, they hear above them the sound of Big Brum striking the hour.

Stamping her booted feet and pulling down her red beanie hat even further, from her vantage point on the Art Gallery steps, Zadie scans the crowded pavements looking for a familiar face. It's officially the first day of spring: the air is sharp and a malicious wind flings cold spray from the nearby fountain. Above her head the clock strikes. One o'clock. He's not usually late. People stream from the library opposite and hurry into the busy warmth of McDonald's, which advertises McPancakes on its steamed up windows.

An assortment of headwear bobs and moves before her, creating an intricate weave of texture and colour. Shiny yellow helmets, vivid turbans, woollen pull-ons, flimsy saris and brightly striped scarves knit a multi-patterned tapestry against the muted grey building of the half-shrouded Town Hall. No one lingers in the cold air.

Her mobile phone plays its sudden tune.

'Zadie?' Andy's apologetic voice in her ear. 'I'll be with you in ten. Promise.'

Ten cold minutes. Zadie's lived here for over nine years, but is often shocked by the sudden sharpness of the weather; perhaps her body still remembers hot yellow sunshine and soft blue skies. She returns up the gallery steps and back into the warmth. It is quiet here. This is where she works – taking art to children, revealing colour and shape and texture. She shows them cranes, the building sites, scaffolding, hoardings, the apartment blocks and shopping centres which jostle in layers like a collage against the sky of this challenging place. She organizes planning workshops, visits, talks, questionnaires and city trails. She loves it.

She climbs the worn mosaic stairs to the Round Room and gazes fondly at *February Fill Dyke* and wonders again how she can use this painting in one of her programmes. A water theme? Painters of weather?

Andy's noisy arrival interrupts her thoughts. He's short, dark and bursting with energy, and his stylish overcoat is discreetly expensive. Recently qualified, Andy works in a light, modern office on the third floor of one of the new buildings on Broad Street. The vast glass window behind his desk creates a living picture of the vibrant city street below. Confidently he grabs Zadie's hand and hustles her out from the gallery back into the unkind wind which snatches her breath. As they run she hears pieces of conversation blown away into fragments: '*See this . . . partnership . . . what do you think?*'

They jump down widely spaced steps where the sculptured nude woman must surely be frozen solid in her waterfall, then they head left into the crowded lunchtime pavements of New Street.

Behind them Iron Man, that vast and modern salute to

Birmingham's industrial wealth, leans into the wind dwarfing the people hurrying beneath. Trying to avoid the solid crowds, Zadie and Andy pass wooden planters trembling with spring flowers, the huddled figure of a *Big Issue* seller and then turn left into Corporation Street.

Andy stops opposite the new Beatties and stands in front of a smart red and white noticeboard. It says simply:

> FELLOWS & FELLOWS
> Pattison's Apartments
> Exclusive City Living
> Safe, Secure, Stylish
> One or Two Bedrooms

Zadie loses her breath again for a different reason. Is she about to face her future?

Andy's key (he has a key?) unlocks a heavy Victorian door with an attractive glass fanlight which opens onto a spacious hall, friendly with pictures and leafy green plants. Silently they enter a smooth lift and alight on the first floor. Bistro Floor. Zadie notices an arrangement of old-fashioned, faded menus in silver frames on the wall. Again Andy, man of surprises, produces an intricate square key. He pushes Zadie forward into an airy, wood-panelled hall – more flourishing plants. A second door to the main apartment reveals a beautifully proportioned living area designed on two levels. Cold spring light streams in from a high, arched window and spills across the polished wooden floors like silk.

Zadie's breath leaves her completely. Her gloved hand is still firmly held in Andy's, and he's speaking to her. Words like 'loving' and 'living' float in the bright space.

She finds herself by the vast arch of the window and thinks how well a window seat would go there.

Below her the city traffic snakes, but she hears no noise.

People cluster into Beatties, and she notices the new patterns and shapes in the city's skyline.

So this is her future: life in this vibrant city with the man she loves. Turning suddenly, she throws her arms around his neck. And is eager now to see the rest of this gorgeous apartment. At the entrance to the kitchen area, Zadie glances back and stares curiously at that high window arch.

Two insubstantial shapes seem to waver against the changing light. Shadows. Clouds. Reflected sky. For a moment she thinks she hears the sound of happy, female laughter, faintly like an echo. Impossible. It must be her own spilling out from her smile. She reaches for Andy's wool-clad arm and they move forward together.

Snake

Luke Brown

The creature in the ceiling was making its noise. It scratched its claws across the plaster above my head, desperate to dig through to get me. I couldn't sleep, wishing it would just crash through; knowing that I deserved whatever it was singling me out for. I felt like a dealer waiting for the door to splinter against a police battering ram. Hours spent awake, listening to the rasps and the thumps, until I was ready to confess everything to Becky, shaking her to wake her up.

'Don't worry,' she said. 'The pest control people are coming tomorrow to get rid of it. Silly. I love you.' And she kissed me and went back to sleep.

That night I tossed and turned in terrible dreams.

When I woke the creature's noise had been replaced by a buzzing coming from outside the window – a dull ringing which made me think of a washing machine, of dirt being atomized. Perhaps there'd been a nuclear explosion.

I felt relieved that the day was over before it'd even had chance to start, and turned over onto my front. I listened to the static in the air as it contracted and expanded, filtering into a pulse. That familiar sound normally hit me in the morning shower, coloured lights strobing in my eyes, a shimmering alcohol soundtrack wrapped around a beat. I

219

opened my eyes and quickly shut them to the steel red glare of my clock radio.

I was woken again by Becky's screams. Only dimly aware of them at first, they intruded into my consciousness as they grew in volume and speed. My eyes opened and I stared with interest at her arms thrashing at some invisible assailant, her mouth twisted in shock. She woke, crying out in resistance, and finding me instead of a monster dived into my chest. I held her tightly, offering consoling words as my cock grew hard.

This wasn't the first time she'd thrown herself into my arms to escape being ripped apart by Rottweilers; or being sentenced to life for mowing down her family in a car; or (a regular one) being beaten by schoolgirl bullies while I looked on, laughing, screwing each of them in turn while they kicked her through her tears. The way she clung to me with a childlike dependency in these moments turned me on – and I'd kiss away the beginnings of tears in her eyes, assuring her I'd never leave her while manoeuvring my hand between her legs.

Afterwards, Becky's eyes bright with reassurance, I lay staring into the shade of the room, listening to that low hum of distant energy I'd heard earlier. I hoped it really was a nuclear explosion so that I wouldn't have to go to work – and I reached over to the curtain, pulling it back with some excitement. The sun wasn't there. But I couldn't see a mushroom cloud either, just an expanse of concrete-grey sky. Drizzle made the street slick and shiny. I opened the window and a damp chill dispersed into the room. The skeleton of a tree outside reached out its fingers to tap at the glass I'd pushed towards it, and I traced the way its branches expanded outwards from its core: a freeze-frame of a gentle explosion. The scratching from the ceiling began again, as the beast continued to dig through the wood and plaster separating us. This life had survived as usual. I tried to come up with a plan to cheat it, but the alarm went off and I found myself in the shower. Colours swam across my eyes.

I headed out into the street, leaving Becky to sleep on her day off from the hospital. I pulled my headphones on under my hood, introducing a slow skittering hip-hop heartbeat and some soaring strings to soundtrack the headlights shining off the wet tarmac; the brick walls filled with the graffiti tags and surreal slogans that'd been there for years. *No Wetherspoons No Peace* – a battle-flag for daytime alcoholics demanding cheap booze in a warm place. I never saw them mobilize unless they were the crew who drank white cider all day in the shelter outside St Mary's Church. But they'd never have wasted good money on paint.

I reached the bus stop, where the calm the music had trickled down my spine was shattered by ragged jags of feedback screaming into the beat. I tore my headphones off as my phone drilled in my pocket. It was a text message – from Jessica, her promise to fuck me hard illuminated in Kryptonite green. I shuddered, feeling sick and excited.

I slid my quid into the chute in front of the silent bus driver and made my way upstairs where I found a seat near the back – close to a group of teenage boys smoking a smelly skunk spliff. The legions of suits and skirts and overalls ignored them. They stared regardless out of holes they had wiped into the misted up windows, or tapped away into their phones at messages or games. The babble of the bus was continually punctuated by a tinny version of a TV theme or pop song, as someone looked embarrassed and hurriedly answered their phone. I put my Walkman back on and was immediately hit with an insect swarm of static from the phone of a pretty girl in front of me. I took it off.

Cruising through Balsall Heath, I watched two bearded guys in baggy trousers entering a mosque. That early and they were already getting ready to pray: an appropriate response to the winter-dark morning, the creeping terror of last night.

My phone went again: a message from Richard, my best mate. It said: Hi m8. Wot u doin 2nite? Meet u 4 footy at PKs l8r?

He knew *all* about my arrangement with Jessica. I sent back: Im screwin Jess 2nite. Maybe l8r?

We swung through the curry restaurants and the kebab shops, and past the German supermarket. I tried listening to my Walkman and was doing well for about five minutes, until we turned round a towerblock and the familiar static began amassing evilly at the edges of the sound. I quickly turned it off as my phone drilled again: a text from Jon, my dealer, from whom I'd ordered some weed and coke for the weekend. All it said was: Stuffs here. But Jon was never awake this early. He can't have gone to bed after scoring, staying up all night on coke or pills or speed, all the while smoking the genetically engineered super-skunk he lived on. I shivered at the thought of those lonely hours: smoke curling around fingers while lungs struggled to find the strength to breathe in. I'd done it many times myself, each time drifting further into the pool of white noise always fizzing at the edge of hearing. I sent Becky a message to tell her I loved her.

I fiddled with my phone, and started playing Snake. With one thumb I ran him round in circles, eating everything in sight. His body curled around the whole screen, until he was so big there was nothing but himself to bite. I winced, remembering the teeth of the creature in the ceiling as they sank into me in my dream last night. My phone jiggled against my thigh when I put it back in my pocket, Rich texting me: Watch out b4 u catch sumthin, haha!

I found myself at work, tiredness switching me on to autopilot, letting me fall through the crowds to the migrating rhythm of the morning. Slipping past the smokers by the front door, I walked into a lift on my own, checking my reflection. I was fairly presentable, red eyes underlined by bags as usual – but sharply suited, and with a nice haircut which I touched up with my hands.

At my desk I felt the familiar despair, worsened when I saw Colin approaching me. A short, obnoxious, bald cockney virgin, Colin – in the perverse distortion of work space – could command respect and favours and make his unfunny jokes and insulting comments with impunity. This was due to his vast and tediously earned experience of how best to make money from the unfortunate. At that moment there were financial problems, looming redundancies, and he'd taken it upon himself to boost flagging morale.

He came at me, beaming. 'Alwight, alwight, you nana – you gonna make some money today?' He left no time to reply, continuing: 'Cos it's out there y'know. It ain't gone away – whatever the facking whingers tell you.'

He pronounced whingers explosively, contemptuously, letting everyone around him hear the scorn he, *Colin*, was pouring on them. And then he continued, 'In fact, I think it's facking exciting right now – everyone's got a chance now to prove that they're worth it – those who stay are gonna be an elite . . . yeah!' And he looked hard at me for a response.

'Like the *A-Team*,' I suggested, trying to take the piss.

He liked this. 'Yes! Like the facking *A-Team*! Fighting gainst the government, giving people a chance, that's the facking bunny.'

Then his face fell. 'But, Joe, you can't make an omelette without breaking eggs.'

The man was clearly insane from all those wasted years

in the same office. His brow furrowed as he searched for a way to extend the metaphor to rousing business effect – one of the skills he'd cultivated in these years was this talent at improvisation – and he finished, triumphantly, emphasizing the point with jabs of his finger. 'But an omelette, it's stronger than all those eggs, cos it sticks . . . *to-geth-a!*'

I had no idea what was singling me out for this special treatment, but I didn't appreciate it, and I raised a counterargument out of annoyance: 'But then it gets eaten . . .'

'Ig-facking-zactly!' he roared, seizing an opportunity, relishing the fascinated attention he was getting from the rest of the office, and hitting his oratory stride. 'It's supposed to be eaten! By RNB Enterprises! It's hungry! It needs its breakfast before it goes to work. But there are rotten eggs making it stink like shit! Not very tasty. There are lazy chickens who can't even be arsed to lay eggs cos they're scared they might be rotten! Chicken shit! And every day RNB Enterprises tries to perform on an empty stomach. It's not fair! So now what we need's a new cook, to weed out all those rotten eggs, wring the necks of all those lazy chickens, and make a smaller omelette, but one that's not all facked up!'

He sounded delighted with himself. I was nodding, my eyes shut, resisting the urge to mutter the words of an Our Father. *Lead us not into temptation but deliver me from evil.* Colin snapped me out of it with a question: 'Are you a good egg, Joe? Ask yourself!'

He snapped his fingers and pointed at me, and with that he ran to his corner and sat down, typing away feverishly, his face contorted with the intellectual effort.

I was now left to check my emails in peace, cheered up slightly by the morning's second instalment of textual filth from Jessica.

Jessica is my ex-girlfriend. We split when I wanted to screw other women and foolishly told her so. I'd tried it on several times without success when we first split, though now she knew I had Becky she was suddenly much more accommodating. Could've been something to do with the demise of her last boyfriend – a wiry, spotty DJ who plays first on the bill at hard house nights to an audience of queers, young girls clutching teddy bears, and Day-Glo clubbing pensioners. Perhaps she became embarrassed by him using words like boshing, mashed, messy and spoonered about ten times in each sentence. But more important, I guess, was the fact he was always too out of it to get it up: highlighting a gap in her life she knew I could fill.

After sending some smut back, I got on the phone and by lunchtime had sold two high-interest loans to housewives on my list of the indecently indebted. I imagined them gliding round town in taxis, slugging back cocktails with shopping bags at their feet. I felt warm inside. Rich is a socialist and criticizes the ethics behind these transactions when I meet him for lunch outside his venture capital firm. But I liked the commission I earned on top of my wage, and the way people's voices would turn from fear and reservation into an edgy, speedy excitement as they relented and decided to sod it and have fun that week.

In high spirits I left the office to walk around town. Firmly at home in the lunchtime city groove, I strolled down New Street – anticipating every opening in the human traffic, spotting every space, and skilfully manoeuvring around the pleading voices of familiar tramps and *Big Issue* sellers. I reached the barrier blocking off the construction site of the new Bullring, and peered over.

I remembered the Reclaim the Streets protest, dancing in this now-vanished space in front of a wall of riot police, delivering huge rants of reason and abuse, fuelled by amphetamine and genuine amazement at their over-reaction to some crusties dancing round an old car. Their faces tried to remain impassive, though you could tell when a point hit home – the weird realization they were human – by the frustration in their faces. They'd suddenly snapped under the pressure, smashing a heavy plastic shield in Rich's face as he shouted 'Peaceful Protest'. It was a good counter-argument: they simultaneously advanced, raining their batons and shields down at a group of middle-class students sat cross-legged at their feet. I'd only been there for the drugs and the dancing, nothing more, but the violence was exhilarating – a huge bonus. Bottles were hurling through the air at the police, who protected themselves by forming a Roman Legion tortoise phalanx with their shields like I'd seen in *Asterix* comics. We got out as the pigs started dragging people off.

That night and the next day, we watched the news eagerly, waiting for the scandal of police brutality to unfold. The tucked-away news item showed a mob of snarling bright-haired crusties, faces full of metal, throwing bottles – and then shots of the police leading them away with considerable restraint. There were no pictures of bloody teenagers, though a friend did get developed a photo of me and Rich taken on the walk back to Selly Oak. We had our arms round each other, the front of Rich's white T-shirt soaked with blood from when the police thug smashed his nose open. We were smiling in the sun, ecstatic, believing for a moment that we had something to fight for.

Now it was just a crater, a vast segment of the city transformed to moon landscape. I watched a crane totter like a drunk tramp, chipping at the ground with its yellow teeth as if prying open a bottle top. Next to me was a Guy Fawkes doll, a loosely human shape made out of blankets – but then it shivered, becoming just another heroin addict, a loser. I watched two builders as they stood, casually chatting and smoking on a girder four or five storeys up on a huge steel frame. They were without ropes, enjoying a cigarette in the biting wind.

'The Parable of the Omelette', the product of Colin's recent labour, lay in my inbox alongside twelve responses, depressing me instantly. After deleting all of them without reading any I felt a bit better. I was on automatic, it was like every other day. I made some calls. I heard Colin raise his voice in conversation to announce: 'My balls are in a facking vice,' and I enjoyed imagining that they really were. I initiated some email flirting with a chubby temp, after complimenting her on her hairstyle when getting a coffee. Perhaps I was on the verge of going too far; it's hard to stop when it's just words on a screen, and it was probably too early in our relationship to suggest the graphic and locally set sexual encounters I had in mind.

I went to the toilet, came back and found three new emails: Becky stuck in a sandwich between the chubby temp and Jessica. She said she was waiting for the pest control man, that she loved me and couldn't wait until I got home. I was appalled at the thought of what pest control might let out on opening the attic-hatch. I made an excuse for why I'd be late (necessary schmoozing to the boss over drinks), and threw myself into my work, though utterly ineffectually.

And all the while I felt a black fear, my head ringing as the whirring of the computers around me rose ever upwards in pitch. Eventually I remembered the other two emails I still had to read. I read them, both requiring a sexy reply I was too flustered to give. I quickly turned my computer off, took a deep breath, grabbed my bag and left the office, watching Colin's glare track me to the door – the first one out.

A loud voice was shouting something unintelligible, and I looked up to see a staggering drunk woman get on the bus.

Everyone concentrated hard on the floor as she continued her tirade, holding onto a railing. I had no idea if she was thirty or fifty, soggy hair all over her face, and I could only make out occasional words: money, niggers, home, pakis, baby, bastard. I squeezed past her as we arrived in Harborne, smelling ammonia.

Jess's flatmate let me in, telling me to go on up, flashing me a look of open contempt. She hated our arrangement, but then she probably wasn't getting any herself. I left her to her morals and bounded upstairs, caught in the moment, already imagining the differences between Jess and Becky's body. Jess's email had told me to be there by six or she'd start without me. I pushed open the door. Jessica sat on her bed, unbuttoning her shirt and kicking off her shoes, stretching out her legs making her skirt climb up her thighs. She stuck out her tongue and beckoned me over.

I really could've gone on for ever. I was elsewhere – worrying about work, wondering if pest control had killed the monster in the attic. After a while Jessica was moaning like she was going to come again, and concentrating hard I managed to as well – by thinking of her flatmate.

I didn't think at all for a long time, then suddenly became aware we'd been silent for an uncomfortable amount of time, at least half an hour in each other's presence with only the most basic of thoughts expressed. The swathe of indistinct noise that'd been bugging me was blanketing the room. We lay on our backs, half undressed, not touching. I recognized elements of her old room: her clock, an Edward Hopper print, a dressing gown. She was looking at me, sadly, concentrating hard as if trying to say something. I said, 'Can I take a shower?'

She nodded, then, as I was putting on her dressing gown, she said, 'You think this doesn't affect you, don't you?'

I shrugged, not knowing what she meant, and walked to

the door. Just before I opened it I heard: 'I slept with Rich a year before we split up.'

Richard is my best friend.

I walked out and across the landing, turned the shower on and got in. It was hot, and I was thorough – scrubbing every part of me with her grape-fruit shower gel, carefully cleaning beneath my nails. I couldn't think of what I'd say when I got back in the room. I stayed there for ages, warm water washing over me, rubbing more and more shower gel over me. I tried to be angry, but my thoughts just floated in the middle of an empty swimming pool.

Back in the room, Jess watched me intently as I got dressed, careful not to catch her eye. She spoke, her voice consciously calm: 'Aren't you going to ask when? Why?'

I stopped still, for a while, then said the most I could. 'Jess, I don't mind, I really don't mind. Just promise me, please, please, if you do one thing for me ever do this. Never let Richard know you told me.'

I got out. There were lots of words from Jessica but I didn't let them connect. Then I thought, that was the last time. It took two bus journeys to get home, but I hardly noticed. Wet smudges of streetlights receded into the distance as I looked out the back window. The bus was quiet and I listened to my Walkman, moody hip-hop blending with the pulse of the streets. I bought a couple of bottles of wine in an off-licence near home and walked past the grafitti tags, getting asked for a quid by the same tall black woman who had patrolled that street every day since I moved in. Walking past the Pat Kav, I saw Rich framed in the window and I hurried past. He still saw me, raising his hand to wave and doing his smile, looking exactly like my best friend. I ran as fast as I could up the street.

I wanted to throw up when I put my key in the lock, with the sudden certainty that Becky had been following me all day and was preparing an interrogation. But she leaped on me in the hall, pushing me against the wall and kissing me hard, unbuttoning my shirt then dropping to her knees to pull off my trousers, lingering there to look up at me with wide eyes and a cheeky grin. Please don't, I thought, not now: but she did. I breathed deeply, fighting panic and after a moment relaxed; Becky looked happy and I led her to bed.

During the sex I felt weary and self-conscious of the absurdity of our motions, the far remove from what we show others. I struggled to stay hard, listening to Becky's moans getting louder, as if from a distance – remembering the cries from a far-off playground on my way to sign on one wet Tuesday afternoon. The muffled cries competed dreamily for my attention with the radiators and the water tank and the car pulling out of the drive, until suddenly there was a huge snap from above followed by frantic banging as something clattered back and forth across the ceiling.

'Fucking hell!' I shouted, heart pounding, trying to get up. I looked to Becky but she pushed my chest down hard with her palms, rubbing herself against me. I lost all sense of order and reason, panicking wildly as the creature continued to smash through the ceiling in a series of wild bangs, Becky holding me down – then she jerked as though it had grabbed back her hair, crying out before falling down on me. Her face rested on mine, and my cheek felt wet.

'That noise, Becky! That fucking noise! It's really pissed off, we've got to go before it comes through,' I shouted, wiping my face with my sleeve.

She looked suddenly sad. 'It was only a squirrel, the pest control man set some traps.'

'Becky, it's a fucking beast!' I cried. 'Listen!'

'Are you drunk? It's just triggered one, hasn't it?' And she mumbled on: 'I'm so glad you came back when you did, though – he set the traps hours ago and I've been sat here waiting for them to go off. He said that it can take hours for them to die sometimes. I didn't want to hear that on my own.'

I was shaking; I didn't want to hear that at all. She stroked my hair and said, 'It's all right, Joe, c'mon it's all right.' Then she sighed contentedly, whispered, '*That* was good.'

I said nothing and we both listened to the silence. I made a prayer, an old habit. *Father, I have sinned, but if it's gone then I'll start over, treat Becky right.*

That night I lay awake in bed, staring at the window – at the dark skeleton of the tree against the moon. And BANG, it was happening again, metal frantically dragged across the wood above. It lasted several violent minutes before stopping. My heartbeat began to steady; during the noise it'd felt like it was me in the steel jaws. But my relief was shattered as it summoned enough strength to smash around again, before stopping just as abruptly. For the next half hour, measured in the red glow of the alarm clock, the squirrel played dead, thinking its cunning could trick the snare into letting it go. I wanted it to live now; awed by the terrible effort with which it clung to life. But each sudden shake after the silence was less forceful than the last. I listened to it die, and fell asleep.

I was woken by Becky mumbling and whining, in pain and afraid somewhere. I was about to rescue her and wake her with a hug, when my phone shivered on the window-sill.

Mr Attwood
Audrey Sandbrook

Statues have never interested me. I served in the police force in Manchester for five years and, during that time, I walked past them at a regulation pace and I drove past them in a patrol car, but I never gave them a second glance.

It was the same when I transferred to Birmingham. I was aware that there were statues in the squares and streets but they meant nothing to me. Until one night about five years ago.

I had only been working in Birmingham for about three months and my partner Joe and I had a call to a disturbance by the Town Hall. When we arrived, there wasn't a soul to be seen, everything was as quiet as the grave.

Joe said, 'You go round one side and I'll go round the other,' and off we went. When I arrived at the back of the Town Hall, I spotted someone sitting on the steps. I went over to take a look and saw that it was a statue: a bronze of a man half lounging on the steps with a quill pen in one hand and a bundle of papers in the other. I was impressed. It looked so natural, as if he was sitting there gathering his thoughts before he wrote the next sentence. One or two bronze pages were lying on the floor behind him as if they were completed. *Full employment* was engraved on one and *Free trade* on the other.

I was looking for the statue's name, when Joe came up behind me. He laughed and said, 'I see you have met Mr Attwood,' and I read aloud: 'Thomas Attwood, 1783–1856, Birmingham's first Member of Parliament.'

'That's right. He was a great guy, way before his time. He believed in universal suffrage, free trade, full employment, you name it.'

'It is a beautiful statue,' I murmured.

'Yes' Joe replied. 'A lot of people think so. But I don't know why it's tucked away here. Hardly anyone sees it.'

The next day, I went to the library and looked up Thomas Attwood. Joe was right: Mr Attwood was a great man and very popular. How strange that a man can be so famous during his lifetime and almost forgotten after his death.

After that first meeting, I often made a detour to see Mr Attwood, sometimes when I was on duty, sometimes not. I found that Joe was wrong about the position of the statue. In the summer, when the city was crowded, Chamberlain Square was full of people watching the free entertainments, eating their lunch or just sitting on the steps in the sunshine. Sometimes there were school parties, and in the holidays parents brought children. Mr Attwood seemed to act as a magnet. Older children took photographs of each other standing at his side. They would place a can of Coke near his hand or put a baseball cap on his head.

And he particularly fascinated smaller children. They would stand in front of him and quite a few of them would talk to him. I remember saying to the father of one small girl, 'She would have a shock if he answered her,' and he replied quite seriously, 'She thinks he does. She told me that he'd asked her if she could read yet. She said that she was on Book 2 and he told her that when she got to Book 3 he'd give her a penny. The funny thing is that when she got to Book 3 she found one of those big old pennies on the garden path on her way in from school. She's convinced Mr Attwood sent it because she told him her address.'

In the evenings, some of Mr Attwood's visitors would be a bit the worse for wear. I often saw drunks haranguing him and I'd tell them to move on. One man was so unpleasant that I took him in.

When the desk sergeant saw him, he said, 'Hello, Bob. At it again are we?' and then he said to me, 'Put him in number two to sleep it off.'

When I returned, I asked the sergeant if Bob always swore at statues. 'Only Mr Attwood,' he replied. 'He doesn't agree with his views on free trade.'

One night, Joe and I were walking across the square on patrol. It was cold and rainy and only a few people were about. We walked round the Town Hall and came down the steps behind Mr Attwood. Sitting at his side was a young man. He was painfully thin and shabbily dressed and rain was glistening on his hair. As we approached, I heard him say, 'As I've said before, I understand what you say about currency reform, but I can't see how it would work. After all, the Germans did that after the First World War and it led to galloping inflation.' Then a pause and: 'Yes, I appreciate that you weren't alive then, but I do think that it's relevant.'

Joe said, 'Hello, Malcolm. Isn't it a bit wet for political discussion?' and the young man got to his feet and wandered away.

'He likes arguing with Mr Attwood,' Joe said, 'but he'll catch his death.'

I laughed. 'Does everyone in this city have discussions with Mr Attwood?' I asked.

'Oh, a lot of people talk to him but the sergeant says he only answers children, drunks and the mentally disturbed,' Joe replied and I think that he was only half joking.

Time passed, and I still called to see Mr Attwood. The children still gathered round him in the daytime and Bob was quite often there in the evenings.

He gradually changed. He no longer ranted and swore at Mr Attwood. Sometimes Bob talked quietly to him and sometimes he just sat at his side, smoking a cigarette. One night I went by and said, 'Good evening, Bob,' and when he replied I realized that he was sober.

I mentioned it to the sergeant and he agreed that it was quite a time since Bob had been brought in to sleep it off.

I also said, in passing, that I hadn't seen Malcolm at all for some months and the sergeant responded that he was probably taking his medication. Apparently, Malcolm was schizophrenic and, when he was taking his medication, he lived with his mother, behaved 'normally' and would hold down a job for a while. Then he'd decide that he was cured, would stop taking his medication, leave home to live on the streets and deteriorate until he was taken back into hospital.

Sure enough, a couple of weeks later, Malcolm was back – telling Mr Attwood that he now had proof that the currency reform idea would never work. Thinner than ever next to Mr Attwood's bronze solidity, he looked almost transparent. I tried to persuade him to go home, but he just kept repeating, 'This is my home. This is where I belong.'

I saw Malcolm several times after that, each time looking skinnier and scruffier than the last. I talked to him and I know other coppers did too, but it was no use. We were all worried and the sergeant even phoned his mother but, like the rest of us, there was nothing she could do.

Then it occurred to me that I hadn't seen Bob at all for some time. I made enquiries, but apparently he'd disappeared altogether. We had almost made up our minds that we would never see him again, when he came to the station. I was talking to the sergeant when a tanned, fit-looking man came in. The sergeant asked if he could help and he said, 'Neither of you recognize me, do you?' We peered at him and realized that he was Bob.

He explained that he'd given up drinking and had managed to get some casual labouring work. He'd found a bedsit, then a more permanent job, and for the last three months he'd been working on a construction site in Leeds – where he was now living in a flat with his new partner.

We were delighted, of course, but also puzzled. 'I had you down as a hopeless case, Bob,' the sergeant said.

Bob laughed. 'So had I,' he replied. 'But then a friend said to me, "You're better than this," and I knew it was true. That was the turning point for me.'

'So no more chatting to Mr Attwood?' I said and immediately knew that I'd made a mistake.

There was a short silence and then Bob asked, 'Who do you think the friend was?' We all laughed and chatted for a few minutes, then Bob said his goodbyes. I walked to the door with him and, just before he left, he whispered, 'I came back to Birmingham to see him again. I thanked him and told him how I was doing, but he didn't say anything. Why do you think that was?' He didn't wait for an answer but walked off quickly.

I told the sergeant what Bob had said and he laughed. 'I've always said that Mr Attwood only talks to children, drunks and the mentally disadvantaged, haven't I?' he said. 'Infants, inebriates and inadequates,' he added rather cuttingly.

One night, about a week later, when I was going off duty, I was hurrying across Chamberlain Square through the rain when someone called out, 'Over here, constable.'

I turned and walked quickly towards the sound and saw, at the side of Mr Attwood, what looked like a heap of sodden clothing. It was a man – unconscious, his face grey and his breathing harsh.

I put my coat around him and called an ambulance, which arrived in a few minutes. I gave the ambulance driver my name and number, but it was only after they had gone and I'd continued on my way that I realized two things. One, they had gone off with my coat; two, I had no idea who had called out to me. It certainly wasn't the sick man and there had been no one else in the square.

The next day, I found out that the man had been taken to Selly Oak Hospital. I telephoned and asked which ward he was on and, when I'd finished my shift, I went to the hospital and enquired about my coat and the welfare of the man. The ward sister apologized and said the ambulance men had thought my coat belonged to the patient. She then said that the patient was still unconscious and they didn't yet know his name.

I asked if I could see him and, of course, it was Malcolm: so thin and ill that I hadn't recognized him in the dark square. As I stood looking down at him, he opened his eyes and a look of understanding crossed his face. I bent towards him and he whispered, 'Tell Mr Attwood.' I nodded and he added urgently, 'Promise.'

'I promise,' I said.

That Friday, Malcolm's mother phoned me. She told me that she'd been with Malcolm when he died but that he hadn't spoken again. (When the sergeant had phoned her to tell her that her son was in hospital, he'd said that Malcolm had asked for her.) She was grateful for what I'd done and I was ashamed that it was so little.

Which was why I felt that I must go and tell Mr Attwood. I knew that it was ridiculous – he was only a statue, after all – but I had to go. I waited until Sunday, which was another wet night, and in the early hours of the morning, I made my way to Chamberlain Square.

I made sure the square was empty and I stood in front of the statue and cleared my throat. 'Mr Attwood,' I said,

'I'm sorry to tell you that Malcolm died in hospital on Tuesday.' Then I turned and walked away.

Suddenly, I was running as I'd never run before. I didn't stop until I was halfway along Colmore Row when a muscular arm reached out and grabbed me. 'Where on earth are you running to?' said Joe. I gasped something about a sudden terrible rainstorm and he said slowly, 'Well, it only seems like drizzle to me, but if it was so bad why didn't you shelter in one of the doorways you've just passed?'

I didn't answer and we turned and walked towards the station. In my mind, I heard the sergeant's voice. *He only talks to infants, inebriates and inadequates*, and there was no way that I was going to tell anyone, not even Joe, that as I'd turned away from Mr Attwood a clear, cultured voice had said, 'Thank you for letting me know, constable. I shall miss him.'

At the Back of the Carriage
Al Hutchins

He was on his own at the back of the carriage, somewhere past Kings Norton. His only company was a gaggle of free newspapers on the seat across and his sight had soaked up enough passing pylons for any mourning mind's eye. If that mind's eye was part of a pair he would have filled its buckets with as much sand as it took to put castles all the way down that beach. But who said there were buckets? Who said this was not a beach of stones? Who in the name of John the Baptist on a mountain bike could move this mountain or make for this mind's eye a pair?

'. . . Tickets or passes please!'

He buried his eyes beyond the window. They saw 'Choppers – the high class butchers' and a rust-wrecked car, sunshone and disused, in a muddy brook. Out in the distance to his right was a Toby Carvery. It was trying to be merry but it felt bleak and the guard for tickets was now gone.

It seemed possible – to the mind of Vincent Leicester it seemed imminent – that he had literally become invisible. All those scrimping youthful postures learnt on London buses to avoid fares had now taken a toll beyond any ken. He'd have free transport for eternity at a price he could afford!

He heard the squawk of a crying and growing child from another carriage and that squawk became the drone of this engine curled round the squealing sound of the wheels of this train as it sped out past Longbridge and Barnt Green over mud-frowned fields towards its usual Redditch destination; frowns which had abandoned the worried lineament of straight front-page headlines and normal contour, frowns whose dance had the sprawl of badly plated spaghetti: a dance he needed now.

For reasons beyond the simple photograph albums of memory, scenes came to mind. Something as ordinary as a pigeon in the upstairs rafters of the Friends Institute on the Moseley Road, circling and disturbing an adult education class, while he delivered chairs.

Or a cocker spaniel in a square in Granada, hurtling and hurtling after low-flying pigeons, ears flapping like wings (turning all heads from the band that played), believing against all odds it could catch them or learn to fly itself; its owner only feigning to bring it back to leash, not wanting this to end.

The latter scene hadn't happened to him but he had lived through it more completely than if he'd been there in flesh and blood. And when they talked it through (how many times talked through?), Vincent and Sarah Leicester on the top-deck back seats of the inner circle they remembered it as if they'd both been there. Any number 8 driver worth his salt would know: 'Cocker spaniel story? Cocker spaniel and low-flying pigeons? Ah, there's the seat. Of a Thursday I'd hear that. Kept getting a different snatch each time mind, but you piece it all together in time, dun't yu? I feel like I was in that square myself. It got so as I could practically hear their every word when they were sat upstairs. I swear I'll come back as a dog when I'm gone – I've already got the hearing!'

It was a tiny part of their history together as man and

wife, thought Vincent, through frost and sleet and shine, one of a thousand tales in the city of a thousand trades. And that city had known the course of every corpuscle through every vein and artery but it did not now know, and nor did he, where for the life of Adam she was nor how she fared.

'Where you off?' A voice was asking him a question.

It belonged to a man whose sideburns were isosceles triangles and whose jacket and hat were so completely covered in butterfly brooches they could moonlight as a butterfly sanctuary. His name was Alf Derry.

'End of the line,' lied Vincent. He was so lost in thought he barely knew he was on a train at all. 'Yourself?'

'I'm going the wrong way,' chuckled the butterfly sanctuary. 'Story of me l-i-f-e from cover to cover. I've written the book, now I'm making the film. It's a disaster movie and I get to play all the characters.'

'Where you heading tho?' Vincent asked, leaning forward. Trying to get a straight answer from this man was like trying to head a square football.

'I didn't know . . . Now I s'ppose I'll have to,' replied the entire cast of the untitled disaster movie.

'Why?' puzzled Vincent aloud. Each answer confused him some more.

'You run out of time. Then there's no choice. There'll only be a few trains left.' And as he said this, for a second Alf Derry looked sad. But sadness wasn't this man's racket. As if to check himself back in, as by some inner reflex, he outstretched his arm to Vincent. (It was then that Vincent realized that the man was blind for Alf Derry's arm leant out in space to greet him but nowhere near. Vincent sidled across his seat to meet it and they shook.)

'Alf Derry's the name, travelling's the . . .' Alf Derry paused and looked perplexed '. . . game. Knew I had it surrounded. Are you in the same line of . . .?'

'Yes,' said Vincent, 'I was trying to keep in motion. There's only the fish that move when I'm parked up. And sometimes I forget to feed them. Gets a bit daft. She'd kill me if she knew. Then Beryl calls. That's her sister. And I feel worse on account of Sarah, that's my missus. She's been bad of late.'

'Don't you realize whichever way we do this it'll work!' exclaimed Sarah Leicester. 'We've got the whole world in our hands!'

'We've got a globe from Lidl in our hands,' replied Vincent. 'It cost £2.99 and at that price it's still more than we can afford. Get in!'

Sarah Leicester froze stock-still. 'Is that all you can say?'

Vincent hated the dramatics of argument and Sarah knew that; Sarah hated his surly deadpan in the heat of argument and he knew that. 'I said get in!' said Vincent, not looking at her.

There were moments in the lives of Vincent and Sarah Leicester when a quality of silence arose amid the blare and hubbub and exhaustion of poverty. It was like bread to hungry birds when it did.

Tonight, in Moseley, on Church Road where you could spot the seasoned alcoholics and trainee drunkards by the Tendercare nappy bags they carried (that's what you were given in the outdoor just up from the Brighton pub), it was a full moon that brought that silence. Once on Colmore Row, it had been a traffic warden that'd stepped in to referee an argument between them. Traffic wardens had thus acquired a heroic status for them both.

But Vincent didn't think it likely that referees would strike lucky for them, not if forty-odd years down the Blues was anything to go by. There'd've been more chance of the young Vincent courting a lass who followed AS**N *I*LA than of having referees among his drinking mates. And, needless to say, the former was a sackable offence.

Vincent remembered another, different kind of silence from an Easter Monday afternoon as he'd looked out from the old Spion Kop to see the team that bore the name of his city go from leading Swindon Town 4–1 after sixty-five minutes to a 6–4 defeat in less than half an hour. From the moment Glenn Hoddle and Mickey Hazard had taken charge of the midfield that day the silence inside St Andrew's had grown and grown to some deafening lurid peak as everyone in the ground watched the unthinkable. But football wasn't more important than *that*. Off the record, Bill Shankly would've said the same. Hadn't the unthinkable happened now? For them both? He tried to remember how he'd felt when he'd lost his mother. He looked out through the window and saw a father leading his young daughter along a wall. Nothing helped.

Alf Derry was asleep.

'Fun! There's the whole world here to rectify and you talk to me about fun!'

She was imitating a line from a film called *The Lost World* as they got into the car. He had bought it for next to nothing and it was nearly worth that. Neither of them could drive. He would start to learn when the work rolled in again. Until such a time, the last legs of this Maestro became an extra wing to their housing association one-bedroomed blues: an alcove, a disused picture house where *they* chose the reels, a crib for the four weeks of Advent like the one he'd seen in Wicklow as a child, a conservatory for the poor. They laughed at the token wild-eyed Latinos in films such as these, always backward and always defending their honour; always inaccurately observed. 'It's the same with Brummies,' Sarah would always say. 'They never get it right, those actors. You know the way a chef gets asked to cook rice when he starts his training. They should do it with actors when they start theirs, get them to perfect the Brummie accent. They're always off-mark.'

'I know how you feel about the fish,' said Alf Derry within three seconds of waking. Vincent had no idea what he was referring to. Alf Derry's response to Vincent spanned a lapse of nearly an hour. It came in reply to nothing in particular, the way much seemed to come from this man: slantwise and benevolent.

The train was approaching New Street. Alf Derry was now going in the direction he'd intended all along. Vincent, who had not been going in any direction, in joining him, was now travelling the other way. But there were no trains left today that gave Alf a chance to go somewhere and get back.

There was nothing for it but to kill time in the city. As they ascended the escalator, Vincent realized what the fish remark had referred to.

Alf turned to look at him: 'It will work itself out, you know.' They were now standing in the ruins of the Bull Ring. There was so much upheaval going on around them that Vincent barely heard what was being said. Alf was still speaking: 'It's like any racket. It can't go on for ever. 'll probably get worse before it gets better but it won't last.' He scratched his nose on his sleeve. 'How long will this take to finish?' asked Alf, scanning the space all around him with his stick. Again, Vincent hardly heard but this time he spoke all the same.

'The wife's brother-in-law had a scar on his left cheek, really pronounced like. He was gonna have an operation to get rid of it. Everyone moaned, urged him to keep it, we've got used to you with it and suchlike. Anyroad, it was his, his scar, he wanted it gone. Just as it came time to 'ave it done, some pimple or spot developed and they had to postpone it, case of infection. When the time came round again, he decided to keep it. That's what I think of when I see that thing over there. It's not pretty but the city wouldn't be the same without it. Some of the kids have never known this place any different.'

He was pointing at the Rotunda. 'Can you see it?'

'I see more than they think,' crackled Alf. 'Let's just say you have your guides. You find they crop up in each city you go to. I can see the shape of it in outline. That seagulls I hear. It's a failed seaside town, isn't it, Birmingham? No, that's how an American would put it. But the way I see it, you're living in a seaside town without the sea, Vincent. Anything can happen – the city's your oyster.'

They had made their way to the Chinese quarter and were stashed inside Mr Yeung's.

'How long have you worn the butterflies?' Vincent asked.

'Ever since Yvonne popped it. She loved them, you see. But I didn't plan to wear them.' He paused. 'Don't really have much time for all that . . . stuff, y'know. I never thought I'd fill the house with them. But everywhere my feet would go I'd seem to find the damn things. Same as when I stopped laying the cables when my eyes baled out on me. I mean, what do you do, Vincent – sit in and get fanatic about the rain? I never knew I'd spend my time going from one place to the next like this. But now it's my life. If I sat in, I'd –' (he searched for the word) '– congeal.' (The word he found contained all the disgust you could get into a word.) 'Now when I reach my front door, I've a tale to tell those butterflies. I've *seen* a bit on me travels, y'know.' Alf Derry's mouth broke into a smirk and the rest of his face followed suit.

The woman who was always there placed two steaming plates of roast duck in black bean sauce on a bed of rice before them. Behind where she sat, perched at the counter, was a shrine with an apple and an orange. Vincent and his wife had come here so often together, and the woman, whose name he didn't know, had often eyed Sarah's bracelets, taking them off and trying them on herself. But when Vincent smiled at her today she didn't respond. As though, without her, without Sarah Leicester there, he was just a blank space. That at least was how Vincent felt about one moment out of thousands in a working day at a Chinese restaurant in Birmingham.

'S'ppose I'm a bloody fool, really.' Vincent sighed. 'I keep coming back to our old haunts, Alf. No woman would do as daft. I catch myself buying things she likes . . . salted peanuts or dark chocolate . . . as if it might put me in touch with her . . . as if she might appear and grab them off me! I don't know what I'm doing, Alf.'

The no-frills restaurant was filling up; all the trappings of courtship and a good time were filing past on the street outside. The beginnings of a usual Friday night in town.

As Vincent settled the bill, he thought one of those irrelevant comic thoughts that strikes in the pith of grief. He realized that he was paying for food alone and not décor; that normally you paid for décor and occasionally good food as well. He imagined a restaurant with both options where you had to turn your face from the walls as you ate, if you only wanted the good food. He pictured the waiters ready; beady of eye to catch you if your own eye strayed.

Alf and Vincent threaded their way past Mr Egg ('Eat like a king for a pound'), over the lights on Queensway, up the hill past Hill Street Q's with its blue-felted pool tables and on again towards New Street. The rain decided to fall, to Vincent's mind like one who'd just remembered to post a letter that had taken root in an overcoat pocket: suddenly but long overdue. It pinned the revellers of this town to shelter and made those others scurry with greater sense to home and hearth.

It was hosing down the black cabs as they re-approached the station.

Alf extended his arm. 'I better get back. My butterflies will be waiting for their bedtime story. I know what it feels like, Vincent. Tonight I'll turn on the radio. It stays on till the end of the shipping forecast. I'll make myself a chop and a plate of greens. When I climb the stairs tonight, I'll still remember details about Yvonne so subtle,' he paused, 'that to give you them in words would be as daft as giving glasses to a blind man.' Alf Derry's throat chuckled in response to his words. He was a kind of one-man Vaudeville show to himself, with the audience thrown in.

He cleared his throat for some space over the station tannoy. 'She's buried a child, Vincent. Your child. It's not in the natural order of things. No one but a mother can know that grief. She'll come back when she's ready. You'll see those broken, punch-drunk eyes laugh again. It won't be the same, my friend . . . it'll be a new life.'

When Vincent Leicester came out of the station concourse the rain had ceased. Hailstones had begun. There were no taxis in sight and on the ground where their wheels had been the day's free newspapers grew more sodden by the second. Vincent stood there for a moment and watched the stones attack the feeble shreds of paper. He looked back at the station doors which could slide open and give him cover. He looked forward at the city that had brought Vincent and Sarah Leicester together. He looked back at the doors again, then faced forward.

Those fish need feeding, Vincent thought.

It would be a long walk home.

Biographical Notes

Simon Broadley has a cat in Walsall, a job in Birmingham and a girlfriend in North London. He plans to produce a landmark documentary about Morrissey's solo career, rebuild the ABC Cinema Walsall brick by brick and front a re-formed Queen for a stadium tour of South America. He still doesn't have someone to press his suits . . .

Luke Brown, 23, grew up in Fleetwood, Lancashire, surrounded on three sides by sea. He moved to Birmingham to study, and now lives in Balsall Heath.

Eldon Davies was born in Swansea, but followed his career as a science teacher in the Birmingham area. He has carried out part-time research at Warwick University, and since retirement has rekindled his interest in creative writing. His other enthusiasms include naval history and classical organ music. He lives in Sutton Coldfield with his wife Carole.

Pauline E. Dungate has been teaching in Birmingham schools for thirty years. Her science fiction, horror and fantasy short stories have been published in both the USA and the UK, including 'Lucy' in *Birmingham Noir*. She also writes critical articles (mostly for American academic volumes), reviews and poems. At night, you might find her out hunting bats.

Anne Dyas was born in West Bromwich, and now lives in Solihull. She attended the Holy Child Convent School in Edgbaston, and Birmingham University, where she studied medicine. After qualification, she worked as a pathologist. Illness intervened, and she retired from work. Her time is now largely occupied by her two children and her garden.

David Hart has worked as an Anglican priest, a theatre critic and arts administrator, now for some five years as a freelance writer. His poetry has been widely published and has won major prizes, including First in the National Poetry Competition. His poems in book form include *Setting the poem to words* (1998) and *Crag Inspector* (2002). His poetry residencies include Worcester Cathedral, South Birmingham Mental Health, the Aldeburgh Poetry Festival, and he was 1997–98 Birmingham Poet Laureate.

Al Hutchins has been writing and performing 'stuff' for nineteen years, most of which lives inside an unreasonable number of Aldi carrier bags. In 1998, thinking these bags should get out more, he formed the rhythm, holler and tune-mongering thing that is the Courtesy Group. He does comedy as Godfrey Salter and his Invisible Ducks. In November 1992, after a miserable 1–0 defeat for the Blues at Barnsley, he walked thirty-four miles after misreading a station timetable giving times for the following year. It doesn't get any better.

Nick Jones was born and raised in Birmingham. He read law at Bristol University and qualified as a corporate lawyer with the Birmingham office of Wragge & Co. A passionate cricketer and golfer and now a legal recruitment consultant by trade, Nick lives with his partner Helen and daughter Ellie in Harborne.

Biographical Notes

M. Idrees Kayani was born in Birmingham, educated at King Edward's School and Sheffield University. Since his release from these institutions of dry, formulaic learning, he has been searching for knowledge on his various travels as an office zero to social care hero and security guard to literary bard, all the while documenting his experiences and refraining from vain, intellectual pretensions.

Sidura Ludwig is a Canadian writer currently living in Birmingham. Her writing has appeared in *Pretext* and *Prairie Fire*. She has also produced a number of radio documentaries for the Canadian Broadcasting Corporation. She is working on a book of linked short stories.

Richard Lutz was born in New York and has been in journalism for most of his life. Since 1983 he has lived in Birmingham and currently works for Carlton TV. Throughout his career he has won numerous awards for reporting both domestically and overseas. He has written for the stage and television, and this is his first published short story. He is married with two sons.

Alan Mahar is the author of two novels, *Flight Patterns* (Gollancz, 1999) and *After the Man Before* (Methuen, 2002) and is working on a third, *Huyton Suite*, for which he won an Arts Council Writers' Award 2002. His short stories and book reviews have appeared in, among others, *Critical Quarterly*, *New Statesman*, *Literary Review* and *Times Literary Supplement*. He founded Tindal Street Fiction Group in 1983 and is currently Publishing Director of Tindal Street Press.

Laura McFall graduated from Goldsmiths' College in 1995 with a BA in drama. She has performed as an actress throughout the UK, including a run at the Old Rep,

Birmingham, which inspired this story. She runs a theatre company called Otherwise Silent, for which she has directed two plays. She attends writing classes at the City Lit, London, which published her first story 'Mama Kan's Kitchen' for Adult Learners Week in 2001. This is her second story.

Ava Ming is a classically trained musician, experienced radio presenter and qualified social worker. Her short stories have been broadcast on BBC Radio 4, published in *Whispers in the Walls* (Tindal Street Press, 2001), and she was a commissioned writer for 'Stories on Stage' at the Midlands Arts Centre. Apart from writing, she lectures in media studies, teaches vocal skills and sings jazz.

John Mulcreevy's first story appeared in *Platform*, a 1970s school magazine. After school he spent time cutting things – steel sheets, grass lawns – and drawing things – cartoon strips, the dole. His second published short story appeared in *Birmingham Noir* (Tindal Street Press, 2002); this is his third. John has spent all his life so far in north Birmingham and will probably continue to do so.

Julie Nugent is thirty-one years old and lives in Hall Green with her husband and daughter. She has recently been awarded a doctorate for research into Birmingham's second-generation Irish community. She is currently employed by the Learning and Skills Council, working in the planning and funding of post-16 education. This is her first piece of published fiction.

Mark Paffard was born in Stoke-on-Trent in 1955 and grew up on the campus of Keele University. He has lived in Birmingham since 1977, working in social care and completing a thesis on Rudyard Kipling's fiction. He's been writing stories since 1990 and is also a member of Cannon Poets. He has three sons.

Audrey Sandbrook is a Brummie born and bred. She worked as a legal executive in the City until retirement twelve years ago. Although she's written stories for most of her life (usually destroying them), this is her first published short story.

Jan Stevens studied fine art at Birmingham Art College, and until recently worked as an art teacher. She has three daughters and lives in an old farmhouse in Worcestershire with her husband and an assortment of animals.

Apart from three years at Loughborough University studying English, **Rachel Taylor** has always lived in Birmingham. Her short story 'Dyed Blonde' was published in *Birmingham Noir* (Tindal Street Press, 2002). Currently, Rachel is learning British Sign Language and working towards a CertHE in creative writing at Birmingham University.

John Wagstaff returned to Birmingham in 1997, forty-three years after he'd left the city at the age of two. He works as a lawyer in the city centre, surrounded by the architecture that plays such a large part in his story. 'An Air Kiss' is his first published piece of fiction.